THE SWORD-WITCH'S HEART

ALSO BY TAVIA LARK

Radiance
The Necromancer's Light
The Paladin's Shadow
The Sword-Witch's Heart

Perilous Courts
Prince and Assassin
Prince in Disguise
Prince and Pawn
Prince and Bodyguard
Prince and Betrothed
Prince of Agony

Fortune Favors the Fae
Bound to the Wild Fae

RADIANCE III

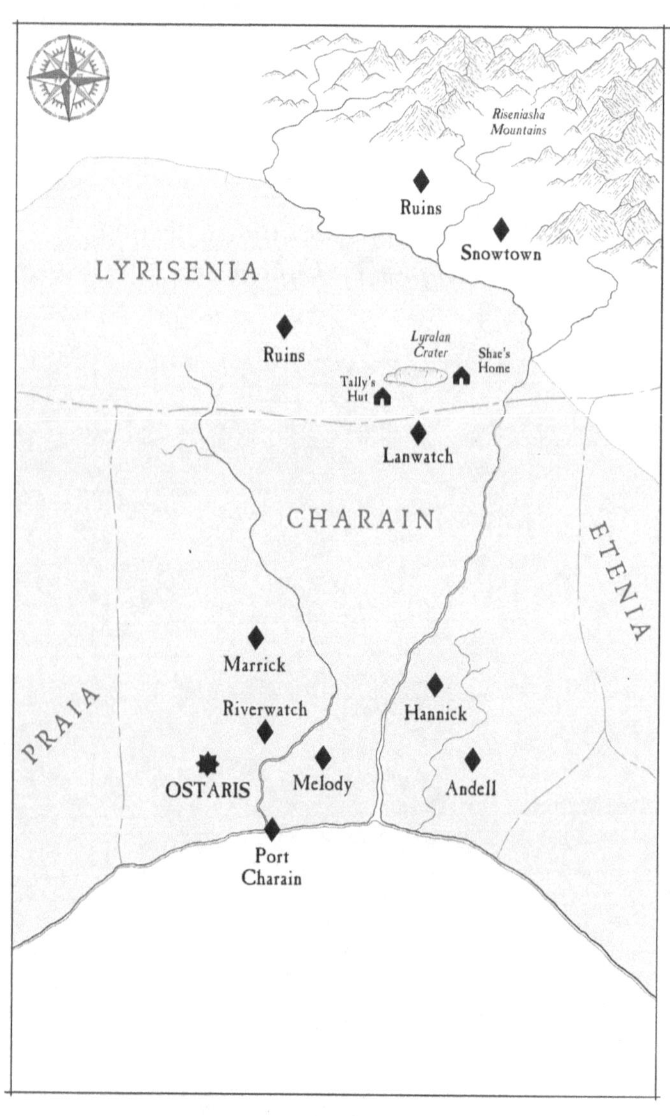

Riseniasha Mountains
Ruins
Snowtown
LYRISENIA
Ruins
Lyralan Crater
Shae's Home
Tally's Hut
Lanwatch
CHARAIN
ETENIA
Marrick
Riverwatch
Hannick
PRAIA
OSTARIS
Melody
Andell
Port Charain

ＰROLOGUE

AFTER THE UNBINDING

Leth hesitates at the silent threshold. He had braced himself for confrontation, but the Tariel family chapel is empty. Trees whisper around him, and the night cuts through his long coat. The divine sword slung across his back sears a line of ice into his skin.

Two hours past midnight, the city of Ostaris is quiet. The day's chaos has ebbed, leaving the people exhausted. In the courtyard of the Bright Cathedral, five bound gods were freed. Thousands of soldiers, paladins, and priests lost their false contracts of divine magic. Two centuries of lies were brought to ruin by the small group calling themselves the Locksmiths.

Leth imagines the rest of the Locksmiths are sleeping, celebrating, or still consulting with the paladin orders. But he has something to take care of alone.

The Tariel chapel to Ka Dravos sits half a mile outside Ostaris, in a stretch of forest owned by the ka Tariels for three hundred years. The stone doors are carved with two snarling wolves. Leth mutters a charm of protection, and one of the onyx spell beads braided into his loose hair flashes silver—but he meets no defensive spells when he touches the door. His family must not have bothered removing him from the wards.

The door creaks open at his touch, revealing the interior. Moonbeams stream from the high windows like blades of light. They reveal the fine layer of dust covering the dark marble floor. Dust covers the single bench by the door, too, where Leth's grandmother used to sit to worship when she became too frail to kneel before the altar.

Leth's lips tighten briefly at the chapel's neglect. He takes a slow breath, holds it, and exhales to center himself. Ka Dravos—the cold, ascetic god of war—rewards strength.

Despite the late hour, Leth expected to find someone else here. His mother, perhaps. His aunts and cousins. His older brother. Even if Anton has spent his career devoted more to politics than faith, surely the Unbinding should have driven him to the chapel.

Did Anton keep his contract or not? Those the gods deemed worthy were allowed to keep their magic. If Ka Dravos judged Anton worthy, then he'll be more powerful than ever. If not, he'll lose all claim to Ka Dravos's Valor.

It's not Leth's place to judge his brother, but he can't help having his own opinions.

The chapel isn't as large as it seemed when Leth was a child, but it's large enough to make him feel small. Statues of men and women line the walls, wielding swords and axes, clad in armor and pelts. A gauntlet of Leth's most esteemed ancestors, staring him down with dead stone eyes as he approaches the altar. Leth grew up on stories of their heroism and strength. The great feats they accomplished with the Valor granted by Ka Dravos.

A waist-high block of marble forms the altar. Leth unstraps the sword from his back. When he grabs the relic's hilt, magic tingles through his glove. The Valor that tempers the war god's acolytes into peerless steel, drumming through his bones. Leth has never wielded Valor, despite his lifetime of training. Before the Unbinding, Valor was falsely restricted to the elite Dravan soldiers within the Charaini army.

Leth's failure to enlist left him only his own meager magic—until now.

He unsheathes the Dravansword and sets both blade and scabbard on the altar. The scabbard is plain leather; the blade is dark steel, and the ruby set in the pommel looks black in the darkness. Uneven blood grooves score the blade like claw marks.

"Release." Leth's minor protection charm shivers away. Nothing stands between him and Ka Dravos.

With another steadying breath, he steps back five feet from the altar and lowers both knees to the night-cold marble. He bows his head, and his shoulder-length hair falls in front of his face. Closing his eyes, he speaks quietly, without ritual or incantation.

"Ka Dravos, I am Leth ka Tariel. I helped free you from the Binding." He doesn't mention his sacrifices. Being faithful to his god required him to betray his family, but Ka Dravos wouldn't care about the cost—only the results. "I ask for your blessing and Valor, in exchange for devoting my heart and sword to you."

He's prayed to Ka Dravos all his life. When he was younger, he thought the god's silence was because Leth wasn't strong enough to deserve an answer. He thought that if he tempered his will and rejected all mortal distractions, trained until his blisters bled, he would earn Ka Dravos's attention.

But nearly two years ago, the Locksmiths' leader told Leth the truth: Ka Dravos *couldn't* answer. Every directive Anton claimed from the god was a lie. Ka Dravos and four other gods were imprisoned two hundred years ago, and if Leth wanted his true birthright, he had to fight for it.

The echoes of his prayer fade from the chapel. Silence holds him captive, and nervousness builds in his throat no matter how steadily he breathes.

Until the air shifts, and the night moves.

Hot-cold *power* crashes down on Leth's shoulders. Forces through his lungs. Willpower alone keeps him on his knees as crushing Valor surrounds him. His joints lock in instinctive resistance, and his vision darkens. For a moment, he's afraid he'll pass out.

The force eases. Gasping for breath, Leth raises his head.

Ka Dravos is tall. At least two feet taller than Leth's five-foot-three. His massive shoulders are made even more massive by his great furred cloak, the length of which dissolves into shadows. A wolf's head helm hangs over half his face, fangs silver in the moonlight.

The god circles behind the altar and runs his fingers along the Dravansword. Steel sings to his touch, and Ka Dravos finally looks at Leth.

"*You ask my blessing.*" Ka Dravos's voice resonates with the steel's uneasy song. Memories of howling nights. "*Yet you reek of demon magic.*"

Leth's blood runs cold. He doesn't. He can't. Unless—

"It isn't mine. I would never contract with a demon."

"*It clings to you like a shroud.*"

Leth clenches his shaking hands against his thighs, hating himself for showing weakness before his god. But he has no hope of hiding his trembling, just like he has no hope of hiding the traces he never thought would be a problem. He's never used demonic magic— but there's a demon-bound mage in the Locksmiths.

Leth's stomach drops. After everything he's been through, everything he's done, if he loses his chance for Valor because of the insufferable Evain Marha—

"*But it matters not.*" Darkness gathers around Ka Dravos. "*Too long have I been a sword locked in its scabbard, and I am weary of all bindings. I will wander now, and while I wander, I will not contract with you. Nor will I contract with any other mortal.*"

His words are cold and final, and ring so loud Leth can't understand them at first. Then he does: Ka Dravos isn't just rejecting him.

Ka Dravos is rejecting *everyone.*

Leth opens his mouth, but the air slams down on him, cutting off his heart's plea before it reaches his lips. Pressure blackens his vision and rings in his ears. Seizes his lungs.

Then vanishes. Ka Dravos is gone.

Leth falls forward, palms on the cold marble. His heart feels cold as marble too as the full truth hits him: he betrayed his family for nothing.

Numb, Leth rises to his feet. He leaves the Dravan-sword on the altar and walks out of the chapel.

$$\text{\Large ☽ ○ ☾}$$

EVAIN LOUNGES ON the rooftop balcony of the third-finest brothel in Ostaris, and inhales. The night sky is rich with power. Answered prayers, contracts formed and broken. Smoke and sky, magic and starlight, crisp as sparkling wine down his throat.

None of it is the sort of power that feeds his own. Evain's needs are far more base than moonlight and prayer; he thrives on human lust. The stronger a person's desire for him, the more powerful he becomes. But the esoteric, divine flavors are interesting, and the ramifications even more so. Far away to the north, he feels a barrier wavering.

For nearly two hundred years, the Northern Barrier has protected Charain from the wild magic and demons that plague neighboring Lyrisenia. But no enchantment made by human hands can last forever.

Evain's unbound black hair scatters over his shoulders, rippling occasionally in the wind. He twists a long strand of it between his fingers. His fingernails are blunt and perfectly manicured, carefully transformed to hide his natural claws. A similar spell conceals his crimson eyes. Though he's alone on the rooftop, he can't be too careful. It wouldn't do for someone to realize Evain isn't actually a human mage sworn to a desire demon. He hasn't killed a demon to keep its powers or locked it safely away in an array.

He's the desire demon himself. His true name, Aevendaris, has never been spoken by human lips.

Evain smiles in anticipation. The Charaini orders will need some time to recover from the shock of the Unbinding. Evain will give them at least a month before making his move.

After two hundred years of traveling the world, it's almost time to return to Lyrisenia. He has some cleaning up to do.

LETH

The winter wind rattles the spell beads in Leth's hair, giving him something to think about besides the way everyone stares at him. Clad in plain black from gloves to boots, he stands out like a blot of ink among the gray and green uniforms outside Fort Tarhaeg. Soldiers hasten to load a caravan of supply carts—enough to support a troop of thirty soldiers.

There are thirty soldiers in Anton's elite guard.

Leth isn't sure what he's doing here. He doesn't know what he wants to say to Anton. But this could be his last chance to clear the air for a long time.

Six weeks after the Unbinding, Fort Tarhaeg looks the same as ever. An imposing compound on the outskirts of Ostaris, half military complex and half ancestral noble home. The great bronze and stone gate is open, and soldiers with green cloaks and bronze wolf's head belt buckles stand guard, their postures stiff with well-trained arrogance.

Perhaps Leth only imagines the dark circles around some soldiers' eyes. Adjusting to the sudden severance of their divine contracts can't be easy.

Their rehearsed postures waver to gawk at Leth. Everyone recognizes him, and Leth imagines their thoughts all echo with the same word: traitor. A few spit on the ground as he passes, but nobody stops him. Leth is almost disappointed to cross the courtyard unimpeded. Maybe his tightly-wound nerves would ease with a good fight.

Past the barracks and stables sits the keep itself, and it's there that Leth is finally stopped.

"Never thought I'd see Leth ka Tariel crawling back home." A lean man crosses his arms in the doorway. A rough blond beard covers his weak chin, and the green and bronze trim on his uniform marks him as an adjutant. "Sorry, have they stripped the name from you yet?"

Revulsion twists Leth's stomach. Javius Orst is Anton's closest friend and most loyal lackey—and the man directly responsible for keeping Leth out of the army six years ago. Now he stands in the doorway of Leth's childhood home, barring him at the threshold.

"Adjutant." Leth keeps his disgust from his face with long practice. "Are my mother and brother in residence?"

"Your brother is. But I don't think he's seeing traitors today."

"He can tell me that himself." Leth rests a hand on his sword hilt, and the way Javius's eyes widen is gratifying. The last thing Leth wants is to lose control and cause a scene, but Javius doesn't know that.

The yard swarms with soldiers, and Leth sees servants past Javius in the entrance hall. Numerically, Leth is at a disadvantage, but he's more than capable of humiliating Javius before anyone subdues him. Especially since Javius no longer has Valor to strengthen his sword.

"Kindly let me pass," Leth says.

Anger spotting red beneath his beard, Javius steps back from the doorway. Leth smells sour beer as he brushes past the man. His shoulders tense, but Javius doesn't try to stop him.

The entrance hall is busy with travel preparations too. Leth stops a servant and asks where in the sprawling keep his brother is. The answer surprises him; Anton never used to frequent the family library like Leth did.

Leth thanks the servant and heads upstairs, ignoring the two guards following him at a distance. The women make no secret of watching him, and Leth isn't trying to hide. They can watch him all they like. Far more unsettling is the familiarity of every stone, candle, and tapestry in these halls. After everything, this is still home.

As a child, Leth loved looking at the great heroes in the tapestries. Men and women in gleaming armor, Valor shining from their swords. Today, Leth can't help but notice the other figures in the tapestries. The vanquished. The dead and dying, demon and human alike.

The guards shadowing him seem winded by the time they reach the fourth floor of the keep. Leth doesn't slow his pace until he reaches the library door. Resting gloved fingertips on the bronze handle, he glances over his shoulder. Spell beads click in his hair.

"You should probably wait in the hallway," he tells the guards. "You don't want to get involved in this."

The younger woman steps forward. "Our orders—"

The other grabs her arm. She looks like she has a few more years of experience. "He's not wrong. This is the general's business, whatever the adjutant says."

Unimpeded, Leth opens the door and steps inside.

The library is the brightest room in Fort Tarhaeg. Tall windows welcome the pale winter sunlight, and expensive mage-lamps illuminate the neat rows of tall bookshelves. Gray curtains cover the shelves of older books, protecting them from the light. The fireplace is unlit, and the room is chilly.

Anton isn't in the main room, but the door beside the fireplace is open. Only ka Tariels have keys to the private room where the family heirlooms and arcane texts are kept. Some are simple instructional texts. Some are half-true, half-myth tales of mages who destroyed cities or found immortality in a demon's contract. Some are histories most ka Tariels would prefer forgotten.

Leth counts his breaths until his pulse steadies. Padding across the plush rugs, he feels smaller and smaller as he passes each tall bookshelf. At the door, dark gray magic flickers at the edge of his vision— wards protecting the valuables within.

The books in this room live in closed cabinets. Anton is locking one of them when Leth enters. Apart from the cabinets lining the walls, the only furniture is a pale wooden table and chairs in the center of the room. A plain leather-bound volume sits on the table.

Anton ka Tariel looks out of place in the library. He's always been big, a head taller than Leth and twice as broad. Born with the natural strength Leth always had to work for, his hands were made to lift greatswords, not books. His hair is the same light brown as Leth's, but he wears it cropped short, with a precisely trimmed beard. Dressed for travel, he's exchanged his usual flashy green cloak for a gray one.

The cabinet lock clicks shut, and Anton turns around. His eyes are the same hazel as Leth's, and they're filled with ice. "What the fuck are you doing here?"

By the tone in Anton's voice, this conversation is already a mistake.

"I heard you were leaving," Leth tries anyway. "I wanted to talk before you rode out."

Anton laughs harshly. The bright lamps show new lines around his eyes. Anton is only six years older than Leth—he turned thirty this year—but the past few months have aged him. "Then talk, little brother."

Leth rests his hands on the back of the chair. "Where are you going? The western border?"

"Not the west." Anton leans against the locked cabinet. Leth tries to remember what books were in that one. The shelves aren't labeled. "Feel free to report that to your spying Praian friends."

Yes, this is a mistake. There's no hope of having a productive conversation when Anton's like this. "I'm not reporting to anyone."

"Cut to the chase," Anton snaps. "Are you here to gloat, or to apologize?"

Leth's fingers tighten around the chair back. "I won't apologize. Breaking the Binding was the right thing to do, and you know it. You've learned our history the same as—"

"To gloat, then," Anton interrupts, with another laugh that doesn't reach his eyes. Walking around the table, his presence pressures Leth backwards. "You're still so arrogant, even when you're slithering in the gutter with criminals and foreign heretics. History? Was that what all this was for—so you could be the next Warlord Prelleth or Kan Aria?"

"It wasn't for me." Leth tamps down the ember of guilt at his own greed.

It wasn't just for him. But he had hopes too.

"You jeopardized our family's entire future with this madness," Anton says. "How much power did those heroes you worship really have? Kan Aria commanded, what, a dozen barbarians? Prelleth held his mountains for two fucking years. The Binding gave us *true* strength. Military. Political. Another twenty years, the right marriages, and we could have ruled the entire country. But you were always too lost in your stupid stories to see that."

"The Binding was a desecration." Leth's voice rises. "How many Dravans did the army have? Five hundred? Valor was so diluted, it took five soldiers to face a single vaidkos. With a true contract, it should be the other way around. The gods' magic isn't meant for a single nation's army. It's meant for the worthy, no matter where—"

Staggering, Leth hears the echoing smack of Anton's backhand first, then feels the blunt impact ringing through his skull. Only then does pain burst through his cheek.

He pivots through his daze, drawing his sword, but Anton has already moved to the table. "If Valor is meant for the worthy, then where is yours?" He flexes his fingers, a slight smile returning to his face, then picks up the book. "Were you not worthy either, little brother?"

Face stinging, Leth can't answer.

Only when Anton strides from the room do Leth's joints unlock. He counts out his breaths and sheathes his sword. Touches the tender skin of his right cheek, wondering how bright the mark is. Wondering how fucking stupid he must be, to still think he could somehow win Anton's approval.

Time to bury that goal, like all his other dreams.

EVAIN

vain inspects himself in the mirror with a slight frown. He'd intended to dress conservatively, so as not to attract undue attention during his visit to the Bright Cathedral. Perhaps the dusky light of his suite in the Veiled Rose is to blame, but his severe braid only highlights his cheekbones and eyebrows, and the coat buttoned to his chin is too well tailored. The tight fit accentuates his shoulders, and the dark red fabric suits the golden tone of his skin. It would suit his natural eyes too if he dared let the crimson show.

What a shame. He winks at his own reflection. *I'm just too attractive.*

He's been avoiding the Bright Cathedral ever since the Unbinding. Paladins sworn to Radiant Vara, a god of sun and truth, have always had a keen sense for demonic magic. Now that Vara is no longer imprisoned, there are fewer paladins with magic—but those that remain are far stronger than they were before. If Evain isn't careful, a clever paladin could figure out his true nature. Abandoning this identity would be very inconvenient.

But he can't avoid the Bright Cathedral forever, and he has a favor to ask of the Varans today. Or a favor to offer them—that's how he'll frame it. The prospect should be mutually beneficial if they accept.

Or mutually disastrous if they don't.

Evain pats his mirror in farewell and picks a pair of black leather gloves, embroidered with red mahr blossoms, from the vanity. He's playing human, after all, and the day is cold.

)O(

MAYBE HE SHOULD have worn a potato sack, Evain reflects as another priest pauses to stare at him. The little rush of power feels good, but he's trying to be low-key here.

Most people in the Bright Cathedral, however, pay more attention to the young man leading Evain through the halls. Karis Cooper is the auburn-haired, freckle-faced Voice of Vara. Just eighteen years old, he might be even better at keeping a secret than Evain himself.

Evain senses absolutely no desire in Karis's gaze, which may have something to do with the flash of metal he spots on the young man's finger. That ring is definitely new, and Evain has lived among humans long enough to recognize the symbol.

Engagement and marriage are strange concepts to Evain. Willingly tying himself down to another person? Pledging his life to theirs? It sounds rather like a binding contract between a mage and a god, or a mage and a demon. Temporary contracts are bad enough, but permanent ones rarely end well for the demon. He ends up either trapped in an array or killed so the mage can use his power unimpeded.

There are advantages to modern Charain's aversion to demons. When Evain first arrived in Lyrisenia, mages were much more eager to summon and bind. There were even some people who thought they could live forever if they shared a demon's lifespan. It never worked, though. Life-sharing requires too much trust and too few boundaries. No demon would be that willing, and no human would be that reckless.

Evain quite likes humans, but tying himself down to one is a bad idea for everyone involved. Better to move on and change his name every ten years or so, before people realize he doesn't age.

He enjoys the friendships while they last, though. That's why he's stayed in this realm so long: he likes people. "Let me see that ring."

Karis's face lights up. "Isn't it nice?" He waves his hand too quickly for Evain to actually look at the ring. "I'm annoyed that it's winter. I don't want to wear gloves over it."

Evain cooperates with an appreciative whistle. "Lovely. And congratulations on locking Ronan down. Not that there's any chance he'd refuse you, of course."

Karis waves the ring around again. "How do you know I proposed first?"

"Because I've met Ronan," Evain answers promptly, and Karis laughs.

They reach a small meeting room with a sunrise mural sweeping across the walls and sheer curtains hanging over the wide windows. A gaudy behemoth of a chair serves as a coat rack in the corner. Plain wooden chairs remain in more regular service around the rectangular table—which hosts a few more people than Evain expected.

He recognizes Ronan Vizia, of course. Leader of the Locksmiths, wanted criminal, and apparently now engaged to the Voice of Vara. Dark hair, bronze skin, and deep eyes that lock onto Karis the moment the door opens. When Karis sits next to him at the head of the table, Ronan smiles so softly that Evain feels a little embarrassed looking at him.

Then there's Captain Edith Tanner, a stout woman with a braided crown of blond hair. She's one of the few ranking members of the Radiant Order who kept her contract with Vara, which has left her mostly in charge. Given that she spent most of the past year hunting Ronan across Charain, seeing the two of them at a table together is amusing.

Evain doesn't recognize the other two people. The woman across from Ronan has deep tan skin, darker than Evain's, and pin-straight black hair to her shoulders. Her eyebrows are sharp, like the longsword at her side, and she wears a crescent moon pendant over her midnight-blue tunic. Beside her, across from Tanner, sits a plump, nervous-looking man with ink-stained fingers. His tunic is Charaini green, and his clothes are very expensive to Evain's discerning eye.

Karis introduces the strangers as Evain lounges at the other end of the table. "This is Sir Haldis, a paladin of Sephine." He gestures to the woman first, then the man. "And this is Telvin, a herald from the palace."

"Pleasure to meet you both," Evain drawls, before remembering himself. He straightens in his chair instead of sensually draping himself over it. "I'm Evain Marha, wandering philanthropist and philanderer. Recent good deeds include risking my charming skin to help unbind your gods from cruel imprisonment. Which I would have done for free, out of the goodness of my heart, but it just so happens you'll want to repay me." Looking at Karis and Tanner, Evain weighs his next words. Their god's jurisdiction includes truth; best to be forthright. "I'll cut to the chase. I need an army."

To Evain's disappointment, nobody gasps with shock.

Haldis's sharp eyebrows draw together, and Telvin shifts in his seat. Ronan opens his mouth as if to say something, then glances at Karis and sits back in his chair.

"Why do you need an army?" Tanner says. "And why in Vara's name should we give one to you?"

Evain spreads his hands on the table, wishing he had a map to dramatically point to. Ronan always had convenient maps to gesture at during Locksmith meetings. Instead, all Evain can do is fix his gaze on each person at the table in turn. "The Northern Barrier was tied to the spell that bound your gods. Without the Binding, it will fail within the year."

This time, the room falls dead silent. Evain's sense of drama is appeased.

Karis's eyes flash with golden Radiance, and he pales under his freckles. "He's telling the truth."

Tanner swears, and Telvin makes a warding gesture. Charain has relied on the Northern Barrier to keep demons out for the past two centuries. Losing it—especially as the country still reels from the Unbinding—is a catastrophic threat.

"I come from Lyrisenia," Evain says, which is partly true. Lyrisenia was the first human land he crossed to, two hundred and fifty years ago. "Things were bad when I left, and they've only gotten worse. Vaidkos, demons, rifts between realms. Without the barrier, no matter how strong your gods are, Charain will face the same fate within the century."

Telvin sits up straight, hands clasped earnestly. "One hundred years? That's plenty of time. We can call our finest mages together and fix the barrier. We can build a better one."

"No," two voices chime in at once. Haldis and Karis, acolytes of the moon and sun.

Haldis continues first at Karis's gesture. "Mother Sephine spoke to me in a dream last night. She told me to come to the Bright Cathedral and listen to the promiscuous man." Evain hears a snort of derision from Ronan. "She also reminded me that my mission is not restricted by arbitrary borders."

Karis props his elbows on the table. "Vara said similar. Plus, Sir Arthur and his necromancer rode in from Lanwatch two days ago, and they had the same concerns about vaidkos activity on both sides of the border. Fuck, I killed a vaidkos myself the other month, just two weeks out from Ostaris."

Tanner winces when the Voice of Vara swears.

"The trouble is the rifts," Evain says. "They allow demons into this realm without the control of a summoning mage, and one rift left untended spawns more in the vicinity. The landscape warps around them, which is very, very bad. Vaidkos are the least of your worries if rifts start popping up across Charain. You'll lose entire harvests to wild magic flares. If you're very unlucky, greater demons will cross over. Demons of death, hunger, desire, and other unsavory elements. Dangerous, intelligent demons. However." Leaning back in his chair, Evain twists the end of his braid around his finger. "I have good news."

A suitably dramatic silence hangs around the table. Much better.

Evain continues with a smile. "I know how to close the rifts, and I can teach others to do it too. Give me a group of capable mages and paladins, and I'll lead them north to start cleaning up Lyrisenia." He looks directly at Karis, who wields the real power in this room. "The barrier will hold for another year. Help me use that year to restore my homeland, and you won't have to worry about yours meeting the same fate."

The Northern Barrier was only ever an awkward splint over the Lyrisenia problem. It's long past time to set the bone.

Karis's eyes gleam gold. "How many mages?"

"We can't just give him an army," Tanner interrupts. "I know you're all used to your clandestine criminal conspiracies—" She glares daggers at Ronan. "—but this is big enough that we need to coordinate with the crown and the military."

"I'll go." Haldis touches her pendant. "I don't need to coordinate with anyone but my god."

Evain says, "At least three mages with a talent for fighting. Or fighters with a talent for magecraft. Send the army after us when you've sorted out the politics."

Settling back with a smile, he listens as they debate. There are logistics to be sorted out and jurisdictions to be determined. Further meetings to be arranged with the crown, council, and military. But Evain knew as soon as Karis asked, "How many mages?" that his demand would be granted.

Within two hours, he has his shopping list checked off. He won't get an entire army; the Radiant Order and—assuming the crown's agreement—Charaini army will stay in Charain, guarding various borders. But Evain will get two Varans, two Sephinians, and a necromancer to lead into the wilderness. A pretty good day at the market.

Haldis leaves first, saying she has a fellow Sephinian to invite. A harried Telvin leaves next, with a sheaf of stressful notes to convey to the High Council. Then Karis, with Tanner at his heels.

Only Evain and Ronan remain in the chamber. Ronan was silent for most of the meeting, but when they're alone, he asks, "Is this why you found me three years ago?"

"Yes," Evain answers. "I knew the barrier was linked to the Binding, and I knew Charain wouldn't help me while the barrier stood."

"Did you consider mentioning that to the rest of us?"

"Not even once."

Ronan laughs. "Fair enough."

Evain stands up and stretches his arms. "I'm not used to you talking so little during strategy parties. You usually save your brooding for after work."

Ronan moves towards the window, where bright winter sunlight diffuses through the sheer curtains. "Karis has things under control. And my skills run more towards infiltration and card tricks than military deployment."

"I suppose pickpocketing isn't very helpful here either," Evain adds. "Or kidnapping."

"Still not sure if I'm good or bad at kidnapping." Ronan pulls aside the curtain to peer out across the courtyard. "Actually, one thing I'm good at is recruitment."

Centuries of finely honed instincts alert Evain to danger. "I'm not going to like what you're about to say, am I?"

Sure enough, Ronan says, "You should take Leth."

"Absolutely not," Evain answers immediately.

Leth ka Tariel is one of the most tedious humans Evain has ever met. No sense of humor. No appreciation of Evain's many charms. No tolerance for demonic anything. Evain likes most humans quite a bit. They're very interesting and fun. That's why he's bothering with this whole altruistic mission to Lyrisenia in the first place; he doesn't want his demonic kindred to eat everyone. But Leth aggravates him like nobody else.

Ronan shrugs. "Suit yourself. But you should really take Leth."

"I really shouldn't. He's boring, and he wants to kill me."

"He only wants to kill you because you're annoying," Ronan says. "He's perfectly polite to everyone else, and he's exactly what you need."

Evain hates how right Ronan is. Leth is just an unbound hedgewitch, without access to greater power, but his grasp of magical theory and experimentation is remarkable. He's also one of the best swordfighters Evain has ever met in the human realm. Evain's looking for mages who can fight, and Leth is exactly that.

And all right, Leth isn't completely boring. He's fun to tease, at least.

"Not that I'm going to ask him," Evain says eventually. "But he won't agree."

Ronan shrugs again. "You don't know unless you ask."

Evain gives an exaggerated sigh. "He won't agree, but where is he these days?"

)O(

HE FINDS LETH eviscerating a training dummy in an otherwise empty practice hall. Dust swirls around the sword-witch's feet. His blade is a silver blur, and his hair whips after him. If the loose strands obstruct his vision, it doesn't slow his ceaseless, violent dance.

A black coat lies discarded in the dust, and Leth's slim figure is clear through his loose gray shirt. Whenever he pauses, half an instant to hold a pose before lunging into the next movement, the fabric clings to his sweat-damp body. Even from across the room, the line of his waist is clear. Evain could practically span it with both hands.

It's a shame such a fine figure is wasted on such an aggravating person.

Every so often, silver magic glitters around Leth. Flashes of light from the spell beads in his hair. The magic strengthens and quickens Leth's movements. His sword gouges through the training dummy's sackcloth skin, and straw and sawdust spill onto the floor.

Leth is scary-quick on his feet, but Evain knows him well enough to see that he's slower than usual. He can't even guess how long Leth's been out here to actually work up a sweat. The sword-witch is tired or focused enough that he hasn't noticed Evain's presence.

Evain considers interrupting Leth's artful, frenzied disembowelment of the training dummy. Then he considers the likelihood of himself getting disemboweled instead. Perhaps he should wait until Leth has sheathed the sword before calling out.

Settling against a pillar, Evain allows himself the luxury of watching. Leth might be annoying, but he's easy on the eyes.

LETH

First Leth imagines the training dummy is Anton. Next, he imagines Javius. Then his muscles and joints melt into the rhythm of his routine, and his mind sails away. He stops thinking and becomes simply a moving body. A flow of breath limned in magic.

A few Varan paladins were training when he arrived at the practice hall. Leth asked if they needed another sword to spar, and they agreed. They recognized him; Leth's been staying in a guest room at the Bright Cathedral since the Unbinding.

He knocked one woman on her ass and sent a man sprawling next. Maybe the other paladins sensed the kind of mood he was in, because suddenly he had the practice room to himself. That's fine. Training dummies last longer, and Leth needs to burn himself out right now. His lungs seize with exertion, and even his well-trained muscles scream with the constant movement. As his exhaustion builds, he can almost forget the stinging bruise around his right eye.

For a delirious moment, he imagines the training dummy has a gray shirt, a sword in its hand, and spell beads in its loose brown hair. Snarling, Leth drives his sword through the vision of himself.

Wood cracks like thunder. The battered dummy slumps on its stake, then falls to the ground. Straw and sackcloth slides from Leth's sword in a puff of dust.

Leth lowers his trembling arm, all his strength suddenly spent. He doesn't have enough spells prepared to drag himself through another routine. Breathing is harder now that he's stopped moving. His shirt sticks to his heaving chest, and even his palms feel wet beneath his gloves. By the sun's angle through the windows, he's been here for hours.

Lightheaded, he sheathes his sword and turns around to find his coat. That's when he realizes he isn't alone. Surprise pierces his exhausted daze, then settles into annoyance.

Evain Marha lounges against a pillar, his dark gaze unwavering. He lacks the decency to look abashed at being caught watching.

Leth's never seen that coat on Evain before. The dark red is eye-catching, which must be why Leth notices the way it outlines Evain's broad shoulders and crossed arms. The way it skims past his hips. An accusation Leth can't refute echoes in his head.

You reek of demon magic. It clings to you like a shroud.

Averting his gaze, Leth makes for his own discarded coat. Not ten paces from the demon-bound witch, but Leth is good at ignoring people.

When he crouches, the change in posture is dizzying. Black sweeps across his vision, and his fingers feel weak and foreign clenched in his coat. He remains crouching, head bowed, and tries to breathe. Clear his head. He refuses to faint in front of anyone, much less Evain.

Footsteps thud on the dusty floor, and Evain's boots appear in front of him. Dark leather wraps around shapely calves, before the red hem curtains off the rest of Evain's legs.

"Need some help?" Evain asks. If he's mocking, it's subtle.

With another deep breath, Leth rises to his feet, coat in hand. This close, it's impossible to ignore Evain's height. The man's at least a foot taller than Leth. Instead of making eye contact, Leth addresses a point of empty air somewhere past Evain's bicep. "What do you want?"

"That's a dangerous question," Evain purrs—the only word for the resonance in his voice. "I wanted to ask—no, before that, what's the matter with you today?"

There's no flirtation in his question, and the change of tone is so abrupt it leaves Leth reeling. When he glances up, Evain's brow furrows in something like confusion or concern.

"Nothing's the matter." Leth ducks away from Evain's piercing gaze. But before he can escape, Evain reaches out.

Leth moves on instinct. The next instant, Evain's gloved fingertips hover an inch away from Leth's chin, and Leth's own hand locks around Evain's wrist, preventing him from getting closer. Adrenaline spikes Leth's pulse, and his mind races with a dozen ways to gain the advantage, using Evain's greater size and mass against him.

But Evain doesn't struggle or move. He just cocks his head. "I see you're as quick as ever, so that's not the problem. Who managed to get a hit on you?"

Leth's mind blanks out.

The bruise shadowing his right eye is still tender when he thinks about it. He knows the purple-black is stark against his skin. He's as quick as ever, but this morning, he just fucking stood there while Anton struck him. As if all the stones of Fort Tarhaeg weighed down his limbs. It never occurred to Leth to try to stop his brother's hand.

"That's none of your concern," Leth snaps, dropping Evain's wrist. He steps back as if that will cool the heat surrounding them. "Get to your point."

He expects Evain to press the matter, but Evain just frowns, then says, "I'm leading an expedition to Lyrisenia. I need mages who can fight, and you're well qualified for that. I'd like to hire you."

"Absolutely not," Leth answers immediately.

Evain laughs at that. The sound is—aggravating. Disorienting. "I pay well."

"The pay isn't the issue." Leth irritably brushes the hair from his forehead and heads for the door.

"I pay *very* well." Evain trails after him. "I assure you, the job description suits your godly moral standards. We'll be cleaning up demons and wild magic in Lyrisenia. Sealing rifts and saving lives."

"Did Ronan put you up to this?" Leth demands as they exit into the courtyard. Winter bites through his sweat-damp shirt, helping to clear his head.

"Of course not," Evain says easily. "Despite our differences, I knew at once you were perfect for this expedition. Your skills are unparalleled and would be a valuable asset, which I am prepared to value monetarily."

Exhaling a frosty cloud, Leth regrets how far away the training hall is from the building his guest room is in. He's certain Ronan put Evain up to this. The Locksmiths have disbanded, but Ronan still acts like he's in charge when he's not bowing to Karis's every whim. Just the other day, he asked if Leth had any plans for a career change. Like he's a parent or teacher, and Leth is his listless, unemployed charge.

Maybe Ronan feels guilty for persuading Leth to join the Locksmiths in the first place. Or maybe Leth just looks so fucking useless right now, Ronan can't help himself.

"I'm not interested." Leth's boots crunch on gravel, and he pauses at a fork in the path. The correct building rises to the left. Will Evain follow him all the way to his room? Maybe he has enough strength left to punch him.

But Evain just halts next to Leth. He's a candle of vivid color in the gray and white cathedral grounds. "Alas, you wound me." Evain's usual flirtatious tone bleeds back into his voice. "The offer stands, though. If you change your mind—or if you simply want to bid us a fond farewell—we'll be departing from the northern gate at dawn, three days from now. You'll want a horse."

"Fuck off."

"See you then," Evain says, and walks away. Leth doesn't know how long his red coat is visible in the distance; he very intentionally doesn't watch him leave.

Back in his borrowed room, the first thing Leth does is pour a glass of water. Afraid to sit down in case he never stands up again, he leans against the table and sips slowly. The room is simple. A bed, table and chairs, and an adjoining bathroom. The only hint of gold is the framed painting of the sun hanging over the bed. He hasn't turned the lamps on, but enough light shines through the wide windows.

The Bright Cathedral's guest rooms are usually reserved for visiting priests. Pilgrims with nowhere else to stay—and that describes Leth himself better than he likes to admit.

Feeling a little more stable, Leth sets the water down and peels off his gloves. His wrists ache from practicing too hard. His whole body is going to ache by tomorrow. Bending over to unlace his boots, he wonders what the fuck he's doing here.

He can't hide in the Bright Cathedral forever, even if Karis would probably let him. He can't return to his family. Anton's left the city, but the rest of the ka Tariels don't think any better of him. Last month's letter to his mother hasn't received a reply.

Besides, Ostaris holds too many memories now. Leth has spent his entire life honing his emotions, digging them deep into safely controlled channels. But his visit home this morning proved he won't be able to maintain that for long if he stays.

He's too weak.

Leth sets his boots by the foot of the bed. After another sip of water, he begins a set of cooldown stretches he's rehearsed since he was a child. He doesn't have to think about the movements, which leaves his mind free to continue ruminating over his future.

That's being generous. He doesn't even know what his present looks like either.

He could join the Riverswords again, like he did after failing to enlist at age eighteen. Lose himself in the mercenary life, following orders, never having to make decisions. Fighting for coin as his only purpose.

Seated on the ground, Leth bends over one outstretched leg. Presses his forehead to his knee, breathes into the stretch, and can't help thinking about Evain's offer.

Leth doesn't like Evain. Some people are inherently incompatible, and Evain annoys him like no one else. But a quest to the fallen empire of Lyrisenia, facing demons and wild magic—Leth has to admit, the idea appeals to him.

It sounds worthy. Heroic.

Maybe if he rides that far north, he'll escape the shadow of Fort Tarhaeg.

"Sparks and ashes," Leth swears, sitting up from the stretch. "I can't actually be considering this." He slumps back against the bedside, arms wrapped around his knees, and can't keep his eyes open anymore.

Exhaustion bleeds the strength from his body. The release of a day's worth—a month's worth—of tension. Huddled on the floor, he drifts off into an uneasy half-sleep, dreamless gray patches of unconsciousness in between idle plans of what he'd pack and where he'd buy a new horse if he wanted to leave within three days. Whether he should stop by the university library and brush up on rift theory. Whether he needs new gloves for the northern winter.

Delirious fantasies, nothing more. He absolutely isn't following Evain to Lyrisenia.

EVAIN

Before dawn on the third day, Evain swans through the perfumed parlor of the Veiled Rose. A set of saddlebags hangs from his shoulder, and he hums a light tune to himself.

The woman at the front desk covers her ears with a groan. "Not you too. All the drunks have been singing that fucking ditty. It's been stuck in my head for weeks."

"Blame the bard-priests for being inspired." Evain flips his long braid over his shoulder. "Their new material is very catchy."

A series of thuds interrupts their conversation: a man walking unsteadily down the stairs. His clothing is rumpled and expensive, his cheeks stubbled and his neck dotted with lipstick and bruises. He pauses at the landing and waves a bejeweled hand up the stairs, calling out, "Goodnight, my beautiful prince!"

Every hungover noble is an opportunity. Evain catches the man's gaze, lifts his chin, and almost-smiles. He doesn't need magic for this—just his own natural charm. The man's gaze drops to Evain's lips, and he wanders over in an unsteady line.

"Don't steal my customers, Marha," the woman at the desks warns.

"I'm just borrowing him for a minute," Evain reassures her, as the hungover man finishes his serpentine journey across the cluttered parlor.

"Hello, my beautiful prince." A cloying blend of wine and roses clings to the man. "What's the price for your name? To kiss your hand? I'll pay ten gold to serve you tea."

Smile deepening, Evain revels in the man's attention. Base, unfettered desire feeds the furnace of his magic. Evain leans in, letting his fingers hover inches from the man's face. He's about to touch when he remembers the last time he tried something like this. Except that time, a slender hand strong as steel grabbed his wrist, and pretty hazel eyes glared up at him through the bruises.

Suddenly, this eager, drunken noble isn't nearly as interesting. Far too easy. Evain drops his hand with a laugh. "You can't afford my name."

The man's chest puffs up. "I'm very rich."

"I'm *very* expensive." Leaving the man stunned, Evain waves goodbye to the woman at the desk and departs the Veiled Rose.

The predawn sky is dark, and the city's rooftops are edged with frost that will melt when the sun rises. Brimming with desire's heat, Evain barely feels the cold. At the northern gate, the guards don't stop him.

They're too blindsided by his smile, followed by the touch of power Evain uses to avert their gazes—a little spell he learned from Ronan. Nobody's watching as he slips from the roadside into the surrounding woods.

The trees around Ostaris keep most of their leaves through the winter. Silver and shadows cover the hushed woods. The forest quiets around him, and the air smells green. Some might call it refreshing; Evain thinks it's just all right. Better than the dark-fogged deserts and abyssal canyons of his homeland, but he far prefers the bustle and energy and *attention* of human cities.

Evain quickly finds a clearing he's used before and sets the saddlebags down. There's a patch of perfectly flattened ground beneath an ancient, sprawling tree. Evain kicks the leaves from the packed dirt, then selects a twig. He crouches, his long coat dragging on the ground, and traces a small, precise array.

A full leather pouch materializes in a puff of smoke. Evain checks that the gold coins inside look legitimate enough, then fastens the pouch to his belt.

The next array is a little more complicated.

With every rune and symbol, the predawn shadows deepen. A poison-sweet song scratches at Evain's soul. Ignoring the familiar call, he retreats several paces. The desire magic he gathered from the hungover nobleman twists like a blood-red ribbon around his arm before he releases it into the array.

The runes pulse like a heartbeat. Smoke rises, swirling and reflecting the red light, then coalesces into concrete form to complete the summoning.

A massive, coal-black stallion stands under the tree. Fully tacked, with long mane and tail flowing gently in the wind. The horse stiffens, startled, then relaxes into his surroundings. His ears flick back and forth curiously, and he turns towards Evain with his—

"That really won't do," Evain says, though the glowing red eyes *are* pretty impressive. Regretfully, he uses a wisp of magic to change the stallion's eyes to a more ordinary deep brown. Then he puts his hands on his hips and finalizes a few orders, power resonating through his voice to enforce obedience. "Now, the rules are different here. You must not kill, eat, or otherwise harm people, unless I tell you to first. Not even accidentally on purpose. I'm not stupid. Understood?"

The demonic stallion snorts, then pushes his nose into Evain's chest.

Evain pats his neck. "Good boy. I'll call you Daziroth."

☽○☾

EVAIN SITS ASTRIDE his new mount as the sun rises and the rest of the party gathers. First to arrive are the Sephinians, including Haldis, whom he met at the Bright Cathedral. Her fellow paladin, Marta, is a wisp of a woman with light brown skin and a few tight curls escaping from her fur-lined hat. Well-wrapped against the cold, she appears half-asleep. She and Haldis arrive on matched bay horses, and Haldis greets Evain before settling into silence. Marta waves slightly, then covers her mouth in a yawn.

Haldis's stoic gaze betrays none of the faint attraction Evain feels from her. He feels nothing at all from Marta—either she's too tired to appreciate his many charms, or her interests don't include men.

Daziroth cranes his neck around to lip at the toe of Evain's boot. "You'll regret biting my foot," Evain warns.

The horse flicks his ears back and forth, then lowers his head.

A third woman rides up not long after. Her sun-emblazoned tunic is clearly visible even from a distance. She stops to talk to one of the gate guards, and a rich laugh rings out before she trots towards the waiting group.

"Are you Evain Marha?" she calls out. The white of her tunic sets off the warmth in her dark skin, and she sits tall in the saddle. A cream-colored scarf is flung around her neck, tails fluttering in the wind.

"You must be Sir Freya." Evain's pretty sure he saw her at the Bright Cathedral on the day of the Unbinding, but they've never met. "Tanner spoke highly of you."

"She better have," Freya says cheerfully. If she's one of the ones who tried to blast the Locksmiths with Radiance, she doesn't show any open animosity at this point. On the contrary—Evain feels the familiar warmth of lust in her appreciative glance.

"I must say Tanner did you one grave disservice," Evain says, with a habitual grin. "She failed to mention how very handsome you are."

Freya laughs loudly. "She always does."

The next members of their party arrive together. Another paladin, a little too blond for Evain's tastes, but a nice set of shoulders. Sir Arthur Davorin is the very picture of the Varan golden boy; Evain can practically see the morality glistening along his chiseled jaw. Beside him rides a dark-haired young man carrying a power far crueler than Evain's. Not all demonic contracts are alike, and death itself sits in the depths of the necromancer's soul.

Shae Nightven seems to have his power well under control, though.

Evain already knew Arthur by reputation—and his history with Ronan—but he officially met the paladin two days ago at Karis's introduction. Shae was busy elsewhere at the time. The pair are to be Evain's guides past the border and into the Lanwatch Riverswords troop.

Arthur rides his impressive chestnut mare over to talk to Freya first, while Shae nudges his dark bay towards Evain. "Is this everyone?"

His gaze is unsettling. None of the paladins have sensed anything awry with Evain's demonic nature, but Shae looks like he's staring straight into Evain's soul.

Any demon-bound human carries a mark in their aura, for those sensitive enough to feel it, just like Evain can sense Shae's own necromancy. But it would take a truly sensitive mage to tell that Evain's aura is innate to him, rather than contracted power, when Evain is as well-shielded as he is.

"We're still waiting on one more," Evain says with confidence, though he's not actually certain the pretty sword-witch will come. Most people don't reject Evain's offers—but Leth isn't most people.

"All right." Brow furrowing briefly, Shae twists one of the rings off his right hand and pockets it. When he speaks again, it's in a language Evain hasn't heard in quite a few years. "Marha, like the flower? Where in Lyrisenia are you from?"

"The east," Evain answers in Lyrisenian as well. "Near the ruins of Aliso. I crossed the border through Etenia, and you could say I'm returning the long way around." Almost true, except Aliso wasn't a ruin when Evain first prowled its streets.

"We've never been neighbors, then." Shae glances at the sky and switches back to Charaini. "It's getting late."

"My little friend may have slept in," Evain says, though the thought of regimented, stickler Leth sleeping in is ludicrous.

He sighs in relief when Shae rides back to Arthur's side. The necromancer doesn't seem to have identified him.

The sun creeps higher above the horizon. Idly unbuttoning his long coat—he'll warm up as he rides—Evain watches slow merchant carts roll past them into the city. A rare emotion wells inside him: disappointment. Which is puzzling. He never thought Leth would agree to this journey in the first place, so why should he be disappointed to be correct?

He's still mulling over this peculiar emotion when trotting hooves catch his ears. A small figure on a pale gray horse approaches. Wrapped from his fingertips to his neck in his usual black, Leth reins in at the edge of the group.

The bruise around his eye has mostly faded.

Evain beams and claps his hands. Daziroth's ears flick towards the sound. "All right, this is everyone. Leth, these are Haldis and Marta. You may have met

Freya already, and this is Arthur and Shae." He points to each person in turn, and his grin deepens as he gestures towards Leth. "Everyone, this is Leth ka Tariel, my charming—"

"Finish that sentence and I walk."

"Suit yourself," Evain says. "But whatever they imagine now will be worse than whatever I would say."

Leth glares. "Somehow I doubt it."

As expected, Leth is no fun at all. But Evain's disappointment is entirely gone.

LETH

Leth doesn't know if this journey is the right decision, but it has to be better than losing himself in the
shadow of Fort Tarhaeg. And he talked with Ronan
and Karis to confirm Evain isn't secretly leading everyone
into some sort of evil demonic ritual. Karis said Radiant
Vara approves, and that's not an opinion Leth takes lightly.

He's not exactly thrilled to be traveling with a
necromancer, but at least Shae is quiet. No constant
flirting and teasing and unbuttoning the top buttons of
his shirt as he—

Leth relaxes his hands on the reins when his new
horse tugs at the bit. She's a steady, sturdy horse, with a
wiry winter coat. Her name at the stable was Star.

At least Evain has the decency to leave Leth alone for
the rest of the morning. Leth tunes out his inane banter
with Freya. They seem to be getting along well.

"Riders ahead," Marta says near noon, her voice thin as a harp string. Leth's ears are a moment slower to pick up the approaching hoofbeats. He doesn't think much of it; they've passed a number of merchant carts, messengers, and pilgrims already. The roads in and out of Ostaris are busy even as winter deepens.

Then soldiers ride into view, and Leth flinches inside at the gray uniforms. The bronze badges glinting on their chests. A dozen Dravan soldiers, led by a captain with green braid at her shoulders.

Just when I was feeling good about getting out of town.

Leth nudges Star farther to the side of the road, eager to let the Dravans pass. Irrational tension claws his stomach. There's no real reason to worry. Dravan captains don't have stop and search authority, so there's no reason for a confrontation.

Except as the two parties cross paths, Leth recognizes Captain Gannet. She served in his uncle's regiment before he retired. By her widening eyes, she recognizes Leth too.

Surprise twisting into an ugly scowl, Gannet reins her horse in. "Leth ka Tariel?" Her soldiers halt behind her. "I want a word with you."

Leth's getting really tired of hearing his full name called out. Reining Star in too, he tells Evain and the others, "Don't wait for me. I'll catch up."

He doesn't want to make a scene, and his new companions don't need to hear about his embarrassing family baggage.

But the party doesn't ride on. Arthur actually nudges his mare towards Leth, as if he's going to act as Leth's protective escort, until Evain drawls, "Over here, brave Sir Arthur, can't you see he wants privacy with the lady?"

Leth isn't used to feeling grateful towards Evain. Schooling his expression, he rides closer to the Dravan troop. "It's been a while, Captain Gannet."

Her scowl deepens. "Don't be fucking polite with me."

"Then how can I help you?" Leth says, which is still probably too polite, judging from her glare.

Behind him, he hears his party riding away. He ignores them, just like he ignores the whispers between the Dravans. Gannet's troop isn't based in Fort Tarhaeg, and few of them should recognize him by sight, but every Dravan in the army knows his name by now. The Tariel traitor who severed them from Valor.

Gannet gives her soldiers a hand signal to hold still. "Your uncle spoke well of you, you know."

That would be news to Leth. Like most of the Tariel elders, his uncle's praise was always directed towards Anton, not the small, bookish failure of a younger brother.

"He thought you had potential, as a kid," Gannet continues. "Dedicated, he called you. I didn't know you well, but I always thought it was a shame you never enlisted." Her scowl softens, and the hurt in her eyes is far worse than the anger. "I want to know why you did it."

Leth takes a deep breath and forces himself to look her square in the eyes.

Ordinary soldiers didn't know the contracts were false before the Unbinding broke them. They weren't at fault. Gannet served and worked hard for decades, building a career and life on the belief her magic was god-given. Leth's not the one who lied to her, but he's the one who took that lie away. Her sword is weaker now, perhaps forever, because of him.

Facing Gannet is harder than facing his brother, who was complicit in the Binding.

"I know this won't help, and you may never believe it," Leth says. "But it was the right thing to do."

Gannet exhales. "You're right. It doesn't help." She lifts her hand, and the Dravans start moving towards Ostaris. After another long moment staring at Leth, she shakes her head and trots away.

Leth counts three breaths to lock up his emotions, then turns Star around.

Most of the group is waiting fifty paces down the road. Only Evain remains in earshot, posed like a portrait on his massive black stallion. His red coat and the horse's tail ripple in the wind. One of Evain's hands is loose on the reins, and the other rests casually against his thigh.

"Are you done chatting?" Evain says, as if he hadn't heard everything. "She was attractive, in a rugged way. But I think she's a little too old for you."

The teasing doesn't annoy Leth as much as usual. He's just grateful Evain isn't asking questions, and that he sent the rest of the party ahead. They're going to be his colleagues for the next few weeks or months, and he'd prefer to keep his baggage private.

So instead of telling Evain to fuck off, Leth says, "Thank you."

The shock on Evain's face is rather rewarding.

FORGETTING THE INCIDENT isn't as easy as riding away, though. Leth is still silently stewing on it by the time they halt for lunch. The riverbank is a common stopping site for travelers, and a handful of guild merchants keep food and supply stalls there to take advantage of the traffic. Rings of benches around fire pits offer a place to sit.

There are other travelers around, which Leth still isn't used to when traveling with Evain. He never went as deep into hiding as Ronan and the rest of the Locksmiths—at least, not until after he stole the Dravansword. But it's still weird being on a quest that isn't a secret.

They picket the horses in range of water and grass, and Evain ties his horse much farther away from the others. The stallion doesn't seem interested in the available grass. His head swivels around, constantly watching.

Leth thinks about Gannet and Anton and everything while he settles next to the rest of the group around one of the firepits. It's stupid. He should be able to let go. But the confrontation gnaws at him, and he finishes his food without tasting it.

He barely hears the others talking. His hand itches for his sword, with the need to hit something. Work himself into exhaustion again, so he can stop thinking. But there are no training dummies here, and he can't drive himself into the ground when he's on a job. He just has to deal with the itch.

The others carry on the conversation just fine without him. Especially Evain and Freya, who seem like two of a kind. Marta becomes much more talkative too when morning's over. Shae doesn't say much from his position plastered under one of Arthur's arms, but he answers Haldis's practical questions about the road to Lyrisenia and the state of the Lanwatch Riverswords.

When he's done eating, Leth stands up. He can't sit still anymore. "I'm going to check on the horses."

Evain catches up to him three steps later. "The horses could use ten more minutes' rest. In the meantime, might I have the tremendous honor of sparring with you, fair sword-witch?"

Temptation halts Leth in his tracks.

This is hardly the first time Evain has asked to spar with him. Back in the Locksmiths, Evain used to ask incessantly, especially after the first time he saw Leth lay Ronan flat on his back. Leth always refused.

But he's in a weird mood today, and maybe taking it out on Evain wouldn't be so bad.

"All right." Leth unbuckles the sword and knife from his belt. "No blades, no magic." He doesn't trust himself with a blade right now, and he doesn't actually want to skewer Evain.

Evain sighs. "Agreed, though dueling to death would be very romantic."

Okay. Maybe he wants to skewer Evain a little bit.

Leth sets his blades down on the bench, already feeling his nerves starting to settle despite Evain's aggravation. He unfastens his coat as well.

"Oh, I love duels," Freya says. "Who wants to bet with me?"

Haldis scoffs. "I don't know about your Radiant Order, but *our* vows forbid gambling."

"Yes, yes, it's very bad." Marta's head bobs, and she moves to sit very close to Freya. "Extremely forbidden."

Then she leans up to whisper into Freya's ear, and Haldis rolls her eyes.

Whatever they're betting, Leth doesn't care. He drops his coat on the bench and looks up in time to see Evain's coat sliding from his shoulders too. The movement pulls Evain's shirt across his shoulders, stretching the collar to bare a broader expanse of tan skin. Next, Evain rolls up his sleeves, revealing well-muscled forearms. His gloves are already gone, and there's something distracting about the precise movements of his hands.

Freya whistles appreciatively, and Leth feels a stab of irritation. He stalks away from the fire pit. "First to the ground?"

"Perfect." Evain follows close, and murmurs for Leth's ears alone: "I've always wanted to see you on your back."

Annoyance flares again. Leth's never sure whether it's better or worse that he knows Evain isn't singling him out. The man's like this with everyone.

"Want me to count you in?" Arthur calls out from the benches. When Leth nods, he doesn't waste time. "On three. Ready? One, two, three."

Neither strikes at first.

Leth circles slowly, light on his feet, and Evain mirrors him. All of Leth's senses sharpen into focus. He doesn't hear the voices of the guild merchants and travelers downriver, but he hears the slight crunch of Evain's boots in the dirt. Leth's blood heats against the winter's chill, all his annoyance gone. Only anticipation remains.

The size advantage is clearly Evain's, but Leth has been fighting people bigger than him since childhood.

He knows how to use his speed and agility to overcome brute strength. What he doesn't know is Evain's hand-to-hand experience. He's only seen Evain fight with magic before, usually at range.

Evain's torso tenses under his shirt, telegraphing his movement an instant early. He lunges forward with an explosive punch—clearly a feint. Leth shifts his weight and spins around the real kick that follows. The world narrows to Evain's shoulder, brushing his in a whisper of friction and heat.

Leth drives an elbow into the other man's back, then barely swings his head away from Evain's tensed fingers. He dances back, excitement brewing in his veins. That wasn't a punch to the head, it was a grab for his hair. Fighting dirty. Evain is clearly more than just a ranged fighter.

A grin curves Leth's lips. This is exactly what he needs today.

They meet again and again, trading blows that rarely land, designed more to test than to harm. Freya and Marta's cheers are a distant accompaniment; all Leth hears is Evain's breath. All he sees is a gleam of sweat on Evain's neck as they both warm with the exertion. Evain's dark hair falls loose from its braid. The tempo quickens until Leth isn't thinking anymore, only moving. Always moving. Always darting back at the last instant. He has to keep his distance to win this.

The next round should be more of the same. Neither of them has tired yet. Leth sidesteps Evain's next move, raising his knee and bracing for—

His mistake is looking at Evain's face.

The intensity of Evain's gaze is arresting. A shocking totality of focus, all centered on Leth. As if the two of them are the only ones in the world. Loose strands of hair flow away from Evain's chiseled features, and sunlight catches in Evain's dark eyes.

Leth falters for half a step, and that's all it takes.

Evain's hand closes burning hot around his shoulder. With a strength far surpassing anything he'd shown before, he shoves Leth down. Leth can't recover and can't resist.

Cold earth knocks the breath from his lungs and the sense from his head. Stunned, Leth blinks at Evain poised above him. Evain's hair falls around them like a curtain, a strand of it tickling Leth's neck. Evain's hand is still hot around his shoulder.

And somehow, Evain's other hand ended up cradled beneath Leth's head. Fingers gently curving into his hair, cushioning his skull from the hard ground.

Leth's blood pulses, and he can't feel anything besides the points of heated contact. He can't think about anything besides the dark light in Evain's eyes. Evain looks just as stunned as Leth feels. Apparently neither of them had expected Evain to win.

Evain shouldn't have won. Except Leth was distracted at just the wrong moment. Except Evain had that inexplicable surge of strength.

Someone applauds. By Marta's musical laugh, she's won the bet.

"I yield," Leth whispers.

Evain's lips part as if he's about to say something unbearable. But he restrains himself, sliding his fingers from Leth's hair before rising to his feet. He offers a hand. "Here."

Ignoring the hand, Leth stands up on his own. "Good fight," he says, more for the others' sake than Evain's. He doesn't need them to think the duel meant anything. That there was anything strange about the result. "I'll check the horses now."

Keeping a wide berth from Evain, Leth gathers his coat and blades. He still feels Evain's touch burning into his shoulder. Gently cradling the back of his head. The bruises are welcome. The tenderness is not.

At least the fight worked. Leth isn't thinking about the Dravans anymore.

EVAIN

Someone wants to fuck Evain. Which would be splendid, except Evain doesn't know *who*.

He's been trying to figure it out ever since his spar with Leth a few days ago. The sensation in the middle of the fight was obvious; that instant rush of power always means someone is laying lascivious eyes on his body. Evain can't blame his mysterious admirer—it's a great body—but maybe he should have kept his coat on to give Leth a fair fight. They agreed not to use blades or magic, after all.

Oh, well. The outcome of the fight wasn't important. Evain had just wanted to get Leth out of whatever bad mood the Dravan woman left him in. It seems to have worked; Leth is back to his ordinary quiet self.

The more important matter remains: who wants to

fuck Evain? Ever since that fight, the sensation has continued, on and off.

Evain contemplates his options as they ride one afternoon. Gray skies hang overhead, layers of heavy clouds threatening rain. The next town is still three hours' ride away. Evain takes up the rear, trying to figure out which of his companions is lusting over him.

Arthur and Shae set the pace ahead, and Evain crosses them off first. The paladin and necromancer are so wrapped up in each other, they can't spare a single thread of desire for anyone else. Whenever they dismount, they're practically glued together.

Leth rides just behind them, and Evain contemplates his slim figure. His posture is perfect, as if he's on parade instead of traipsing through the woods. If anything, Leth seems colder and quieter now than before the Unbinding. He hasn't warmed up to the paladins and Shae yet—though to be fair, Evain can't remember how long it took the rest of the Locksmiths to befriend him.

And Leth never warmed up to Evain.

No, definitely not Leth. Evain continues his contemplation. Perhaps Freya? She's three pints of fun poured into a single glass, and certainly not shy. Evain has a feeling there wouldn't be any question about whether she was ogling him, if she was.

Marta shows no sign of interest in men, whether she's half-asleep before lunch or wide awake after. Her partner Haldis would certainly be fun—she seems like the sort of law-abiding stickler who turns into a kinky, glorious mess behind closed doors. Evain won't rule Haldis out completely.

His musings end abruptly when Daziroth veers towards the side of the road. Swearing, Evain jerks on the reins and hooks back his heel, far more roughly than he'd treat a mortal horse. A fat rabbit darts to safety through the underbrush.

"I'll feed you later," Evain hisses under his breath. Summoning demon mounts has certain inconveniences; Daziroth is more carnivorous than expected.

The horse snorts in annoyance but continues along the road. Before Evain can resume contemplating the mystery of who wants to fuck him, Freya slows her mount to keep pace with him, well behind the others.

"Beautiful day, isn't it?" She gestures to the clouds.

"Don't tempt the storm gods," Evain says. "How can I help you, Sir Paladin?"

Freya nudges her horse closer and lowers her voice. "I just wanted to make it clear that I'm calling dibs."

Raising an eyebrow, Evain follows her gaze. She's looking at Haldis and Marta—not Leth, which is a strange relief. Evain is certain she and Leth would be a bad fit. "Which one?"

Freya's grin widens. "Both."

Evain laughs. He's always admired ambition. "They're all yours, if you can catch them."

Movement catches his attention ahead, and Evain looks up to see Leth twisting around in the saddle, looking back. Their eyes meet.

Then Daziroth takes advantage of Evain's distraction and lunges towards the side of the road. Evain swears loudly, while Freya laughs even louder. By the time Evain wrestles Daziroth into obedience again, all he sees up ahead is Leth's back, straight and unyielding as a sword.

) O (

THE STORM CRASHES into them an hour from town. At the first few raindrops, the entire party breaks into a trot without discussion beyond Marta's colorful swearing. Evain tips his head back, enjoying the icy rain. Not quite cold enough for snow, but bone-chilling. Refreshing.

They don't have rain like this where he comes from.

Then the clouds shatter and unleash the rest of the storm. Evain's coat keeps the worst of it away, but the cold pounds against his shoulders. He exerts the faintest hint of demonic power to protect himself from the worst of it. By the flashes of pearl and gold light ahead, the rest of the party is casting weather charms too. Radiant Vara's heat and Cold Sephine's reflection. Everyone except—Evain doesn't sense any magic from Leth. He rides up as Leth tugs his hood up over his head.

"Did you forget to braid a weather charm into your pretty hair?"

Leth's mare pays no heed to Daziroth's wagging ears, and Leth doesn't look up at Evain's question. The black hood hides his eyes.

"I could help," Evain says. "Just sit still, and let me—"

"Don't." Leth nudges his mare another foot away. "I don't need your demon magic to deal with a bit of rain."

Evain grits his teeth. "Suit yourself." He kicks Daziroth forward, taking the lead. The demon horse's great hooves splash across the road, and Evain pulls his hood over his head to keep his eyes clear.

Leth's distaste shouldn't bother him as much as it does. Evain is used to getting side-eyed, even when people believe he's human. Many cultures he's dabbled in hold suspicion towards demon-bound mages. The Charaini save most of their distrust for necromancers, for historically understandable reasons, but certain pockets of society still prefer not to associate with anyone with a demon contract.

Strangely, Leth doesn't seem to hate Shae nearly as much as he hates Evain, and Evain hasn't the faintest clue why. Logic and custom should surely dictate that he give the necromancer a far wider berth.

Humans can be so peculiar. Evain should be used to that by now.

$$\mathbf{)O(}$$

THEY'RE ALL SOAKED by the time they reach town. None of them are weather-witches, and their charms can only do so much against rain whipping from every direction. Evain's shoulders are heavy with the constant downpour, and cold droplets slide past his hood, along his jaw, down the back of his neck. He would kill for a hot bath—literally, if he had to.

"If the inn is full, I'm taking drastic measures," he mutters darkly.

Daziroth is the only one close enough to hear him through the rain. The horse ignores him, his own ears tucked back against the wet. His luxurious mane plastered against his neck, he gives off an air of feeling betrayed by the mortal world.

The Dancing Hog Inn is rather nicer than the hovels the Locksmiths used to board in. Judging by a glimpse through the windows, the tavern downstairs is bustling with travelers and locals avoiding the rain. The stables out back are spacious, and the stablehands very polite, though they have to shout over the rattle of water on the roof. They usher the party into the wide-open barn aisle instead of making them dismount in the drenched yard.

"Please tell me there are rooms available." Evain dismounts. "Lie if you have to—I can afford to kick someone out." He can always summon more gold, after all.

"No need for that," says the stablehand who hurries towards him. The young woman has a crooked nose and easy smile. Evain feels a flush of desire from her as soon as they make eye contact. "Normally we'd make you rent the room before taking a stall, but with this weather, well. Let's get this beautiful boy—whoa there!"

The young woman jumps a step back as Daziroth swings his head around. No flash of teeth, but the menacing aura is unmistakable.

"Daisy doesn't bite." Evain pats Daziroth's neck in warning. "But if you can point me to a stall, I'll put him away myself."

Relieved, the stablehand points out everything Evain needs, then rushes off to help take care of Freya's horse, who's fussing at the clattering raindrops but looks much more manageable than Daziroth. The Sephinians' matched bays and Arthur and Shae's horses are perfectly calm. Evain can't see Leth or his horse past the rest of the group.

Arthur walks over. "I can head inside to rent rooms for us. Looks like you're a bit busy with this one."

Evain wrangles Daziroth's head away from the horse in the stall next door, where he's trying to make friends again. "You're a fair and just man, truly worthy of your contract." The compliments flow easily from Evain's lips. "That would be lovely."

Shae catches up, carrying his saddle. "You're leaving Duchess alone?" he asks Arthur. "Who are you, and what have you done with my paladin?"

Very few things make Evain feel like a voyeur. The way Arthur smiles at *my paladin* is one for the list. Like a sunrise, like sugar, so sweet Evain's teeth hurt. "I trust you to take care of her. Unless you want to go in and talk to the innkeeper instead?"

"No, thanks," Shae replies immediately. "Go do your talking-to-people thing. Charm a discount out of them. I'll stay out with the horses."

Arthur laughs and leans over the saddle in Shae's arms to kiss him. Evain turns away as Shae's eyes flutter closed, feeling strangely—envious.

Until he catches a glimpse of the man walking past him down the aisle, and the sight stuns him so badly, he can't feel anything else.

Evain has spent two hundred and fifty years wandering the human realm. He spent an entire year once luxuriating on Etenian pleasure boats, and he's watched a thousand Ellaran veil dances. Men, women, people who are both or neither. Evain has tasted the full gamut of humanity, but somehow nobody has ever fascinated him quite like the drenched and bedraggled Leth ka Tariel.

All of them are soaked by the rain, and Leth worst of all. His hood is down around his shoulders, and his hair plasters dark to his skull, outlining the elegant silhouette of his neck. A few strands stick against his cheek. Water beads along his skin, reflecting lamplight. He looks ethereal, inhuman, against the dusty stable backdrop.

Evain's arms itch with the urge to wrap around Leth's thin shoulders. He craves the chance to lick the raindrops from Leth's jaw, and exhale heat between his lips. To warm him up, from the inside out.

As if he feels the pressure of Evain's gaze, Leth glances up. His delicate brow furrows in a glare, which Evain meets with a lazy salute. Leth's frown only deepens.

Sighing, Evain returns to scraping the water off Daziroth's coat. It must have been too long since he last fucked anyone, if he's having wild, unwelcome thoughts about Leth. He needs a good flirt, or something more, to take the edge off.

Luckily, there's a busy tavern just waiting for him across the stableyard. Plenty of tipsy strangers to help him forget about tedious sword-witches for the night.

LETH

Leth has never been so grateful to squeeze his way into a crowded tavern. The shock of warmth and laughter is welcome after the cold rain. He'd be more grateful if he could fall straight into bed, but he needs a key and a room number from whoever has them. And he could probably do with a bite to eat first.

He flags down a serving boy and orders whatever they have that's hot. Then he stands at the edge of the room and searches for a familiar face.

The Dancing Hog's tavern is a wide, spacious hall, with a bar on either side of the room. A truly magnificent fireplace crackles away on the back wall. On each side of the ornate brick chimney, a painted hog cavorts in dancer's ribbons. They have little wings. Plush chairs and round tables circle around the fireplace, while the rest of the hall hosts rows of trestle tables.

Crowds of locals and travelers converge, some sitting on the benches, some sitting on the tables themselves. Mingled voices fill the space up to the rafters. Far too many people for Leth's comfort, but he doesn't need to be comfortable. He just needs a place to sit.

Evain is nowhere in sight. Not that Leth cares where Evain is.

Movement catches his eye—Sir Arthur waving at him from a trestle table. His hair is wet and his shoulders dark with rain, but otherwise he appears surprisingly unaffected by the downpour. Shae sits beside him, his pale face reddened from the cold outside or the heat within. They already have food, and there's a space clear on the bench across from them.

"Thanks for saving me a seat." Leth dumps his waterproof bag under the bench and peels off his wet coat. He drapes the drenched garment over the bench next to him, letting it drip onto the floor.

"Of course," Arthur says. "I grabbed us the last few rooms in the inn too. Did you order already?"

Leth nods.

Shae looks up from his dinner, his gray eyes startlingly clear. "Haldis and Marta went upstairs already. Freya and Evain are still down here somewhere."

"Thanks," Leth says again, unsure why Shae felt the need to tell him that. Just because he looked around for Evain earlier, doesn't mean he actually needs to know where he is.

By all rights, Shae should bother Leth more than he does. He's demon-bound, and he traffics in death. Necromancy is legal in Charain—with many restrictions—but Leth was always taught that law and morality were separate, overlapping concepts. Just because something is legal doesn't make it right, and associating with demons pollutes the soul.

But Shae is quiet, not overbearing. Leth appreciates that. He's not inherently, constantly infuriating, like—

"Oh, Evain's over there." Arthur points. Then a frown crosses his golden brow. "Huh."

Leth twists around. A group of patrons has cleared out from their end of the table, and past the empty tankards and mostly-empty trays of food, Leth sees Evain.

The man's red coat is gone, uncovering a white silk shirt that makes his skin seem to glow. Everything makes his skin seem to glow. He lounges in one of the plush chairs by the fireplace, his knee hooked over the arm of it and the tail of his hair draped over his shoulder. The damp strands give him a lazy, seductive look. One hand props up his chin, and the other holds a tankard of something.

And he's giving his signature smirk to the handsome farmer in the chair next to him. Like a moth drawn to a flame, the farmer leans forward. He sits so close to the edge of his seat, Leth thinks he might fall off it.

Evain lifts his tankard to his lips, baring the long line of his throat to the firelight. Leth turns around in disgust as the farmer leans in closer.

"I don't mean to pry," Arthur says carefully, "but are you all right with that?" He has an odd expression on his face. Beside him, Shae focuses intently on his stew.

"Why wouldn't I be?" Leth winces at the sharpness of his voice. He takes a slow breath and adjusts his tone. "Evain always does that. It's how his magic works."

Arthur glances over Leth's shoulder, and Leth refuses to imagine what Evain is doing that makes Arthur frown like that. Then he can't imagine anything anyway, because Arthur's next words make Leth completely blank out: "I just thought you two were together."

The tavern noise muffles beneath Leth's shocked disbelief.

"We're not," Leth says when his brain revives. "Assuredly not. That would be ridiculous." The serving boy appears at his elbow before Arthur can answer. Leth leans back to make room for the tray and fishes a couple coppers from his belt. "Thank you—could you get me a pint of your strongest, please?"

He doesn't drink much. Another thing his ancestors disapprove of. But he could really use a beer right now—to chase the cold from his bones, and the idea of being *together* with Evain from his head.

The three of them eat quietly until Leth's beer appears. After he's taken the first sip of the heavy stout, Shae looks up from across the table. "How long have you known Evain, anyway? Do you know him well?"

Leth takes a larger sip. "Almost two years. We only worked together. He joined Ronan before I did." Too late, Leth remembers Arthur's history with Ronan. "Sorry, I shouldn't have…"

Arthur waves his hand. "It's fine. Ronan and I have talked."

"You call that talking?" Shae pushes his empty bowl aside. "You just stood next to him in the garden for half an hour and then clapped his shoulder."

Leth chokes on his next gulp of beer.

Arthur laughs. "That was enough for now." He sets his fork down too, making eye contact with Shae. After whatever silent communication they engage in, Shae stands up, and Arthur tells Leth, "Your room is number thirty-seven, by the way, on the third floor. Your key is—" He lays a few out on the table, checking the engravings, and slides the correct one over. "—this one."

"Thanks," Leth says.

Arthur pauses after standing. Another odd expression crosses his face. "About the rooms. When I rented them, I was under the impression—"

Shae yanks his sleeve. "Don't be a hero."

"Right," Arthur says. He looks—guilty? "See you in the morning."

Leth bids them farewell, baffled but too tired and uncomfortable to pay much mind to whatever Arthur wanted to say. Whatever's wrong with the room, Leth is sure he can deal with it. He might have grown up in luxury, but he worked for the Riverswords too. He can sleep just about anywhere if he has to.

His damp clothes itch against his skin. Maybe he'll order a bath, if the inn offers it.

Familiar laughter rings behind him, and Leth can't help turning around. Evain is perched on the arm of his chair now, one leg crossed over the other. The handsome farmer is gone, and Evain accepts a fresh tankard from a big, broad-shouldered mercenary instead. Evain brushes his hair back behind his ear. A clearly calculated move, Leth thinks darkly, showing off the long lines of his fingers, his strong wrist—

Evain's eyes widen. He starts looking around the room, and Leth turns before they can make eye contact.

Irritation prickling under his skin, Leth flags down the serving boy to order another beer.

))O((

TWO HOURS AND too many beers later, Leth fumbles with the lock of room thirty-seven. Muffled rain drums the roof above. The key doesn't fit on his first few attempts; Leth's still floating on the bubbles of his last tankard. Probably a bad idea—but he doesn't feel cold anymore.

The door swings open, and humid air washes over Leth's face.

Wait, why is the light on?

A shadow moves behind a translucent screen at the far end of the room. Dropping his bag and coat, Leth touches his sword hilt just as a familiar, sultry voice calls out.

"I thought I only ordered a bath tonight, not company." Evain steps out from behind the bathing screen, clad only in a towel around his hips. "But I don't mind if—Leth?"

Rain patters on the windowpane outside. Inside, Evain's wet hair is a dark river to his waist. Water clings to every curve of muscle, steam gilding his chest and full droplets sliding down his neck and arms. What ranged mage needs an abdomen like that? Chiseled lines disappear beneath the precarious edge of the towel.

A gold and ruby barbell gleams in his left nipple.

"Like my catalyst?" Evain touches the piercing.

No wonder Leth never sees Evain touching a focus object when he casts magic. Averting his gaze, Leth clutches his sword hilt like a security blanket and addresses the floorboards. "What are you doing in my room?"

"Clearly I'm taking a bath," Evain says. "And this is *my* room."

A few key memories surface through Leth's floaty, hazy shock. Justice-sworn paladin Arthur saying, *About the rooms…* Water drips from Evain's hair to the hardwood floor, louder than the rain outside. *I thought you two were together.*

Leth releases his sword and scrubs his hand over his face. "Fuck. I'm too tired right now. I'll challenge Arthur to a duel in the morning."

"Will you?" Evain asks. "Why?"

Leth nods solemnly. "To the death."

Evain laughs. Nothing like his sultry, seductive laughter from down in the tavern hall. This is light. Natural. Leth forgets what else he wanted to say.

Room thirty-seven is spacious for an inn. Geometric tapestries in green and orange soften the walls. The wash basin is painted with a cheerful row of dancing pigs. A large mirror hangs over the washstand, and the pale wooden frame matches the table, chairs, and bed.

There's nothing wrong with the bed, except that there's only one of it.

Evain retreats behind the bathing screen. Watching his silhouette moving behind the silk paper is less annoying than looking at him directly. "How drunk are you?" Evain asks from behind the screen.

There's no good answer to that, so Leth doesn't give one. He kicks his bag and coat further into the room and slumps at the table. Peeling off his gloves requires more concentration than it should. The mirror across the room reflects his red-rimmed eyes and the weird clumps his hair has dried into. Leth resolves to rebraid his spell beads in the morning too, before he challenges the treacherous paladin.

Bootlaces are more difficult than gloves. Leth has only gotten one boot off by the time Evain reemerges, dressed in flowing red. He fails to concentrate on his second boot as Evain walks towards him. The bootlace gets less cooperative the closer Evain gets, until the hem of Evain's robe sweeps the floor in front of him.

"You're very drunk, aren't you?"

Evain's presence weighs down the air, replacing the dissipating steam with greater heat. Vision blurring, Leth loses purchase on the bootlace. He suddenly remembers another time he drank too much. Mind swimming from strangely strong wine, a thinner figure than Evain looming too close—

Evain takes a step back. "You can keep the room. I'll reserve another."

The pressure eases from Leth's lungs. He remembers where he is and who he's with, and there's something weirdly reassuring about arguing with Evain. "Can't." He finally kicks his boot away and starts pulling his socks off. "Arthur said he got us the last rooms in the inn."

Evain sighs dramatically. "A minor complication. I have my ways."

As Evain disappears behind the screen again, Leth's grip on his damp socks tightens. He had been certain Evain would insist on Leth leaving. Or he'd make lascivious jokes about sharing the room. Leth was ready for that argument. But this easy accommodation?

Frustrating. Useless. Like swinging his fist and striking cotton.

Evain reemerges with his saddlebags, and he's wearing boots under his silk robe. He stops at the mirror to mess with his still-damp hair. Apparently, he truly means to relinquish the room to Leth, and like everything else about Evain, the consideration is irritating.

Almost as irritating as the idea of Evain going downstairs and finding someone else to sleep with tonight. The handsome farmer or the broad-shouldered mercenary.

"I don't care if you stay," Leth says on impulse, flinging his socks aside. "We've shared a room before."

Evain pauses, his fingers half-through another rake of his hair. "Hiding out at the Veiled Rose with everyone else? I think that's a little different."

"Since when were you such a prude?" Leth laughs. When he stands up, the alcohol spins through his blood again, threatening his balance. Fuck, he's going to have another headache in the morning, in addition to the headache named Evain Marha. "Stay or leave. I really don't care. Just don't talk to me about it."

"Fuck, you *are* drunk." After a long moment, Evain drops his bags again. "Fine. Someone should supervise you anyway. But I look forward to saying 'I told you so' in the morning."

"Said not to talk to me," Leth mutters, rummaging for a change of clothes.

Evain's answering laugh violates the spirit of the law, if not the letter of it. But he remains satisfactorily quiet and distant while Leth changes behind the screen. When Leth emerges—still chilly, his hair still a mess, because fuck if he's taking a bath tonight, but at least his clothes are dry and clean—Evain shoves a mug into his hand.

"Drink this," Evain says sternly.

Maybe it's the firm resonance of his voice. Maybe Leth's just too drunk and tired to argue more. He puts the mug to his lips without question and finds plain water inside.

Evain is across the room by the time he finishes it, and Leth's head is too fuzzy to process how fucking weird Evain is being. He sets the mug down and grabs his dagger before crawling into bed. The bedding is soft and the pillow thick enough he can't feel the lump of the dagger underneath it. He curls up facing the window, his back to Evain.

The lamps click, and darkness blankets the room. Leth's eyelids are too heavy, his body too loose and comfortable. He's barely awake by the time the mattress dips and Evain's body heat radiates through the quilt.

)O(

LETH WAKES TO a dry mouth and throbbing head. He's also very warm. Somehow the quilt twisted around him overnight, looping around his waist and pressing against his back. Leth melts under the comfortable warmth, tempted to drift to sleep again. Delay his morning prayers and the full assault of his hangover. There's something soft and secure about being enclosed like this, with the gentle sigh of breath on the back of his neck.

Wait—breath?

Leth goes rigid, suddenly wide awake. That's not just the quilt wrapped around him: a strong arm encircles his waist, palm draped against his chest. *Evain's* arm. That's Evain's entire body plastered against his, chest to back, thigh to thigh. Evain's knees tucked behind Leth's.

That's Evain's cock, unmistakably hard against Leth's ass.

Evain mumbles something in a language Leth has never heard before. The words stir in Leth's hair. Then Evain's arms tighten, and he *nuzzles* the back of Leth's neck.

The tiny movement shatters through Leth's every nerve and jolts him into action. He shoves his hand under the pillow as he drives his elbow back into Evain's stomach. Evain's surprised, sleepy grunt doesn't stop him. In one surge of movement, he flips over onto Evain. His dagger's scabbard clatters to the floorboards.

Blinking beneath him, Evain doesn't resist. His unbound hair spreads across the pillow, and his red robe falls open to bare most of his chest. The collar catches on the shape of his piercing. Urgent heat pools under Leth's skin. A wash of something that must be fury, or embarrassment. Surely nothing else.

"What the fuck were you doing?" Leth snarls, his knife kissing the apple of Evain's throat. Against Leth's thigh, Evain's erection doesn't subside in the slightest.

EVAIN

Blood and power simmer through Evain's soul, mapping out the revelation of Leth's desire. The human's lust is overwhelming. Undeniable. Evain never imagined Leth could desire so strongly, much less that his desire would ever stray towards *him*. But Leth's gaze is molten shadow along Evain's skin, melting under the edge of his robe.

Harvest Lord's balls, Evain has never felt this powerful. With fuel like this, he could bind and banish a dozen demons. Cast and control a thousand shadow-swords. If he contracted himself to a heart like this, he would never go hungry again.

The way Leth looks above him is captivating. That pretty face flushed in the gray light, all dawn's fire caught as fury in his eyes. A pillow mark on his cheek, and his hair a mess. Morning wood is no explanation for how hard Evain is.

And if Evain breathes a word of this revelation, Leth's knife will slice straight through his jugular. Which would be both very messy and suspiciously nonfatal.

"I was sleeping," Evain says carefully. He's good at languages, but remembering his Charaini is difficult with the distraction of Leth's thigh against his cock. "Sometimes I hug a pillow in my sleep."

Leth doesn't move. "Do I look like a pillow?"

"A very sharp pillow."

The knife falls away from his neck, and Leth swings off of him, to Evain's relief and regret. Lying back, he fixes the memory in his mind as he listens to Leth moving around the room. He needs to memorize the precise weight of Leth on his thighs, the way his collar fell open around his neck. And before that, Evain's too-brief, half-awake awareness of Leth's narrow waist under his arm, the scent of his skin. How well they fit together. His ass.

Evain already misses Leth's ass.

The door opens. Evain calls out, "See you at breakfast."

The door closes.

As Leth's footsteps disappear down the hall, Evain's hand disappears under his robe. So much for his plan to forget about Leth. Until Evain has him, he's going to think of nothing else.

☽○☾

EVAIN DESCENDS TO a tavern hall much emptier than the night before. Sleepy servers bring food to sleepier guests scattered along the trestle tables. The fireplace with its dancing pigs gives the room a lazy, comfortable warmth compared t*o the slate-gray skies outside. Evain finds Freya across from Marta and Haldis at one end of a table, closest to the fire. No sign of Arthur, Shae, or Leth. Evain flags down a serving woman to reserve breakfast for two, then sits next to Freya.

"Arthur and that necromancer are out checking the horses and the roads," Freya tells him, stretching over the table for the jug of water. Glowing with unmistakable satisfaction, she's probably the most awake person in the room. "The rain didn't last the night, so it shouldn't be too muddy out."

"It's rude to keep calling him a necromancer like that." Wrapped up like usual, Marta tugs her cream-colored scarf down enough to sip from a steaming mug. The scarf suits the light brown of her skin.

Freya sighs. "Well, he is one, isn't he?" Marta just stares over the rim of her mug, until Freya sighs again. "You're right, you're right. I'm trying to be better about that."

Marta's lips curve in a tiny smile. "Of course."

Evain is pretty sure he's seen that particular scarf around Freya's neck before. "Late night?" he asks Haldis across from him.

Haldis glares daggers over her porridge. Her eyes are puffy with lack of sleep, and her hair isn't washed, just braided back. Evain would wager five gold that Marta is the one who braided her hair; Haldis looks like she woke up as a walking corpse.

"Very late," Marta answers on Haldis's behalf. She rummages in her coat and produces a dark glass bottle. After tipping a few drops into her own mug, she pushes the mug towards Haldis. "Here, this will help your head."

Haldis drinks from Marta's mug without a word.

Between bites of his mediocre porridge and very acceptable ham and potatoes, Evain pulls out a notebook and pencil. He precisely tears six pages from the notebook.

Freya leans over. "What's that for?"

"Study cards," Evain replies, just as desire magic tingles under his skin. His pencil pauses over the first page before he starts drawing.

"Study cards? What are you studying?" Freya looks over his shoulder and waves. "Leth, over here! Your food's been ready."

Suppressing his smirk is an act of supreme willpower, but Evain has centuries of practice. He finishes the drawing and passes it to Freya. "I'm not the one who needs to study," he says, before permitting himself to glance at Leth, who looks—

Perfect.

That isn't necessarily a compliment.

Leth found a chance to bathe somewhere, and his hair hangs straight and smooth to his shoulders, loose except for the neat new braids of spell beads. His black coat is buttoned to his chin, without a single wrinkle, and the slender hands that so recently held a dagger to Evain's throat are hidden in dark leather gloves. Cold and forbidding as the blades he wields, Leth looks as tightly-wound as ever.

The only difference is how badly Evain wants to unravel him. "Did you sleep late this morning?" Evain says cheerfully, because all right, his willpower isn't *that* amazing.

The remaining breakfast tray is next to Evain. Rather than sitting beside him, Leth very deliberately sits next to Haldis on the other side of the table, then pulls the tray over. He doesn't answer Evain's question.

"Why do I need to study?" Freya turns the paper around. She has it upside down, then rotates it to be ninety degrees off. "I barely passed my magecraft classes as a squire. Give this to Leth or Marta."

"They'll get their own." Evain starts drawing the same array on the next sheet. The runes are complicated and require precision; one wouldn't want to forget the last line of a banishing rune and turn the subject invisible instead. Banishing from sight and place and realm are all distinct. "This is an array to seal wild magic rifts. It's likely we'll split the work. Some of us will seal the rifts while the rest stand guard against the nasty beasties drawn to the wild magic. But I want everyone to know the array."

He passes the next sheet to Marta, who holds it close to her scarf-encircled face to examine. "What pretty runes. Where did you learn calligraphy?"

Evain grins and faux-whispers behind his hand, "You don't want to know."

"Scandalous," Freya says, drawing out the syllables.

Leth's gloved hand tightens on his spoon. Evain resumes drawing before he gets caught staring. "I'll explain the theory and process when we stop for lunch today, and we can practice along our little jaunt. But I don't fancy practicing my penmanship on a log or rock."

He gives the next array to Haldis, who's made more progress on her porridge after taking the medicine from Marta. The next goes to Leth, who's barely touched his breakfast. A teasing admonishment dances on the tip of Evain's tongue. *Eat up, I paid good copper for that.* But that sounds a little too… doting. And if Leth knew Evain bought his breakfast, he probably wouldn't touch another bite.

Evain smiles to himself as he draws arrays to save for Arthur and Shae. Leth's attraction to him changes everything and nothing. Desire alone can't overcome all differences.

Not without a little effort.

)O(

THE ROADS PROVE safe to ride. They'd have been taking a risk with heavy cargo, but Charaini dirt roads are better than some paved roads Evain has traveled in other lands. The party makes good time in the morning, despite the number of hangovers between them.

Daziroth is a pain in the ass—sometimes literally—as he attempts to investigate all the new scents brought forth by the previous day's rain. Sometimes Evain thinks he accidentally summoned a giant demonic puppy instead of a horse.

They pull over for lunch an hour past noon, at a place where the road is slightly wider, with few other redeeming qualities.

"I could spread out the picnic blanket," Marta suggests.

"You're not getting the picnic blanket dirty," Haldis says.

"You brought a—" Shae starts, but Freya interrupts, exclaiming, "What a great idea, Marta!"

Evain snorts. Freya clearly already scored last night; she doesn't need to keep trying so hard. It's cute, though. Humans can be so enthusiastic.

The picnic blanket remains safely packed, and the party eats their lunch standing while the horses rest and graze at the roadside. Evain takes the opportunity for a theory lesson, as promised. "First, have any of you encountered rifts before?" he addresses his gathered audience. Once again, he wishes he had a table with a good, comprehensive map to point at, like Ronan always managed. Natural leader, Ronan. "Nightven?"

"Not many, and I'm grateful for it." Shae stands close enough to Arthur that their arms brush. "One opened up nearby when I was a child. My father kept me inside while my mother warded our homestead against the vaidkos. She was out there for three days before the rift closed. More recently, Arthur and I have seen two while riding with the Riverswords."

"We turned tail and ran," Arthur says, without shame. "Radiance, those things feel nasty."

Rifts surely would feel nasty to an acolyte of Vara. Evain would prefer to be repulsed by them too. Instead, he's drawn to them, like his homeland's hateful claws are trying to drag him back.

"All right, and has anyone besides Shae summoned a demon before?" Evain shoots a glance at the sword-witch leaning against a nearby tree. "Not you, Leth. I know you would never do something so crass."

"I've banished plenty." Marta squints at her copy of the array. "The core circle of this looks very similar to banishing arrays I've used before, but not quite."

"It's banishing a place, instead of a being," Leth suddenly says from the edge of the group. "The array doesn't just close the door. It disperses the energy safely and banishes the slice of the demonic realm that made it through the rift."

Evain's heart thuds. Why is it so fucking sexy for someone to read his array correctly? "Exactly."

Leth's voice lowers. "It's cleverly done."

With Leth's gaze fixed on the ground, Evain is free to beam at the praise. "Leth has it right. I prefer to think of the rifts not as an open door, but an invasion. If a ship has a hole in the bottom, plugging the hole isn't sufficient, is it? You have to bail out the water that's already flooded in."

"And the water has sharks," Freya says.

"Clever as it is, does this array actually work?" Haldis asks. All traces of her earlier exhaustion gone, she's back to her usual no-nonsense self. "Have you used it? I was under the impression you haven't returned to Lyrisenia in years."

"A fine question, Sir Haldis." A fine question Evain will have to answer carefully. Who knows how much falsehood the Varans can sense without an active truth spell? "I sealed a rift once when I was younger, using a far worse array. The drawing in your hands is a refined version. Fewer side effects. If it doesn't work, I'll owe you a fancy dinner."

A far worse array is a tremendous understatement.

Two hundred fifty years ago, he was indeed younger than he is now. A rift spat him out in a dark Lyrisenian forest. Before it could suck him back in, Evain cut a plain circle into the ground. Unused to the mortal realm, with only that bare-bones symbol to guide his powers, sealing the rift nearly killed him. The backlash felled every tree in a half-mile radius.

"It should work." Marta leans against Haldis's shoulder.

Evain glances towards Leth again, half-expecting more input. Spell theory is one of his specialties. But Leth just leans silently against the tree. His lashes are lowered, and his face is paler than usual. Strange. A mild hangover should be better by now. Evain has never had a hangover himself, but he knows how they work for humans.

"Anyway, just practice drawing the array when you have a chance," Evain says. "We should move on for now, so we can make the next town by dark."

As they all gather their horses and mount up, Evain pays covert attention to Leth. He's the only one who sees that when Leth hooks his foot into the stirrup and jumps up, he fails to make it into the saddle. Staggering back to the wet earth splatters flecks of mud onto his boots and the hem of his coat. Leth's back heaves with a deep breath. He makes it into the saddle on his second try, his hands barely trembling on the reins.

Evain swings onto Daziroth and rides up next to him. "Are you all right?"

"Of course," Leth snaps, kicking his mare forward.

Unconvinced, Evain frowns and follows.

LETH

The ache in Leth's head only worsens as the day continues. Thankfully, Star is well-behaved and happy to follow the rest of the horses. Leth's attention keeps straying away from the road, catching on a particular tree clawing at the sky, or the long ends of Marta's scarf flapping in the breeze. The memory of red silk, slipping beneath his hand and thighs, threatening and promising to fall away completely.

Leth doesn't believe Evain embraced him on purpose. For all Evain's teasing, he's never crossed boundaries like that. Why bother, when there are plenty of fools ready and willing to bed him? No, now that his shock has cooled, he's merely annoyed with Evain. He reserves his anger and disgust for himself, for not waking up sooner. For his first thought upon waking being how *comfortable* he was.

He's not at all comfortable now. Winter cuts to his shivering bones. Damp sweat at his temples only makes it worse. Pulling his coat tighter doesn't do anything, and Leth wonders how the others are standing this. They don't seem to be feeling the cold like he is.

How pathetic. A few beers and he's useless the entire next day. As weak as he's ever been—as weak as Anton always said he was.

Leth exerts all his strength to remain properly upright in the saddle, determined to conceal his weakness from his companions. A lifetime of overheard gossip loops through his head, cutting deeper than the cold. Leth ka Tariel, the worthless runt. At least his parents have their firstborn to depend on. At least he never enlisted. At least he's gone now.

Maybe this isn't just a hangover. He doesn't usually indulge in this much self-flagellation.

Distracted and dazed, he hears Evain call something out, but he doesn't process the meaning until everyone else halts around him. Star obligingly halts too, without any input from Leth's stiff hands. Leth struggles to concentrate on Evain's next words.

"Let's stretch out for a few minutes here." Evain's voice is smooth and warm. A sound to sink into. "My horse could use a rest, as could my gorgeous, world-renowned ass."

Dismounting is a mistake. Leth's knees buckle when his feet hit the ground, and only his death-grip on the saddle keeps him upright. He inhales, barely smelling the scent of leather and horse.

Evain's voice catches his attention again. A barely audible hum as he asks Marta something.

"Oh, of course." Her voice carries. "Are you not feeling well?"

"Just a little under the weather," Evain says.

Leth leads Star away from the others, trying to get his feet back under him. Metaphorically and literally—just walking in a straight line is a feat of concentration. He tethers Star near a scraggly patch of year-round grass and leans against a nearby tree.

All the trees around him are bare. Muted brown branches stretch upwards, losing the last of their color to the gray sky. Leth watches the thinner branches sway in the wind, and realizes he forgot to pray this morning.

A branch snaps close by. Leth's head whips up to find Evain ten feet away, dropping a twig to the ground. He clearly snapped it on purpose.

"Is it time to go?" Leth isn't sure how long they've been stopped, or whether he'll be able to reach the saddle again. His legs feel even weaker than before.

"Not yet. How are you feeling?"

Leth looks away as Evain's shadow falls over him. "I'm fine."

"Really." Evain removes the glove from his right hand. "I'm no Varan, but I can tell when you're lying, little Leth."

"I'm *fine*," Leth hisses. A beat later, he remembers to add, "Don't call me that."

Evain steps forward, and Leth instinctively steps back—forgetting he's already leaning against a tree. His head knocks against the trunk, and rough bark pricks into his shoulder blades. The air around him closes in with a scent like smoke and cinnamon. He can't see or breathe anything except Evain. When Evain lifts his hand, Leth's reflexes are too muddled to knock him away. The back of Evain's hand presses to Leth's forehead.

"Your hand is too cold," Leth says quietly.

"You're burning up." Evain's sculpted brow furrows. His hair is in a single long plait again, draped in front of his shoulder to draw Leth's attention to Evain's throat. The angle of his jaw, the movement of his lips. "Take this. Marta says to just let it melt under your tongue. She's no Dansa, but she has half an apothecary packed up with that picnic blanket."

His hand falls away from Leth's forehead. He pulls his glove back on, then offers a paper-wrapped pill.

Craning his neck up to meet Evain's eyes is too much effort, so Leth addresses one of Evain's flower-carved coat buttons instead. "I'll be fine soon. I won't slow us down."

"Of course you won't slow us down." Evain's voice lowers in a dangerously comforting tone. "Because if you don't take this, I'm going to tie you up and sling you over my horse's shoulders, so I don't have to worry about you falling out of the saddle. Understand?"

Leth's head snaps up.

For an instant, red flashes in the depths of Evain's eyes. "So defiant," he says with a smile. "Think you can beat me right now?"

Leth knows he can't. And he must truly be feverish, because he doesn't twist away as Evain unwraps the paper. The tablet leaves grains of chalk-white dust on his leather gloves. Evain lifts his fingers to Leth's lips, and a shockingly familiar sensation sweeps through Leth's entire body. The same sensation he woke up to this morning: the feeling of being held close and kept safe.

Closing his eyes, Leth doesn't resist as Evain pushes the pill into his mouth. Evain's breath brushes over his forehead. Soft leather nudges his dry lips, and his lungs fill with smoke and cinnamon.

The pill slides tasteless under his tongue. Tingling spreads through his veins, but Leth doesn't know if he can blame it on the medication.

"We'll ride on in five minutes," Evain says. "Let me know if you need help mounting up."

He leaves Leth against the tree, no longer shivering but just as dizzy as before.

)O(

LETH PULLS UP alongside Shae. "Can I talk to you?"

The medication kicked in quickly. An hour later, the dizziness and shivers are gone. All that remains is bone-deep exhaustion and the taste of leather on his lips.

"All right," Shae answers, surprise clear in his eyes. He turns to Arthur on the other side of him. "You ride ahead."

"As you command, beloved." Arthur nudges his magnificent horse closer and slides half out of the saddle to press a kiss to the top of Shae's head. Shae's only reaction is a slight smile—he's clearly accustomed to this. Arthur heaves himself back into position and trots his mare forward, towards Evain and the women.

Up ahead, Freya is recounting some story that requires a lot of arm gestures, drawing laughter from Evain and Marta. Back here with Leth and Shae, every-thing is quieter. Just steady hoofbeats in soft earth and whispering wind through bare trees.

Shae rides silently next to him, glancing over from time to time. He wears fingerless gloves despite the cold, baring his silver rings. When the wind whips his dark hair away, more silver glitters at his ears. If there's a more dangerous power to wrest from a demon than necromancy, Leth's never heard of it. The number of charms and spells Shae needs to simply survive from day to day must be exhausting.

"I apologize if this is rude," Leth says eventually. "But I wanted to ask why you contracted with a demon."

Shae gives him a long, unreadable look. "You don't want to know that."

"I'm sorry. I overstepped. You don't need to—"

"That's not what I meant," Shae interrupts. "I meant, what you really want to know is why *Evain* contracted with a demon, right?"

The question dizzies him like a blow to the head. Leth isn't used to being seen through so easily. "I suppose I do."

Fitting Evain into his worldview was easier when Leth thought the man was entirely immoral. A hedonist indulging in demonic magic and human extravagance. Provocative and irritating on purpose. Leth prides himself on his self-control, but Evain drives him to distraction as easily as rolling up his sleeves. Half the time Leth was in the Locksmiths, Evain was out somewhere unaccounted for, which Ronan accepted but Leth always distrusted. And Leth knows the constant philandering is necessary for Evain's magic, but it bothers him anyway.

Disliking Evain used to be simple, but now, Leth doesn't know how to deal with how reliable Evain is in a fight. How much care and preparation he's put into this quest—the worthiness of the quest itself. He doesn't know how to deal with a demonic mage making study cards, and he itches to ask more about the theory behind the array.

Evain was as aggravating as ever today, forcing Leth to take the medication. But he was also considerate enough to use some other excuse to stop the party, so nobody else would see Leth's weakness. Has Evain changed? Or was he always like this, and Leth too caught up in his family baggage to see it?

The gap between Leth and Shae and the rest of the party widens. Shae leans forward and pats his little gelding's neck. "You'll have to ask him directly. Everyone has their own reason for it."

"Does it…" Leth trails off. It would certainly be overstepping to ask if Shae thought a demonic contract made him more evil. "Nevermind. Thank you."

"Don't mention it." They ride together in silence for a while, until Shae suddenly adds, "Now I might be the one overstepping, but what's it like following Ka Dravos? He seems, hm. Stricter than Vara."

Leth considers his answer. "Unrewarding."

)O(

IN THE NEXT town, Evain reserves their rooms for the night. Leth braces himself for the arrangement, and his palm tingles beneath his glove when Evain drops a key into it.

"You get your own room tonight," Evain tells him.

The key is heavier than it should be in Leth's fist. He tells himself he isn't disappointed. He tells himself he isn't cold, saying his prayers without answers and curling into bed alone.

EVAIN

Evain tastes old magic in the air as they ride into Lanwatch two weeks later. The Northern Barrier stretches miles into the sky, far taller than the mountain range that crowns Charain. The spell is invisible, save for the occasional dark shimmer against the gray winter sky.

Last time Evain left Lyrisenia, the Northern Barrier didn't exist. He admires the scope and scale of the spell—humans can be ingenious with the limited means available to them. Binding gods, casting out demons, building enchantments that endure far past their own limited lifespans.

Ingenious, yet short-sighted. The Northern Barrier only protects Charain. It does nothing to solve the problem of Lyrisenia.

Daziroth snorts nervously as they ride through town. He senses the Northern Barrier too. Evain pats his shoulder, unable to reassure him out loud. Someone could overhear. But they *will* cross into Lyrisenia unimpeded. The barrier is fracturing, after all. And thanks to a certain someone's covert attention, Evain is very strong right now.

The ring of steel on steel greets them at the River-swords outpost. Evain rides in next to Arthur and Shae, finding a well-used courtyard surrounding the barracks and office. A painted wooden sign swings above the outpost door, with half a dozen arrows sticking from the center. To the right of the door, a ring of men and women circle two combatants wielding practice swords. A woman perches on a throne of barrels, overlooking the fight with a brown paper bag in her hand.

At the sound of hoofbeats, she swings down from her wooden throne. "Hello, darlings! Took you long enough. Did you take a nap every mile?"

On approach, she proves to be only a few inches shorter than Evain. She wears a loose brown shirt under a tightly-laced leather vest, and there's a wide streak of Riverswords-blue in her black hair. Her skin has an unhealthy pallor, like she's spent too long out of the sun, but her dark eyes are bright. The paper bag in her hand smells like candied nuts.

"Good to see you too, Georgia," Arthur answers with a grin. He swings down from the saddle and gestures. "This is Evain Marha. Evain, this is Captain Georgia Oakven."

Another Lyrisenian name.

"Delighted to meet you." Evain dismounts as well. "Arthur and Shae told me you were charged with protecting the roads north of the border, and I'd love to talk about a collaboration, if you're amenable."

"I'm amenable." Georgia cocks her head. "But I'm not cheap."

"Conveniently, I'm not stingy," Evain says. "But I'm not desperate either, and I know the Lanwatch council's already paying you."

Georgia laughs. "Never enough, my friend, never enough."

Evain points to the rest of the crew in turn. "Sir Freya, of the Radiant Order. Sir Haldis and Sir Marta, of the Sephinian Order. And Leth…" He trails off, suddenly unsure how to label Leth. A ka Tariel? A Locksmith? A sword-witch?

Leth dismounts and leads his mare forward. "I worked for the Port Charain company for a few years, under Captain Bry." Right. He was a Riversword too.

Georgia looks Leth up and down. "Guess you're older than you look, pipsqueak. You must not have served recently, because I hear it's Commander Bry now. He was always a kiss-ass."

Leth doesn't seem bothered by the dig on his height—or if he's bothered, he doesn't show it. He's always so polite with people who aren't Evain. What would happen if Evain called him pipsqueak? Could be fun to find out.

A lean, silver-haired man emerges from the outpost and joins them. "Nightven, could you meet with Georgia first? I'll get your friends and horses settled."

Georgia winks at him. "You worry too much, sweetheart. But sure. You lot, this is Reed, my second in command and fretting nursemaid. He'll set you up. Nightven?"

Shae hands his reins to Arthur. "Of course."

"And take these." Georgia shoves the paper bag into Shae's hands. "I'm sick of just smelling them all day."

Clutching the bag of candied nuts, Shae follows Georgia into the outpost. A breeze picks up, and Evain catches the sickly-sweet smell of blood. Interesting. There are very few reasons someone would need a necromancer to check them over.

"We're going to stay at the Mother's church," Haldis says. "We'll meet you back here when we've stabled our horses and spoken with our priests."

"Bye bye," Marta adds with a little wave, and kicks her horse away.

Haldis lingers another moment and points at Freya, who's half out of her saddle already. "You're staying with us tonight, too," she declares, then rides after Marta.

Freya freezes, then swings back into her saddle with a laugh. "Am I good or what?"

)O(

A FEW HOURS later, everyone gathers in the Riverswords meeting room: a comfortable collection of frayed armchairs and sofas around a crackling fire. Reed comes around with beers for everyone, and only Leth and Haldis decline.

Arthur and Shae take one oversized chair, and Freya and her Sephinians pile onto the sofa. Evain perches on the arm of the other chair, wondering if Leth will dare take the only remaining seat—until Leth pulls a wooden chair over from the card table across the room. He sets it across from Evain, never once making eye contact.

He doesn't need to, for Evain to feel the desire wafting from him. Only centuries of practice keep Evain's expression unchanged, and if anyone notices the tightening in his trousers, well, that's their fault for staring at his cock.

Georgia sits on the low table, the firelight bringing some color to her pallid cheeks. On the rest of the table spreads a map of Lyrisenia, weighted down with empty bottles on the corners. Maybe Evain could buy it off her for use in his own important meetings.

"Your hospitality is much appreciated." Evain raises his beer in salute. "As for our purpose in Lanwatch..."

Lanwatch's council has already hired Georgia's company to keep the roads clear between Lanwatch and the nearest Lyrisenian settlements. There's still some trade between the groups, though it's getting more dangerous by the day. Evain explains the wavering of the Northern Barrier, the pending military reinforcement, and his own scheme to seal the rifts.

"That'd be a lot of help," Georgia says when he finishes. "As sweet as the hazard pay is, I'd rather my darlings start getting their beauty sleep again. Mother knows some of them need it. What do you want from us?"

"Guides and backup." Evain shifts in his seat. The way Leth watches him is only getting more distracting.

"Shae says you've been tracking the wild magic flares. Rifts tend to open in the same places, so guiding us to known hot-spots would help."

Georgia nods. "Easy enough. We've been working with a few Lyrisenians too. They know their backyard better than we do."

"Are any of them witches?" Haldis asks. "Any of your mercenaries, too?"

"Yes and yes, a few of them at least."

Evain's eyes stray once again to Leth, who's sitting perfectly straight in his wooden chair. His face looks softer in the firelight, and the chair is a bit too tall for him. The tips of his toes don't quite touch the floor.

"I'd like to split into two groups, so we can hit multiple regions at once." Evain's attention returns to Georgia. "Each group with a few of us and a few of you. How many can you spare? I want to spread out, but not spread you too thin."

"I need to talk with Reed and the council before I make any promises, but two squads should be doable." Georgia taps her map again. "You and I can talk about geography, but one squad should focus on the area around Sasana. There's fifty stubborn Lyrisenians still living there, and the vaidkos are getting bad. How are you lot dividing up?"

Two squads. This is the part where Ronan would discuss who wants to go where. Get everyone's input on their own strengths and interests. But Evain isn't Ronan. He doesn't have maps to point at, and he doesn't need feedback on personnel distribution.

The only one he's not sure about is Freya. She's definitely been fucking Haldis and Marta, but Evain's inhuman intuition tells him she's not looking to settle down. Forcing further proximity might be more fraught than fun.

"Arthur, Shae, and Freya are one group," Evain decides. Sure enough, Marta looks a little disappointed, but Freya and Haldis seem content with the arrangement. Pleased with himself, Evain holds Leth's gaze next. "Haldis, Marta, and Leth are with me."

He could have let Leth choose. Ronan would have. Each group already had two paladins and—ostensibly—a demon-bound mage. Leth was the odd one out. But Evain is very selfish. He wants the power Leth gives him, and he wants to be able to admire Leth at his leisure.

Leth looks away without saying anything, and Evain claps his hands. "Well, it looks like any further planning will have to await Georgia's budget discussions. Shall we adjourn, and reconvene tomorrow? I'd planned on staying in Lanwatch for a week anyway."

Everyone disperses except for Evain, Leth, and Georgia. "We're going to seal *way* more rifts than you," Marta says as they leave.

Freya shakes her fist. "Want to bet?"

Reed appears out of nowhere, silent as Georgia's shadow. He sets a fresh tray of beers on a vacated chair, and this time Leth takes one.

"Are those marks rifts?" Leth asks, moving to the couch for a better view of the map.

"Aye," Georgia says. "Crosses are confirmed, and circles are approximate, or hearsay from locals." She cracks her neck with a sharp snap. "This should be the army's job. They've been ignoring the north for too long, as if Praia's ever going to actually invade the west."

"They won't ignore it for much longer," Evain says. "Like I said, the crown and churches are sending troops north soon. The Radiant Order's new prophet is—" Reckless. Impulsive. Idealistic. All of eighteen years old, with the energy to prove it. "—not the type to get bogged down by bureaucracy."

"I'll believe it when I see it." Georgia grabs a tankard but doesn't drink. Just holds it, like a habit. "A troop of soldiers rode through here not a week ago. Fool me, I thought the crown had finally taken heed of my messages and sent that lot to help, but no. Their limp cock of a commander didn't even have time to meet with me. Fucking Dravans."

Alarm zings through Evain as Leth's tankard clatters to the ground.

Beer spills over the floor, and Leth scrambles up, pale-faced. "I'm so sorry. Could you get me a towel? I'll clean this up."

"Sit back down," Georgia says, unperturbed. She leans forward and presses her own untouched tankard into Leth's hands. "Reed will get it."

"Will he?" Reed mutters, but disappears into another room anyway. He returns with a rag of indeterminate color and drops it in the puddle, then just leaves it to soak without wiping it at all.

"Sorry," Leth says again.

Evain waits, but it doesn't seem like Leth's going to say anything else. So it's Evain who asks what he thinks Leth wants to. "Do you know who was leading the Dravans?"

Leth's fingers tighten on the tankard.

"How could I not?" Georgia rolls her eyes. "His aides were very clear that the illustrious General ka Tariel didn't have time to talk to Riverswords ruffians. The new General ka Tariel, that is. Anton. His mother retired years ago."

Evain isn't being considerate, asking questions on Leth's behalf. His motives are purely selfish: he doesn't want anyone else to see Leth vulnerable. "Where were they going? What were they doing, if they weren't answering your messages?"

"No idea what they were doing, but they rode north." Georgia grimaces. "Maybe they're demon-hunting like us. I know there was a vaidkos incident outside Melody a few months ago, and the Dravans are dicks but they're not stupid. Hunting at the source is better. But if they're demon-hunting, they're not being team players about it."

"What a shame," Evain says. "I love being a team player. The more the merrier."

A clatter sounds from outside, joined by raised voices. Georgia swings to her feet. "Speaking of merry, it sounds like my darlings are having too much fun. We'll talk tomorrow—Reed showed you rooms already, right? Perfect."

"This was a delight," Evain says smoothly. "I look forward to continuing."

Georgia exits with Reed at her heels, leaving only Evain and Leth with the fire, map, and empty tankards.

Not all empty. Evain snags the last full mug from the tray and moves to the arm of the couch. "What are you worried about?"

Leth leans forward, elbows on his knees, seemingly focused on the map. His hair falls forward to conceal his expression, so Evain has to admire the slim lines of his waist instead. The curve of his ass as his trousers stretch taut. "I spoke with Anton before he left," Leth says. "We argued, and he wouldn't tell me where he was going. I didn't expect him to be heading north too."

Suspicion rises in Evain's heart. "When did you argue?"

"The day you proposed this job," Leth answers, then goes rigid. That was the day Evain found Leth throwing himself at a training dummy, well past the limits of exhaustion, with a vicious bruise around his eye.

Did your brother hit you?

Evain doesn't need to ask, and he won't force Leth to answer. With every moment Evain stays quiet, tension eases from Leth's thin shoulders. They sit in silence until Leth leans back against the couch. "Don't you need to go out?"

The firelight is so pretty along Leth's jaw. "Go out?"

"You know." Leth's gaze slides away.

Evain knows. But he doesn't have to go out and flirt with mercenaries or townsfolk to replenish his magic. He gets quite enough from the deceptively frigid sword-witch on the couch next to him. "Maybe later." Evain plays with the end of his braid. "Does my promiscuity really bother you so much?"

"It doesn't."

"I think it does," Evain muses. "But why?"

Leth jumps to his feet. "I'm going to rest now."

In the instant before he turns away, Evain catches a faint pink flush along his cheeks. Maybe chasing this prey won't take as long as he expected after all. Evain savors the view of Leth's departure, then finishes his beer.

He needs to find Georgia and ask if there's a tailor in town.

LETH

Leth kneels on cold floorboards and tries to pray. Dawn hasn't broken yet, and the room is still gray with the remnants of night. The outpost's insulation isn't bad, but Leth's only half-dressed, and goosebumps prickle down his bare arms.

He's prayed to Ka Dravos almost every morning for as long as he can remember, but ever since the Unbinding, it's been harder to think what to say.

"God of war, grant me strength," he says eventually, leaning on impersonal ritual words. Hollow and insincere, but that's all he can offer this morning. His voice sounds thin in the tiny room. "Grant me Valor. Guide my blade."

The prayer feels insufficient. Leth wants so much more than strength from Ka Dravos, but he'll get even less than that. Maybe it's time to stop praying at all.

He wonders if Anton is looking for more now, too.

A knock on the door scatters his dismal thoughts. Leth jumps to his feet. "One moment!"

He grabs a shirt quickly, but nobody's at the door when he opens it. Just a bundle wrapped in burlap and tied in twine. Leth looks both ways down the barracks hall and doesn't see or hear anything except for some mercenary snoring in the next room.

The room lacks a table, so Leth sets the bundle on the bed he just made. He'll straighten the blankets again later. He cuts the twine with his knife and unwraps a brand-new set of winter clothes. Coat, gloves, under-clothes, socks, and scarf. Leth's hand clenches around the knife, and then he turns the lamp on. The coat is black, similar to his current coat, but a different material. Warmer, and the lining is dense red wool. The scarf is bright red too, with a plain steel pin to keep it from blowing away or falling off in a fight.

Nothing Leth would normally wear. But today isn't a normal day.

Today is the day he leaves Charain for the first time in his twenty-four years. They've rested a week in Lanwatch, arranging supplies and preparing for the journey ahead. Evain spent yesterday morning drilling them all in the rift-sealing array. They drew circle after circle, rune after rune, in the dirt of the Riverswords' yard, until Georgia came out to scold them for scaring her darlings with all the witchcraft.

Leth got it right the first time, and Evain told him, "Well done," which shouldn't have felt so good to hear.

Leth's fingertips sink into the soft red scarf, and a strange feeling surges up in him. Something like flower petals gently brushing against glass. The clothes surely aren't anything personal. He remembers Reed saying he had more supplies waiting for them, and maybe everyone got new clothes.

Even so. It's nice to feel cared for, just a little.

☽ ◯ ☾

THE SUN RISES reluctantly over the Riverswords' yard, and night's frost still gleams along rooftops. Leth joins the rest of the group for one last gathering together. Arthur, Shae, and Freya won't leave town until later today, but Evain wanted to talk to everyone. Arthur looks half-asleep, and Marta looks fully asleep. She's wrapped in so many scarves and furs, she resembles a fluffy ball more than a person. Everyone's breath rises in clouds.

Leth doesn't feel the cold at all. His new clothes are warm and fit him perfectly. So perfectly he would think they were tailored to his exact measurements, if he didn't know better.

Evain is cheerful and animated despite the early hour. Leth hasn't seen him this happy outside of wine and cheese night at the Locksmiths' base, or holding flirtatious court at random taverns. A hint of a smile lingers at the corners of his lips, the curve of his eyes, and the glance he gives Leth is almost as warm as the red scarf around his neck.

Fingering the end of the scarf, Leth looks away.

"Gather round, gather round." Evain has a dark velvet pouch in his hands. "I have a gift for everyone. A token of my appreciation and affection."

He turns to Leth first and presses a small object into his palm. They're both wearing gloves, but Leth still feels the heat of his too-brief touch. As Evain moves onto the others, Leth inspects the token. A silver disc the size of a coin, strung on a thin leather cord. A very familiar pattern is etched onto the face of the disc.

Freya swears loudly. "Fucking ashes, Evain, why did we have to memorize the fucking array if you were just going to give us these?"

"What if you lose the pendant?" Evain says. "You lost your scarf to Sir Marta already."

Blinking awake, Marta touches the cream-colored scarf around her neck.

"You're lucky we're splitting up," Freya says darkly, and Arthur laughs. Even Shae beside him cracks a smile.

Leth focuses on the pendant as the others chat and say their farewells. The artisanship is exact, every rune precise in miniature. The sort of artisanship Leth recognizes as *very* expensive. Whether he went to a silversmith or a craft-witch, Evain spent a lot of money in preparation for this quest, even beyond the travel expenses and wages. It's hard to imagine all this preparation took place just within the months after the Unbinding. Evain must have been planning this for years.

A shadow crosses over him. Leth looks up—and up—at Evain.

"Are you ready to go?" Evain doesn't wait for Leth's answer before plucking the pendant from Leth's hands.

His hands are bare now, his gloves hanging out of his coat pocket. "Here, let me."

He moves slowly enough that Leth could knock his hand away if he wanted. And he should want to, because nothing has truly changed. Evain is still demon-bound, and Leth should still hate that. But he stands stone-still as Evain unwinds his scarf and slides the leather string around his neck. His bare fingers brush Leth's throat, searing hot, as he tucks the pendant into his coat.

That cinnamon smoke scent twists into Leth's lungs and hooks like thorns. Red flashes through Evain's eyes, a trick of the rising sun.

"Don't lose this." Evain's voice is steady, as if what he's doing to Leth is ordinary. As if it's *nothing*. He rewraps Leth's scarf too. "Let's head out."

The pendant weighs heavy against Leth's chest, and he fears it will rattle against his ribs with the furious pounding of his heart. He clenches his fists, then relaxes them. Takes three deep breaths before bidding the others farewell and following Evain from the outpost.

)O(

TWO OF GEORGIA'S darlings wait at the Lanwatch stables with the horses. One of them, a woman in her fifties with silver-blond hair and weathered skin, introduces herself as Bricks. She's supervising a string of shaggy pack ponies, while another pony in a riding saddle stands behind her and lips at her hair.

The other Riversword is a young man who can't be older than twenty. His mop of black hair ruffles in the wind, and his beard is the faintest shadow against his russet brown skin. A bow and quiver sit over his shoulder. "You can call me Darkblade," he says, offering his hand.

"Not this again." Bricks rolls her eyes. "You can call him *Darren*."

"Or Darren," Darren says with a sigh, though his grin stays bright.

Marta produces a hand from her bundling of coats and mumbles sleepily, "Marta. Nice to meet you, Darkblade."

Leth reaches out next. "I'm Leth. Ah…"

"Darren is fine." Darren's grin widens. "I saw you practicing outside last night. I'd love to spar with you sometime."

"Of course." Leth rarely turns down the chance to spar with someone new; every new opponent is a chance to become stronger, or to share his own skills with others. "That would be nice."

He's barely let go of Darren when another hand closes over Leth's shoulder. Squeezing lightly, Evain looms over. "We met yesterday, of course, but it's a pleasure to see you again, Darren." Evain leans forward into the space between Leth and Darren.

Annoyance pricks through Leth. Does Evain really need to flirt with everyone they meet?

But it seems not to work this time. Darren's eyes flick to Evain's hand on Leth's shoulder, and his smile doesn't fade but he takes a step back. "Of course, I look forward to working with all of you. Professionally. And I'd love to spar with you too?"

"Sounds lovely," Evain says. "Oh, there are our horses."

He squeezes Leth's shoulder one more time—a warning? A habit? Surely he doesn't know the way it sends dizzying flutters through Leth's veins—and saunters away.

Darren coughs and runs his hand through his floppy hair. "I think he might have misunderstood me. We're very professional in the Riverswords."

"Of course," Leth says, baffled. He has no idea what Darren thinks Evain might have misunderstood.

As Leth checks over Star's tack, Bricks calls out to Evain. "Are you sure you don't want a pony?" Her lips purse, the expression calling attention to a white scar along her jaw. The frown is directed at Evain's flashy black stallion. "Your boy isn't suited to the weather we'll hit north of the border."

From the way Daziroth turns his head, ears pricking forward, then back, Leth would swear the horse understood her. It's an eerie moment—until the horse turns again to rub his face on Evain's shoulder.

Evain shoves Daziroth's face away. "I know Daisy doesn't look it, but he'll handle the cold just fine."

Daziroth really doesn't look it. Star and the Sephinians' bays aren't as rugged as the shaggy Lanwatch ponies, but they've all grown in thick winter coats. Daziroth, however, is as sleek and glossy as if it's the height of summer.

Bricks frowns and pushes the point. "The folks here will take good care of him while we're away. The weather's mild now, but our winters get real rough real quick. Storms blow up out of nowhere."

"They're my winters too," Evain says. "I lived outside Aliso for twenty years."

Leth's gloved fingers pause beneath Star's girth.

"Radiance, did you really?" Bricks laughs. "You'd know better than me, then. Don't mind me, I always have to check. We get the occasional summer flower up here, badly dressed and badly mounted."

Evain laughs too. "Then I can only be grateful you didn't criticize my dress."

After checking the girth's tension, Leth mounts up. His new clothes fit perfectly, allowing enough movement even though they're thicker than his old clothes. What doesn't fit perfectly, though, is Evain's casual mention of twenty years.

Leth doesn't know much about Evain's past. He's never asked or wanted to ask. But they were in the Locksmiths together for almost two years, and Leth picked up a thing or two. He knows Evain joined the Locksmiths three years ago, though he doesn't know why. He knows Evain has traveled. Evain once mentioned having visited Dansa's medicine temple in Praia, though he used the sacred hot springs for rather non-medical purposes.

Leth was in the kitchen once when, over a bottle of wine, Evain told Melanne he spent ten years in the Scasca Isles. And he once mentioned a year spent hopping between Etenian pleasure boats. A year seducing priests in Ellaroc, the city of waterfalls.

A year here, a year there. The years add up, and they add up to at least fifty with the addition of twenty years outside Aliso—while Evain doesn't look a day over thirty.

"Everyone ready?" Evain stands in his stirrups, overlooking them all, and his half-bound hair streams behind him. "The tender embrace of my homeland awaits. The mountains of Lyrisenia are pining for my return."

The years add up, but so do Evain's exaggerations. Leth should know better than to take anything Evain says seriously. Shaking his head, he nudges Star forward with his calves.

Morning brightens over Lanwatch's sharp-slanting roofs and the shopkeepers salting their doorsteps. Centuries ago, when Lyrisenia was a vibrant empire, Lanwatch sat astride a bustling trade route. As the empire splintered and demonic incursions escalated, Lanwatch's merchants fell back in favor of soldiers. The barracks and garrisons from that era still stand today, but the soldiers have since moved to other regions, leaving Lanwatch quiet.

Two gates mark the border. Sleepy guards crank open the wooden inner gate as Leth and the others approach. Bricks pauses her string of ponies to chat briefly. The second gate towers above the first. Its great stone wings spread wide open against the city wall, held fast by years of climbing vines and built-up earth and frost. Centuries have passed since the stone gate last closed, because what protects Lanwatch and the rest of Charain isn't the gates, but the occasional shimmer in the sky overhead.

Leth nudges Star to a quicker walk as they pass through the gates. Stone columns mark the border and the base of the Northern Barrier a hundred feet from the city gates, and Leth finds himself eager to press forward.

He catches up to Evain at the head of the group, just before he leaves his homeland for the first time in his life.

The trees are the same on either side of the border. Whip-thin, resolute evergreens, dark-needled and glittering with frost. The road is the same hard-packed earth, and Leth doesn't even feel the magic of the barrier. The only change is that one moment, the ancient border posts are in front of him; the next moment, they're behind, and a brand-new land spreads out before him. A land where nobody knows Leth ka Tariel, or the man he's failed to be.

Leth inhales a breath of winter, and something loosens around his heart.

Two years ago, he joined the Locksmiths for a reason. A belief that gods shouldn't be bound to one place and one purpose. Maybe he shouldn't be bound either, shackled to family traditions nobody else seems to follow and chained to divine teachings his god won't reward him for. Maybe out here, he could learn to do something crazy like want something nobody told him to want.

"Never thought I'd see the day." Evain's half-bound hair sways behind him, and a strange, contemplative look crosses his handsome face.

"What is it?" Leth's eyes dart to the horizon, then back to Evain. For some reason, he doesn't want to look away.

"You're smiling."

Leth tugs his scarf closer around his neck. The red wool is soft under his chin. "It's not like I never smile."

"Not like this," Evain says, so softly Leth would miss it if he were listening any less intently. "Also, that scarf looks good on you."

Leth shakes his head and turns back to the snow-swept forest. Underneath the soft warmth of the scarf, another heat tingles against his throat. The memory of Evain's fingers placing the silver pendant around his neck. The heat rises through his face, and Leth hopes he isn't flushing.

That's another thing that doesn't change from one side of the border to the next. Evain still has a way of getting under his skin.

EVAIN

There's nothing magical about the sight of Leth wearing the clothes Evain bought for him. Evain's possessiveness is pure animal instinct, something even more primal than his transmutation of desire into magic. He has one intense regret: that in his two and a half centuries among mortals, he never learned the tailor's trade, to make the clothes himself.

There might be something magical in Leth's flush. Evain's blood rushes downward so quickly a lesser man might pass out. Even he feels somewhat weak in the saddle.

All right, some of his weakness is due to the effort of crossing the Northern Barrier unscathed and unnoticed. He expended a significant amount of his gathered power to shield himself and Daziroth for the crossing. Apparently it worked; neither Haldis nor Marta drew their holy swords against the unmasked demonic threat, and the barrier itself didn't repel them. Evain felt only an unpleasant tingle crawling along his skin.

At least replenishing his power is easy, even if Leth's still in denial about his own desires.

Darren rides up on his sturdy pony. "We'll meet Tally an hour from here. I'll point out the trail when we get to it—it's a little hard to see from this direction."

"Thank you... Darren." Evain chooses his own names because they sound nice, so he has little room to judge. But Darkblade really is a bit much.

Darren is tall, handsome, and attracted to Evain in a passing sort of way. Evain would appreciate that more if the young mercenary wasn't also clearly attracted to Leth. That's fine as long as Darren keeps that attraction to himself and doesn't keep proposing lascivious activities like sparring. Or shaking hands for too long.

Humans might call Evain hypocritical; Evain doesn't fucking care. He just appreciates Darren's ability to take a hint and back away from Evain's... whatever Leth is.

Pale gray blankets the sky above, and dark forest lines the road they travel. A tall, dark mountain range rises to the east. Evain has never traveled this region of Lyrisenia before. From his perspective in Aliso, the Riseniasha mountains rose to the west. The old empire sprawled over mountains and forests, river valleys and vast plains, sharing borders with Etenia, Charain, and Praia to the south.

It should have been large enough and old enough to withstand the incursions of wild magic. But for some reason, it didn't. Evain has heard many stories why but doesn't know which are true. Two centuries ago, he was far too caught up in the thrill of human lives, the prospect of an entire vital world waiting for him, to pay attention to politics and unnatural disasters.

Evain is about to ask Leth something—anything, he just wants to make him blush again—when a faint chill tugs on his awareness. Evain's fingers tighten on the reins, and Daziroth lifts his head too.

A new rift has opened. None of the humans sense it, so Evain keeps quiet.

After Darren points out the new trail, they arrive at a thatched cottage tucked away in a clearing. A row of wooden sheds blends with the tree line, flanked by flower beds. Red mahr always blooms in winter, but the pale shaflowers are out of season.

Darren dismounts and makes for the cottage, but the door swings open before he can knock. The man who emerges is neither short nor tall, with dark brown hair instead of black like most Lyrisenians. His cloak is patched, and he pulls his hood over his head just as Evain catches a glimpse of dark green eyes.

"How've you been, Tally?" Darren says. "Long time no see."

"Spare the introductions. There's a rift brewing five miles from here," Tally says to the group, then pauses next to Darren. "Also, it's been three days."

"A long time, right," Darren says, while Tally strides towards the string of ponies. Bricks is already unloading one of them. "Well, everyone, this is Talirasell Ivha. Tally, this is Evain Marha, and that's—"

"Where should I put these?" Bricks asks Tally, indicating the unloaded packs.

Tally takes the reins and leads the pony towards a tree stump to mount up. "The door's unlocked."

Darren's the one who ends up carrying the packs into the cottage and locking up before the party sets off again. He continues the introductions as he works, and Evain is honestly impressed he got everyone's names right. Tally himself seems distracted, head cocked as if listening to something nobody else can hear.

"Yes, it's this way," he says. "Follow me."

🌙○🌙

THEY DISMOUNT A mile out from the rift, when the horses begin dancing nervously against the reins. Evain feels the uneasy pull of magic too. It's unnerving. Enticing. Bricks makes sure the mounts are secure, and Tally gives a final set of directions. "Skirt around the hill, don't go up it." His eyes flash a lighter green. "The sooner you get there, the better. It's calling vaidkos already."

"You're not coming with us?" Marta shucks off one of her coats and two of her scarves. She still looks like a stuffed animal.

Tally adjusts his hood. "I'm no fighter."

"I could—" Darren starts, but Bricks interrupts him.

"You could stay with the horses like you're told," she says sternly.

"Definitely what I was going to say." Darren's grin doesn't falter.

When Evain negotiated help from Georgia, she was adamant that she didn't want her darlings getting close to the rifts if they could avoid it. Her mercenaries are well-trained, and they know the area, but fighting other humans or even the occasional stray vaidkos is one thing. Diving into wild magic is quite another. There was steel in Georgia's voice and painful fire in her eyes. Evain didn't need to ask to know she'd already lost people to Lyrisenia's dangers.

Leth fingers his scarf as if about to take it off, and Evain's eyes narrow—but in the end Leth adjusts the steel pin and leaves the scarf on.

"If we're not back by nightfall," Evain starts, then grins. "We're having too much fun, and we'll see you by dawn." He grabs Daziroth by the nose, staring deep into his eyes. "Behave." Daziroth's ears flick back and forth, before he wrestles out of Evain's grip to continue inspecting the tree next to him. That's as much of an agreement as Evain's going to get.

Evain flips his hair over his shoulder and stalks off through the forest. He doesn't really need Tally's directions. This close, he could find the rift with his eyes closed.

Leth, Haldis, and Marta fall in behind him.

"This is very exciting," Marta says. "I bet Freya and the others haven't found a rift so quickly."

"Do you miss her already?" Evain tosses back a wink.

"None of your business," Haldis says.

But Marta laughs. "We'll see her again. She's not one to settle down, but, hm. Sometimes that's fun too." Her voice takes on a dreamy quality. "Such nice arms… Of course, your arms are the best, Haldis my love."

A surge of power interrupts their conversation. As if the earth rises and falls around them, except nothing moves. Wild magic shivers through Evain's soul. It's worse for the humans. Leth staggers next to him, and Evain instinctively catches him by the elbow. Their bodies press together, and the moment of contact burns Leth's attraction into Evain's nerves. Evain lets go before he gives into the urge to pull him even closer.

One of the beads in Leth's hair flashes silver, a prepared charm activating. "I suppose we're close."

"Very," Evain says. "When we get there, which of you wants to try the spell first?"

He really means the question for Leth, and he watches those pretty eyes light up. But Leth takes too long to reply, and Marta answers first. "Could we? I assumed you would want to do it, since it's your array and all."

"I'll take over if anything goes awry," Evain says. "But hopefully, we'll be doing a lot of this. I want to make sure everyone knows the spell, and what better way to practice than to practice?"

"I'd really love to." Marta's smile dimples.

"Then we'll defend you valiantly, Sir Marta." Evain sweeps a bow. He's a little disappointed Leth didn't speak up, when he can tell Leth wanted to, but now's not the time to push. "Let's go."

Moments later, Haldis calls out, "Vaidkos ahead."

White light flares. Sephine's protective magic. "Two of them," Marta adds.

"We'll fight our way to the rift, then," Evain says. "You two stick together, and Leth, stick with me. Whoever gets to the rift first, start the spell."

"See you there," Marta says, and follows Haldis into the trees. She moves with surprising grace considering her layers of coats.

With a soft exhalation, Evain releases his magic and manifests a sword of red shadows in the air. He grips the hilt, and the shadows smoke away to leave dark red steel. "How about a kiss for luck, little Leth?"

"Shut up," Leth says, with the same annoyed vehemence as usual. It sounds sweeter every day. Sword in hand, he darts away at a different angle than the Sephinians.

Excitement buzzes under Evain's skin. Leth's retorts haven't changed, but the way he glanced at Evain's lips at the word *kiss* was definitely new—and a welcome rush of power. This vaidkos is going to be a piece of cake.

Evain sees the serpentine bulk ahead as the first wave of corrosive magic hits. It washes off of him like water. Another spell flashes in Leth's hair, and the demonic miasma doesn't slow him at all.

The vaidkos is huge, twelve feet at the shoulders, and its sinuous body winds through the trees. Its massive, wedge-shaped head lacks eyes, instead lined with three rows of flaring nostrils and an unholy number of needle-like teeth. The creature is too big for this stretch of forest, and on every side of it, the trees bear splintered scars of its passing.

Leth looks tiny against the vaidkos's bulk, but he flings himself forward like the monster is just another training dummy. Evain flings himself forward as well, sparks and shadows streaming in his wake.

The eyeless head swings towards Leth first. Evain takes advantage of its distraction to fling out his left hand. Five long shadow-knives manifest in motion, piercing towards the vaidkos's hindquarters.

"Over here," Evain calls out, and meets the swinging head with his sword. Steel and fang screech together.

Impact rings through Evain's shoulder as he dances away. Green-black blood steams away from deep wounds in the beast's chest and shoulders. Souvenirs of Leth's artistry.

The blur in the corner of his vision is Leth too, circling around. His witchcraft amplifies his speed past human ability. Without verbal coordination, Evain spins towards the vaidkos again. Red light flares around his hands. The eyeless vaidkos can't see the light, but the power and heat draw its attention. Evain laughs aloud and dodges back just enough. Needle fangs snap scant inches from the hem of his coat, and acidic saliva burns into the frosty dirt. The vaidkos rears back, then lunges—

And Leth's sword flashes silver, slicing upward under its throat.

Blood sizzles, and the gurgling, serpentine body spasms. Leth stumbles backwards, and Evain grabs him by the shoulder. They duck behind a tree just before a thick curve of flesh slams into the other side of the trunk. Soft needles shower onto them from the shaking branches above. Wood crunches and splinters from the dying demon's convulsions.

Then there's silence. No sound but the rustling trees, and no movement but Leth's breath frosting the air between them. Two hearts drumming in tandem. Adrenaline surges through Evain, not Leth's desire but his own.

Evain is on the cusp of reaching out when Leth's gaze lowers, and he ducks away. Evain sighs and steps out too. Now's not the time. The rift still pulls at him.

Leth stoops to pull his sword from the smoking ashes, all that remains of the vaidkos's corpse. "I don't hear the others," he says, moving forward with his sword in hand. The direction of the rift is clear from this distance, even for humans.

"They've probably beaten us to it," Evain says with a sigh, just as a burst of power radiates from in front of them. Evain throws up a shield on instinct, red sparks weaving through the air in front of them—

But the foreign power dissipates harmlessly, with no more impact than the wind fluttering through their hair. A whoop of laughter echoes through the frosty landscape: Marta's high voice, with a lower echo from Haldis.

Leth sheathes his sword. "I guess your array worked."

Grinning, Evain lowers his hand and releases the shield. "I guess it did."

☽○☾

THE SEVEN OF them make camp for the night with a rocky hillside to their east and a thick copse of trees to their west, blocking off most of the wind. The sky is still clear of snow, but the temperature drops when the sun sets. Haldis walks the protective wards around the camp, and Evain makes sure he's well within the boundary before her spell sets.

She's warding against demons, among other things, but it's easy enough to escape detection when he's already within the spell.

Darren hunted a few rabbits while the party was separated, and Evain takes charge of cooking them while the others set up camp and tend the horses. The savory scent draws everyone together again by the time dinner is ready. They sit on rocks and empty tent covers, and Haldis and Marta cuddle on Marta's picnic blanket.

Evain is pleased when Leth sits next to him, leaning against the same hulking boulder. Sure, there's an entire two feet of space between them, but a year ago, Leth would have sat across the fire, as far away as possible.

Of course, a year ago, Evain wouldn't have cared where Leth sat.

"Drink, anyone?" Tally asks from across the low fire. He twists in his seat and produces a leather-wrapped bottle and a stack of small wooden cups from one of the packs. "It's strong, mind you."

"He's not joking." Darren takes the bottle next. "He brews it himself." He pours some directly into his own flask, then passes it onto Bricks, who takes a cup.

"Maybe you shouldn't," Haldis starts, but sighs and pours a cup when Marta pouts.

"I deserve a drink," Marta says earnestly. "I deserve at least five, but I'll stop at one. Probably."

Even in the unsteady firelight, Evain can read the exasperation on Haldis's face. She holds onto the bottle for a long moment before pouring a cup for herself as well.

There are two cups left when the bottle reaches Evain. He casually hides one in the shadows next to him, while asking, "Who's your contract with, Tally?"

Tally takes a sip, his slight smile unchanging. His hood is thrown back around his shoulders, but his expression still feels hidden. "That's a delicate question around these parts. What if it's some fell demon?"

"I'd be in no position to judge if you were demon bound." Evain pours until the little wooden cup is nearly full. The liquid is thick, clear in the firelight, and smells like spice and vanilla. "But I know what divinity feels like."

"You don't have to answer him," Leth says suddenly. He's done with his food, sitting with his knees up and his arms around them. "He's always like this."

Evain leans a little closer. "Like what?"

Firelight dances in Leth's glare, but he doesn't retreat.

Tally laughs. "Pass the bottle back, will you? I'm an acolyte of Edren. The Wild Mother."

Carefully balancing his cup, Evain stretches to return the bottle via Haldis. Ever-curious Marta takes up the questions about Tally's practice. Whether he can talk to plants—not quite—or if he's immune to poison—yes. The local foliage is also how he locates rifts so precisely.

While they talk, Evain looks over to find Leth watching him again. This time, it takes Leth a moment longer to look away.

Already tipsy from the breath of Leth's attraction, Evain shifts on the ground and lounges a little closer. He says just for the two of them, "Did you want a drink?"

"All right," Leth answers, just as quietly.

Evain takes a sip first. The liquor is honey-sweet and burns down his throat. The vanilla lingers on his lips as he passes the cup to Leth. Their bare fingers don't quite touch. Somehow, the knowledge they *almost* touched burns even hotter than the alcohol.

"What about you, Leth?" Darren asks from across the fire. "The way you fought back at the outpost looked a little like Reed. Did you serve in the military like he used to?"

Leth's lips tighten almost imperceptibly, but his voice is steady in reply. "No, I've just trained with a lot of soldiers over the years. I spent a few years with the Port Charain Riverswords." His gaze lowers. "What brought you and Bricks to Captain Oakven's company?"

Darren takes the change of topic and runs with it, without seeming to notice Leth was deflecting. But maybe Evain shouldn't feel so smug about knowing Leth better than any of them, because he has no idea why Leth *didn't* join the military.

Logically, Leth should have enlisted. When Evain first passed through Ostaris two centuries ago, the ka Tariels already ran the Charaini military. Combine Leth's rigid work ethic and religious fervor with his pathological devotion to duty, and Ronan should have been recruiting him out of the army instead of a tiny mercenary troop.

But he didn't enlist. Evain wonders if Leth will deflect his questions too, if he asks.

Leth brings the wooden cup to his lips. The movement slows in the firelight, and Evain can focus on nothing else. Leth's lower lip indents at the wooden rim, and the angle of his neck makes Evain's fingers itch to touch him. The knowledge that Leth's mouth is pressed to the same cup that Evain just drank from makes Evain's blood quicken, and his heart drums with the staccato beat of obsession.

Like a brand-new rift, pulling him closer and closer. Evain is all too willing to be dragged in.

LETH

"Who's on watch tonight?" The liquor's as strong as Tally promised. Leth passes the cup back to Evain after a single sip. "I can take a shift."

From the corner of his eye, he watches Evain rub his thumb over the rim of the cup.

"I'll take the first shift," Darren says quickly. "I'm useless for late shifts."

"Darkblade here sleeps like a fucking log once he's out," Bricks confirms.

Evain takes a tiny sip, lips curling in a smirk for some unknown reason. "All right, how about Darren, Bricks, me, then Leth?" He raises his cup to the paladins and Tally. "You three can take turns tomorrow—I think dashing Sir Marta needs her beauty sleep tonight."

"That rift was a bastard," Marta agrees sleepily.

Leth sits back against the rocks as the others chat. The rock is cold through his coat, and the hard ground is a far cry from the inns they've been staying at through Charain. But Leth is more comfortable than he's been in a long time. He hadn't had a true fight since the Unbinding. Only when his blade sliced into the vaidkos's neck had he realized how much he needed this. Adrenaline. Purpose. The *safety* of combat, when he knows what to do, and he knows his companion has his back.

There was something different about fighting with Evain today. They've fought together before—infiltrating Fort Tarhaeg, breaking into the Bright Cathedral. Evain was always competent and powerful.

But he hadn't seamlessly adapted to Leth's fighting style the way he did today. He was so attuned to Leth's movements that at every step, he placed himself exactly where Leth needed him. Drawing the vaidkos's attention, distracting, repositioning. Giving Leth the perfect opening for slaughter.

The memory is almost as warm as the red scarf around his neck.

Maybe working with Evain isn't so bad, even if he's demon-bound. As long as Evain's not hurting anyone, and as long as they're working towards a worthy cause, Leth wouldn't mind letting Evain watch his back a while longer.

After helping clean up, Leth sits by the fire again and watches as everyone settles for the night. Darren moves his bedroll to a tent, then climbs a little ways up the hill to get a better vantage for his watch shift. Bricks checks on the horses, then disappears into the same tent as Darren.

Tally disappears behind a wide-trunked tree, and after a subtle flux of magic, doesn't emerge from the other side. Leth knows very little about Wild Edren, but disappearing into a tree seems like a plausible aspect of her jurisdiction. He'll have to ask Tally about that later.

Marta giggles as Haldis half-pulls, half-carries her into their tent. The giggling continues after the tent flap closes, then ends abruptly. Leth looks away—and meets Evain's eyes. Evain's expression doesn't change. He just holds Leth's gaze a moment before disappearing into the third tent. The canvas illuminates faintly red.

A fact Leth has been skating around all night is manifestly clear: it's far too cold to sleep outdoors, and there are only three tents. There's no question of where he's sleeping.

The thought of sharing an enclosed space with Evain makes Leth more nervous than throwing himself at a vaidkos. But he's trained all his life to suppress unease and irrational fears; he gathers his bedroll and nerves, and slips into the tent.

Evain's sitting on his own bedroll, rebraiding his long hair. He doesn't look up from the steady movements of his long fingers. A coin-sized mote of light hovers at the apex of the tent, illuminating everything in soft, intimate red.

Silence hangs between them, taut as a bowstring.

Or maybe that's just Leth, his shoulders tensing as he lays out his bedroll. Unbuttons his coat and unlaces his boots. Maybe Evain doesn't notice how small the tent is, low enough that Leth almost has to duck. It's wide enough for three people, but not wide enough for Leth to forget the steady sound of Evain's breath.

Evain finally breaks the silence when Leth is halfway into his bedroll.

"I was wondering something." Evain's voice is low, his eyes dark and unreadable. They're only two feet apart. If Leth leaned in, and Evain leaned in, they could touch.

Leth wrestles down his wayward thoughts. "What were you wondering?"

"Why didn't you join the army?" Evain snaps his fingers, and the floating light dims. "I thought I knew you pretty well, but I realized when Darren asked that I don't know that."

Leth's hard-won calm scatters. His fingernails dig into his thighs. "It wasn't a good fit."

"I don't believe that." Evain leans back on his arms. "You don't have to tell me if you don't want to, of course. I'm only curious. But rest assured, nothing you say could possibly scandalize me."

"Can anything scandalize you?"

Evain grins. "I live in hope."

Leth leans back on his hands, mirroring Evain. Something about the dim light and Evain's careful interest, the lingering sense of security from their battle together, makes him feel safe enough to talk about this. Maybe it's silly to hide it. Secrets can be a weakness too.

"I'll have to disappoint you, because this isn't scandalous at all." Leth keeps his voice down, remembering how far Marta's giggles carried. "I was due to enlist when I was eighteen. I'd completed almost all of the initial recruitment trials."

"Recruitment trials? I assumed your family just lifted a finger and got in."

Leth's mouth ticks up in a wry smile. "Everyone has to serve one year as an ordinary soldier before being promoted, even legacy recruits, and everyone has to pass all the tests. Though you're right, there's not much suspense for ka Tariels." His smile fades. "I suppose I'm truly exceptional in that regard. The last step is a swearing-in ceremony. It's held twice a year, every summer and winter. You have to attend to formalize your enlistment, and if you miss the initiation, your enlistment is canceled."

His was supposed to be midsummer. The sweltering, humid night only spiked his nausea, intensified the pounding in his head.

"I can't imagine you being late for anything," Evain says.

"I was careless." Leth takes a few breaths and forces the emotion from his voice—but he can't stop the twisting pain between his ribs. He hasn't talked about this in years. "Some friends invited me out the night before. I didn't drink much, but my wine was drugged. I didn't realize in time, and I was too incapacitated to attend the ceremony the next day."

"Who was it?"

The question startles Leth. Evain's voice is colder than he's ever heard it.

Who was it? Is that the problem? "It doesn't matter." Leth's chest hurts. He shouldn't have talked about this.

"I shouldn't have been out the night before the ceremony. The responsibility was—"

"I don't care if you were responsible or not," Evain says, still dangerously calm and cold. "I just want to know who it was."

Assuming responsibility is simpler. But Leth should have known Evain wouldn't let things stay simple. "Javius Orst. My brother's adjutant."

Evain's gaze glitters sharp in the red light. "Did he hurt you?"

Leth's nails dig into his thighs again. "Nothing happened."

Head spinning and limbs faltering, he managed to get home and lock himself in his room before anything happened. *If* anything would have happened—he'll never know. Maybe Javius really was just trying to help him walk home. The uncertainty may be the strangest part to process.

But in the end, nothing happened that night. The next day is what ruined Leth's life.

Evain looks away first this time. The cold echo leaves his voice. "I wouldn't think any less of you if something had happened," he says lightly. "But I apologize for prying."

Leth's fingers unclench. "It's fine." To his surprise, it's true. He's fine. Not happy, but fine. He survived this trial of emotion, and Evain neither dismissed nor pitied him. "Anyway, I had no evidence of anything, and I missed the initiation ceremony. My brother refused to make an exception, and he forbade me from enlisting that season. Or ever. He said he didn't want to give the appearance of nepotism."

"That was cruel of him."

Leth has never thought of it as cruel before. At the time, he thought Anton was being harsh but fair, in keeping with Ka Dravos's teachings. But when else has Anton ever been so faithful to Ka Dravos?

"That's the ka Tariels for you," Leth says eventually, lying down.

Evain snaps his fingers, and the red light winks out. Leth thinks they're done talking, but minutes later, when Leth's stomach has done twisting, Evain says into the darkness, "I'm glad Ronan recruited you."

Leth doesn't have to count his breaths for calm anymore. "I'm glad too."

☽○☾

LETH HALF-WAKES TO a tap on the tent frame, and Bricks calling through the darkness, "Evain? Your watch is next."

When Leth fell asleep, he was in his bedroll, several feet away from Evain. Now, he's moved over, his own bedroll discarded, his cheek on Evain's chest. His arm rests on Evain's stomach, and Evain's arm drapes loose around his shoulders. Evain's chest rumbles underneath Leth's ear as he answers, "Just a moment."

Evain strokes Leth's arm, fingers barely-there through Leth's sleeve. Leth doesn't hate the touch. He's warm and comfortable—and he'll ruin it if he wakes up. So, he keeps his eyes closed as Evain sighs a warm gust through his hair. As Evain strokes his arm one more time, then extricates himself.

Leth is colder without Evain beneath him, until fabric rustles through the darkness. Warm weight settles over him, and fingertips touch his forehead like burning feathers. Light as clouds and searing as the sun.

Only when Evain leaves the tent does Leth reach down and confirm that Evain covered him in his own discarded bedding too, wrapping him doubly warm before leaving him alone in the tent. That light, burning sensation tickles his heart. Pulling the bedding closer, Leth waits for his pulse to calm down. It's a long time before he falls back asleep.

)O(

THEY COME ACROSS the next rift five days later, after checking several inactive sites of previous rifts. Evain's horse is reacting to something unseen, snorting plumes of frosty breath into the air, when Tally calls out that he senses a rift a mile away.

Leth recalls Georgia Oakven's map. "That's a new location."

"Careful, everyone." Evain pulls his horse under control. His handsome features draw into an uncharacteristic frown. "New isn't a good thing."

Does Leth imagine the way Evain's gaze lingers on him? He's been imagining a lot of things, the past few nights.

They leave most of the horses with Bricks, Darren, and Tally, but this time Evain brings Daziroth along. Bricks just mutters, "Better you than me." She's obviously no longer concerned for Daziroth's wellbeing; the overly cuddly stallion has proven impervious to the cold.

Marta recites a prayer-spell over herself and Haldis. Leth adjusts the pin on his red scarf and buttons the ends under his coat, then activates a spell bead for speed and agility.

Daziroth follows like he's attached to Evain's shadow, with an eerie amount of focus. For such a large horse, he makes surprisingly little noise winding through the narrow forest trails.

"Do you sense any vaidkos?" Leth asks. His own magic isn't enough to sense demons without a deliberate, time-consuming spell, so he has to rely on the three contracted mages.

"None," Haldis says.

"The woods are too quiet," Marta adds, then hisses through her teeth.

A moment later, Leth feels the sick change in the air. Nauseating, frightening. A burned-hair taste that hooks into his hindbrain, triggering primal instincts that scream *run*.

Marta casts another prayer-spell, and this one washes over Leth too. Mother Sephine's clarity doesn't erase the fear but eases it enough that Leth can think through the miasma as they continue.

The woods give way abruptly to a ruined village. Stone and log walls broken, roofs gone, piles of rubble smoothed over by snow. Black-red magic flickers beyond half-standing buildings.

Empty, snow-crusted streets lead them to the shelter of a tall, lone-standing stone wall. Evain's horse hangs behind them, as if guarding their backs. When they stop, Leth says, "I'd like to try sealing the rift this time."

"By all means," Evain says.

So Leth doesn't draw his sword as they approach the frayed edge of another world. Instead, he fumbles under his coat for the pendant Evain gave him. He can't feel the engraving through his glove, but he knows the runes by heart, and the silver map of a solution gives him courage to face the rift itself.

Which he needs, because the rift is *wrong*.

What was once the village's main street is now a gash of twisting shadows, twenty feet high and thirty feet long. Leth's brain instinctively rejects the visuals. False. Wrong. Not of this world. Red and black fog—or yellow and gray—a sickening green—pools in the great gap of it, swirling too thickly for Leth to see anything of the realm beyond. If he squints, maybe he can make sense of the moving shapes.

Evain squeezes the back of his neck, the touch muffled through his glove and Leth's scarf. "Don't look too close."

"Fuck off," Leth mutters, but his retort lacks heat. He's annoyed by how unannoyed he is. How stupidly comforting he finds Evain's low laugh in response.

"The first vaidkos is crossing over," Evain says, as the rift pulses ominously. "Start the spell—we've got your back."

He steps away, but Leth still feels his touch on the back of his neck. Lights flash against the rift: Marta's magic shield and Haldis's shining blade. Leth clutches his pendant and focuses inward. Tapping into the depths of his own magic, the only small strength he was born with, he begins to chant.

The words have a grammarless pattern. Names of runes in Charaini and Lyrisenian. Layers of denotation and connotation, familiar and foreign, overlap and echo each other. Leth's eyes are open, but he sees little besides flashing lights and swirling power. Wild rift magic rushes towards him, a gust of scouring wind—

The next line of the spell is *protection*, and Leth shakes not from the force of the rift but from the force of his own spell. Evain's spell, pouring from his lips, surrounding him.

Silver light pierces the cracks between his fingers as the pendant glows. Leth sees the array etched in his vision, overlaying the rest of the world. The rift. The paladins chasing a vaidkos back into the void. The demon-mage standing close by, supporting the paladins at range and never leaving Leth's side.

Leth doesn't have time to wonder where Evain found so much power, when he hasn't flirted with anyone in days. He speaks the final line, and the rift implodes. The smoke and terror suck back into the vanishing gap, until all that remains is the empty street.

Still clasping the pendant, Leth stands stunned. That was… easier than he expected.

Light snowflakes glitter in the pearlescence of Marta's shield spell. Daziroth trots over, great hooves muffled, and butts his head affectionately against Evain's back.

Evain turns to Leth, a faint smirk on his lips. Some strands of hair have fallen loose from his braid, fluttering with sparks of lingering magic. "How was it?"

Leth's heart thuds, and his daze has nothing to do with exhaustion. He's not nearly as tired as he should be from working a spell that powerful—and that's due to the skill of the spellcrafting, the efficient harnessing and dispersal of power. The spell mostly used the rift's own magic instead of drawing too deep on the caster's reserves.

Conservation of magic isn't a consideration for most mages, because the truly powerful all have access to divine or demonic power. Crafting a spell like this with uncontracted mages in mind is highly unusual.

Leth unclenches his hand from the pendant. "How long did it take you to write this?"

"I know, I'm very impressive, aren't I?" Evain's smirk deepens, and in his daze, Leth doesn't even mind. "Why don't I tell you over—"

Daziroth's scream breaks through the peace, and dark power explodes behind Evain. Smoke and fear, light and despair. A new rift severs the veil between realms.

Evain swears and starts to chant, but there's no time. It's too close. Leth moves on instinct, dodging Daziroth's scrambling retreat, and seizes hold of Evain's arm. He needs to pull Evain out of harm's way—but the rift is still too close. There's still no time. Evain can't finish the spell, and Leth can't drag either of them to safety.

Dark magic pulses and sweeps them away.

EVAIN

Oh, fuck no. Evain is *not* going home.

The rift isn't full-formed yet. Just a swirl of wild magic flaring along the faults between worlds. Evain, Leth, and Daziroth tumble through roiling clouds of black and red, waves of magnetic terror, spiraling towards—even the gods don't know.

Evain refuses to follow. Not just for himself, but for the pretty sword-witch gripping his forearm with iron strength. Leth's face is bloodless white, but his lips move in a spell Evain can't hear. A bead in his hair flashes, and a shield shimmers around them, weaving silver through the blood-red of Evain's magic.

Nothing else happens. There's no way Leth knows how to counter this, but Leth's grip doesn't waver. He doesn't stop trying to fight the magical onslaught. Evain can't waver either, because he's the reason Leth is in this mess. The rift only draws in creatures of demonic origin like Evain and Daziroth. Even demon-contracted mages wouldn't be dragged in so easily. Had Leth not leaped towards him, had Leth not grabbed his arm and tried to protect him, he would still be safe with Marta and Haldis in the mortal world.

But Leth did leap towards him, because that's the kind of person Leth is. It would be heartwarming, if the results weren't so terrifying.

Drawing on his last reserves of power, Evain stabilizes their tumbling and yanks them away from the yawning abyss of the demonic realm. He hooks a strand of power around Daziroth, tethering him close, and takes Leth into his arms. The embrace leaves no space between them. His heart stumbles when Leth clutches his coat. Their echoing heartbeats are the only living things in the swirling void.

Evain can keep them from falling further, but they're still stuck in the rift itself. He doesn't have enough power left to throw them back to the mortal realm.

But there's an easy way to get more.

Evain works one hand between them and touches Leth's chin. Tilts his face up, and stares into his wide hazel eyes. Sparks and ashes, Leth is beautiful. Evain regrets desperately that he can't take the time to chase Leth like he wanted to—to court him for weeks, months, years if need be, until Leth's walls of restraint and distrust erode away.

Neither of them is ready, but Evain's out of options. At least he's always loved a dramatic gesture.

"Hey gorgeous," Evain drawls, and from the way Leth's eyes widen, Leth hears him even through the roar of the rift. "What's a pretty thing like you doing in a place like this?"

"Evain, this isn't the—"

Leth's voice chokes off when Evain runs his thumb along the thin curve of his lip. Desire pulses around them, a bright new wave in the sea of power.

Not enough yet. Evain drops his other hand to Leth's narrow waist. The layers in the way don't help, but Leth's breath hitches even so—and again when Evain tightens his grip. "I'd apologize for being forward," Evain says, his voice resonating with the rush of power. "But we both know I'm really not sorry for this."

He leans down, and as his lips meet Leth's, he closes his eyes. For a moment, all the wild magic falls away, and all Evain feels is the electric point of contact. Leth's shock. His own. He licks the curve of Leth's lips, and Leth tilts his head in subtle surrender.

A new storm consumes Evain. Desire thunders through his bones and arcs like lightning through his veins. Leth's desire or his own, it's impossible to tell. The taste of dry lips and warm breath is a catalyst like no other.

All Evain wants is to deepen the kiss, but he breaks it instead. With his new surge of power, he forces a path back to the mortal world.

LETH

Between one breath and the next, the wild magic vanishes. Leth staggers as solid ground appears under his feet. Mostly solid—his boots sink into snow. He would have fallen if not for Evain's arms still around him. Evain's hand still at his waist.

Leth rests stunned for a moment against the steady heat of Evain's body, then shoves away. Evain lets him go, and Leth does fall this time. One knee lands in the snow, which is fine. He needs the space. He can't think.

Evain stumbles a few steps away and leans over, hands braced on his knees. His hair's fallen half out of its braid, a night-black curtain hiding his expression. Daziroth trembles next to him, his ears pinned back, looking just as shocked as the two men.

A white and black world surrounds them. A foot of snow, soft beneath the icy crust, blankets the jagged hillscape. Leth can't tell if the stone shapes to the south are rock formations or ruins. Snow-covered earth rises around them in every direction, cupping them in a shallow valley. Few trees break up the landscape, and the sky above is heavy and gray.

The snow-bitten wind whisks away Leth's gasping breaths. His mind is a mess. He can't meditate his way through so many shocks at once. Falling into the rift. His magic burning away uselessly against a challenge he couldn't face with a sword. Evain's strength pulling them out. Evain's kiss. Perhaps most shocking of all: Leth didn't hate it, and he didn't want it to end.

He can't handle that right now.

Daziroth snorts and knocks his head against Evain's back, nearly sending Evain to his knees too. "Thanks, Daisy, I really appreciate that." Evain straightens up and leans against Daziroth's shoulder. Exhaustion grays his face.

Leth sucks in a breath of frigid air and shoves to his feet. He pulls his scarf higher over his mouth and nose. "Where are we?"

Evain tucks his hair behind his ear. The wind immediately whips it free again. "Still in Lyrisenia, praise Sephine's blessed tits." He points to a mountain range, its jagged peaks faintly visible through the clouds. "But we're at least a week north and east of where we should be. I think."

Without any sun peeking through the clouds, Leth can't confirm the direction Evain's pointing. He'll just have to trust him on that. Leth squints through the wind, his vision a little clearer now that his dizziness has faded. "We should take shelter. The ruins over there look like the best option."

The wind cuts sharper by the moment, and snow falls more heavily.

"My thoughts exactly." Evain crunches through the snow towards him, Daziroth at his back. "Let me give you a leg up." His voice is as smooth as ever, but his gaze is strangely indirect. If Evain was anyone else, Leth would call him nervous.

"Don't worry about me." Leth's pulse quickens as the distance between them lessens. He's trying to think about survival here, not the heat of Evain's lips on his. "You can ride." Shoving his hands in his pockets, he strides off before Evain can continue the argument.

The sky darkens above as they walk. Evain follows behind him, not too near and not too far. He sends Daziroth ahead, letting the glossy dark horse break a path through the snow. Almost prancing in excitement, Daziroth seems completely unperturbed by the cold winds. Leth envies the horse's energy.

Snow-heavy wind buffets him, and even Leth's thick coat can't keep him warm. He regrets using up most of his saved charms in the rift; a shield spell might help with the weather, but he needs to sleep before he can prepare another. His dwindling endurance is all that's pushing him through the snow.

Concentrating on putting one foot in front of the other, Leth uses the waving flag of Daziroth's tail as a guide. The closer they get, the harder the ruins are to see.

Leth catches himself the first time he stumbles.

The second time, he falls to one knee. His head spins before he shoves to his feet again and continues forward, lungs aching with the cold.

The third time, Evain catches him by the elbow. "This is stupid." Evain raises his voice over the wind. "You're riding the rest of the way, and nothing you say or do will prevent that from happening, so why don't we skip the rest of the argument?"

Leth finds it difficult to think, much less argue, when Evain stands this close to him. The firm, gentle grip on his elbow is an anchor. "Fine, then. If your monster horse will let me."

"Of course he will." Evain whistles, and Daziroth stops up ahead. "Daisy's a good boy."

Daziroth looks about as skeptical as Leth feels, but obediently stands still. Leth reaches for the saddle, wishing he had a rock to mount from, or that Daziroth was much shorter. Instead, he tucks his knee in Evain's cupped hands. They don't count off; he just jumps when Evain lifts in perfect coordination. Leth settles onto the cold leather of the saddle, hyperaware of Evain's absence. The brief warmth of his touch is gone, so there's no reason for Leth's skin to be tingling like this.

The stirrups are too long, but Leth doesn't intend to take his gloves off to adjust the leathers, so he'll have to go without. Taking the reins, he's about to suggest they switch spots halfway, when Evain grabs the low front and back of the saddle.

Evain's wrist rubs the inside of Leth's thigh. Stepping into the stirrup presses his leg right behind Leth's, and the sudden friction shorts out Leth's thoughts. Leth only processes what Evain is doing when the whole saddle tilts, and Evain swings up behind him.

The force of the wind cuts off, replaced with Evain's body sheltering him in warmth. Chest against back, thighs behind thighs. Evain reaches forward to take the reins from Leth's slack hands, caging Leth in his arms. He says into Leth's ear, "Let's skip this argument too, all right?"

Leth can't muster a response when his heart pounds so violently in his throat. He sits ramrod-straight, refusing to lean back as Evain nudges Daziroth forward, as if any speck of distance will make a difference.

Whether he's leaning against Evain or walking far away doesn't matter. He still feels Evain's tongue swiping at the seam of his lips.

Leth knows the parameters of Evain's magic. Evain draws power not from touch, but from lust. A touch or kiss is simply the means to the end, and the end is *emotion*. Desire. If Leth had felt no attraction in response, Evain's magic would have failed, and the tempest of wild magic would have torn them to shreds.

A shiver wracks through Leth, and he knows he's being childishly stubborn. His ideals of self-control and restraint used to be a crutch—now they're a tether. Evain has taken care of Leth, despite Leth's best or worst intentions, ever since they left Ostaris. Maybe taking shelter from the wind isn't weakness after all.

Ten minutes later, Leth allows himself to melt against Evain's chest. His frozen joints unlock one by one. Only then does Evain ask, directly into his ear, "Are you mad that I kissed you?"

"No. It was necessary." Leth pulls his scarf up against a fresh slice of wind. He's not mad that Evain kissed him. He's mad that it worked. That he can't keep denying how much he wants Evain.

That it still says nothing about how Evain feels about him.

This might, though: the way Evain moves the reins to one hand and wraps the other arm around Leth's waist. "It's all right if you're mad." Evain tightens his arm, and his sigh is lost to the wind. "But I'm glad that you're not."

Winter swirls around them, and the ruins rise before them. Leth's fingers curl in his perfectly fitting new gloves.

Nobody else got new clothes the morning they left Lanwatch. Just him.

EVAIN

Evain has never been so aware of how fragile humans are. Hopefully his panic doesn't show in his voice. Leth was shivering when Evain threw him onto the horse, and Evain doesn't know nearly enough about frostbite. He can't help his ridiculous fear that if he lets go, Leth will be blown away into the storm. The blizzard is very strong, after all, and Leth is very small.

That holding onto him has its own benefits is beside the point.

Evain isn't impervious to the weather, but his internal heat is much stronger than a human's. He and Daziroth can last much longer than Leth in the cold. Luckily, Leth hasn't seemed to notice anything strange about that yet.

Leth is preoccupied with other matters, apparently. He turns his head slightly, the angle still wrong to face each other, and his snow-streaked hair paints ice against Evain's jaw. "How did you get my measurements, by the way?"

There's a riveting softness to his voice. Not a quality Evain often associates with Leth. If Evain had known such softness was hiding under Leth's prickly shell, he would have tried to break into him months ago. Years ago.

"I have a very good eye." Evain hesitates, though *hesitation* is not a quality he often associates with himself. "And I've spent a lot of time looking at you."

Leth's hair moves against his jaw again. If he doesn't stop moving, Evain won't be able to conceal his reaction. "Why just for me? Did the others have better winter gear already?"

"I wouldn't know. I don't pay as much attention to them."

Maybe the blizzard is affecting him after all. Dizzying him into madness. He swears he hears Leth reply, "That's good." He definitely hears Leth's next words: "I was wrong about you. You aren't that bad a person."

An unfamiliar pang of guilt tempers Evain's reaction. Leth wouldn't say that if he knew the truth. Cradling his fragile human, Evain says, "You weren't wrong." His chin leans more heavily on Leth's narrow shoulder. "I'm a terrible person."

)O(

BY THE TIME they reach the ruins, Leth is shivering again, and Evain's worry reaches a fever pitch. He keeps it to himself, but nudges Daziroth faster past the first few shards of wall.

The ruins aren't on any map Evain has ever seen. Through a half-arched gateway waits the largest building left standing: a hewn-rock chapel. Snow piles along its walls, and any glass is long since shattered and scattered, but its roof is intact. Evain doesn't sense any danger at the archway threshold. Glassy gouges mar the carvings around the door and the gateway pillars. The people who last worshiped at this chapel cleaned up their spells before they left.

Evain rides Daziroth up the snow-swept steps, and the wind cuts off as they enter the chapel. The sudden stillness roars in Evain's ears. He gestures a mote of light into being above them, chasing the darkness away.

Vestibules branch off in each cardinal direction, and the central chamber is circular and plain. No altars or benches. Just a flat black-rock circle slightly raised in the center of the floor. Time and weather have pock-marked the rest of the flagstone floor, but the center circle remains untouched.

Evain doesn't think it's a coincidence the rift led them to a Lyrisenian summoning chapel. At least this one has been properly disarmed, and its careful construction likely makes it the safest shelter in the forgotten town.

Reluctantly, Evain unwraps his arms from Leth and dismounts. Leth slides down too, without protesting the supportive hand at his waist. Shivers vibrate through both of them as Evain doesn't let go, and Leth doesn't shake him off.

"Let's move to a smaller chamber," Evain says. "Easier to keep warm." *And a bit less creepy.*

The first chamber is useless, empty except for shards of broken glass and ceramic debris. The second was once a library, and it's good enough. Nothing remains of the books but dust and scraps of leather gathered in the corners. Tipped-over chairs and tables scatter between tipped-over shelves. The fireplace is the important part.

"These carvings were destroyed by magic, not the elements." Leth reaches towards a wall but doesn't quite touch. "No god was worshiped here."

Evain tugs Leth away by the shoulder. "Explore *after* you've stopped shivering."

"How are you not cold?" Leth asks.

"I am, though. I'm very, very cold. If only I had someone to warm me up." Evain pulls Leth to the empty fireplace. "Stay put. I'll get the firestone from the saddle bags."

Leth's face is red from the cold, his hair bedraggled. Evain leaves him reluctantly, reassuring himself that his human probably won't freeze to death in his absence. He swiftly untacks Daziroth in the central chamber, where the horse's ears swivel in every direction. Faint scurrying sounds can be heard now and then.

Evain tells his horse, "You can eat the rats, as long as you don't let Leth see you, all right?"

Daziroth rubs his head against Evain's chest, then stalks away into the shadows. His hooves are eerily quiet against the broken flagstones.

Back in the library, Leth hasn't stayed put; he's feeding pieces of a broken bookshelf into the fireplace. He doesn't move away when Evain approaches, and their shoulders brush as Evain squats with the firestones. Sending his mote of light up the chimney confirms there's a clear vent for the smoke. Evain extinguishes it once the fire catches hold.

Pocketing the firestones, Evain is at a loss for what to do next. The urgency of the ride is over. The howling wind has quieted. Leth's red-rimmed eyes are fixed on him. Instinct draws Evain forward to brush melting snow from Leth's hair, and he teases on reflex, "We should get you out of those wet clothes."

Leth's gaze flicks down. Firelight gilds the tips of his eyelashes. "You *are* terrible." He starts unfastening his gloves.

"Practical," Evain insists. "My motives are purely practical." Anticipation swells on a wave of giddy desire.

He watches Leth undress as he strips off his own coat. He likes Leth in any amount of clothing, but less is definitely more. Boots and daggers, gloves and coats pile together by the hearth, until Evain and Leth are only dressed in shirts and trousers. Then it's the easiest thing in the world to pull Leth to the ground with him.

They sit nestled together, facing the fire, Leth's back against Evain's chest. Just like sharing a saddle in the storm, except it's quiet now. There's no howling wind to distract Evain from Leth's unsteady pulse. Evain takes Leth's ice-cold hands in his and intertwines their fingers.

Only then, with Leth's hands warming against his, does the band of tension ease from Evain's heart.

Outside, the blizzard still rages, but it can't touch them here. The fire slowly heats the ancient library, and the pretty human in Evain's arms has finally stopped shivering. Evain presses his cheek against Leth's damp hair. A spell bead digs into his skin.

A beautiful man in his arms, a romantic fireside cuddle. Evain's physical reaction is inevitable. He doesn't notice his cock hardening, but he notices the moment Leth feels him. Leth goes rigid, and his fingers tighten between Evain's.

Evain nuzzles his hair. "If you want to stab me, your knife is over there."

Leth's muscles unlock, and he melts back against Evain again. "It's too cold, and you're too warm. You're safe until the blizzard is over."

"May the bard-priests sing of your mercy for centuries to come." Evain nuzzles his hair again. Disengages his fingers and slides his hands up Leth's arms. "Turn around."

Leth twists around to kneel in front of Evain. His eyes glitter in the firelight, and there's a wary edge to his gaze, but no dismay or disgust. "What?"

Evain tucks a strand of hair behind Leth's ear, lingering against the delicate shell. "I need to kiss you."

Leth's eyes drop to his lips. "For the magic?"

"If you'd like the excuse." Evain leans in, and Leth doesn't pull away.

LETH

Their second kiss is far more intense than their first. The only storm is the thundering of Leth's heart; the only wild magic is the fire cascading through his nerves. Evain's lips are slow and steady against his, grounding him in the moment. As the last of his reservations shatter, Leth can't deny himself anymore. He's out of excuses not to want this.

Miles away from everywhere he's ever known, this insistent, infuriating man tastes like home. Better. Leth never belonged at home the way he belongs in Evain's arms right now.

Evain touches Leth's ear again, and the sparks of pleasure race straight to his cock. Leth never knew his ear could be so sensitive. Then Evain's palm curves over the back of his neck, and Leth's breath punches out of him. Overwhelmed by the simplicity of the touch,

Leth doesn't know how he'll survive anything more than this.

But he wants to find out.

Leth pulls away, panting, and tries to wrestle his breathing under control. Evain's hand tightens on the back of his neck, keeping him close enough that their breath mingles between their lips.

"Don't do that," Evain says, his voice like heated silk.

"What?"

Evain grins. "Don't control yourself. I want to drive you crazy."

Leth's breath shudders away as Evain seizes his mouth again. There's nothing slow or steady about this kiss. Evain pushes, and Leth follows until he lies flat on the dusty floor. Evain's hand rests protectively behind his head, and his tongue delves deep, igniting every nerve in Leth's body. Leth groans into the kiss, and the next slick movement of Evain's lips drives away his momentary embarrassment.

Evain maps out his ribs, waist, arms with leisurely, exhilarating touches. Leth bucks up reflexively, and Evain grins against his mouth. "Like that, gorgeous."

"Do you ever stop talking?" Leth gasps, tangling his own hands in Evain's long hair and yanking him down. Evain just laughs, until Leth silences him in another kiss.

He's not as good at this as Evain is. His experience is limited, and Evain's is obviously not. A tiny, insecure corner of Leth's mind—one of the few corners not over-whelmed by Evain's touch—worries Evain can tell. Maybe he'll regret starting this because Leth isn't good at it.

Leth doesn't know when he started to care what Evain thought of him, but he can't help it. He's never been good enough at anything. Why should this be any different?

"You're distracted." Evain sighs, sitting back. "I must be losing my touch."

"Sorry." A stupid, childish fear spikes through Leth—that by worrying about fucking up, he's ruined this anyway. His family didn't want him; his god didn't want him. Why should Evain?

"Tell me what's wrong," Evain says, as if that's an easy thing to ask. Maybe for him it is. "I don't want to wake up to… Actually, the last time I woke up to a knife at my throat was pretty hot."

Nothing's wrong, Leth wants to say. He wants to don his denial like armor, hiding his weak points. But exhaustion and desire have shattered his defenses. "I guess I was just wondering what you see in me."

Evain stares, like one or both of them truly has gone insane, then leans in to kiss just the corner of Leth's mouth. "I see you," Evain says. "That's all I want to see. Come here."

Leth leans back in Evain's arms again, and this time Evain pushes his hair away to kiss the back of his neck. Tenderness tingles across his skin. Then Evain bites, and Leth's thoughts scatter with a groan.

"I can feel how much you want me, you know," Evain says against his nape. His hand wanders towards Leth's trouser laces. "I've felt it for ages, but I didn't realize it was you until that morning at the Dancing Hog."

Evain really doesn't shut up. Leth can't focus on his insecurities when Evain's hand is at his waistband, and Evain's cock is hard against his ass.

"You're like nobody I've ever met," Evain continues. "Do you know how much effort I've spent restraining myself the past few weeks? Every part of you entices me."

The heat of the crackling fire is nothing compared to Leth's burning blood. The last of the ice melts from his veins, and he's surprised his breath doesn't rise like steam. His hips buck up as Evain gets his trousers open.

"I wish I could share my power with you," Evain says as he draws out Leth's cock. "So you could feel in your soul exactly how much I want you too."

Leth's breath stutters. Surrounded by Evain's honeyed voice and the confident fingers encircling his cock, he can't think about anything else. Every expert touch ignites his nerves, and he arches into Evain's grasp. He doesn't know what to do with his hands and ends up clawing bruises into Evain's thighs on either side of him.

Spurred on by the bruises, Evain twists his fingers to the base of Leth's cock, then reaches farther to palm Leth's balls. Leth's toes curl, and his eyes roll back—and Evain stops moving. Just *holds* him, as Leth jerks up instinctively against his grip. He's desperate for more. Everything is so much, so intense, his eyes start to sting.

"Evain," he whispers, the closest he can get to begging.

"That name sounds good on your lips." The smugness in Evain's voice is equal parts maddening and delicious. "Say it again?"

Leth just sucks in air through his teeth as Evain resumes stroking his cock. It's easier with his eyes closed. Easier still when Evain brings his other hand up to cover Leth's eyes, like a living blindfold, blocking out the rest of the world. Keeping Leth pinned in place with his head against Evain's shoulder, even as he squirms with every movement.

Each time he squirms, he feels Evain's cock rock-hard against his backside. Evain's breath grows more ragged in his ear as well.

"Call my name, pretty Leth," Evain purrs. "I'll let you come either way. I'm a gentleman. But I really want to hear it."

"You are *not* a—" Leth breaks into a moan. Evain's grip tightens, and Leth's mind blanks out in pleasure. Safe in the darkness behind Evain's palm, he shudders through his release.

Whether he calls out Evain's name or merely thinks it, he isn't sure. But when his mind clears, Evain is murmuring smug nonsense into his ear. So maybe he did call out. Leth's too exhausted and spent to care either way.

Not too exhausted to remember his sense of fairness. Evain is still hard behind him. Leth isn't going to be any good at this, but he should still—

There's a wet sound next to his ear. Leth pulls Evain's hand from his eyes and turns to find Evain leisurely licking Leth's come off his long fingers. The curl of his tongue seeking every last drop makes Leth's softening cock twitch briefly. Evain's eyelids lower, and he sighs in pleasure.

Leth touches Evain's chest. His belt. "Let me take care of you too."

Evain covers his hand. His skin is damp where they touch, and the visual of him licking come off his hand spikes through Leth's hindbrain again. "I'm too tired for more tonight. Let's just sleep, all right?"

"You mean you think *I'm* too tired," Leth accuses. But he can't deny it. His eyelids are heavier with every moment, and the sweet warmth of the fire and his post-orgasm languor combine into a powerful sleeping drug. "I can stay awake."

Evain kisses the corner of his lips, then tilts his head and takes his mouth fully, devouring the last shred of resistance from Leth's breath. "Don't think I'm being polite," Evain says when he breaks away. He unfolds his long legs and rises to his feet. "I'm keeping track, and I expect to settle the score next time."

He reaches down. Distracted by the mention of *next time*, Leth doesn't even think before taking his hand and letting Evain pull him to his feet.

They don't have much in the way of supplies, only what Evain had packed on Daziroth. A few days of travel food. Evain's ridiculous, impractical red silk robe. No tent, and only one bedroll, which Evain spreads out by the fire. Leth is asleep as soon as his head touches the ground.

)O(

LETH WAKES TO comfort and warmth. Evain's steady heartbeat under his ear, and Evain's wicked hand wandering lower and lower down his back. Leth's eyes crack open just as Evain finishes his journey with a gentle squeeze of Leth's ass.

"Didn't realize you were a morning person." Leth's voice is rough with sleep, and he makes no attempt at moving. One night's sleep wasn't quite enough to restore him after yesterday's ordeal.

Low laughter vibrates through Evain's chest, into Leth's bones. "I most assuredly am not a morning person." He gives Leth's ass another lingering squeeze. "I much prefer to stay in bed until noon."

His hand stays firmly in place as Leth half sits, bracing himself on one arm over Evain. There are no windows in the ancient library, and the fire has burned low. The enclosed space holds the heat well, but the light is dim. Spread out on the rough bedroll, Evain looks like a painting. His ink-black hair scatters loose all around him, somehow just as smooth and glossy as ever. Reflected firelight suffuses his tanned-gold skin, and the red silk robe falls open over half his chest. The gold and ruby piercing gleams against his nipple.

But surely no painting could capture the intensity in Evain's eyes. Leth senses that behind the sensual facade waits a ravenous predator, fixed on his prey. With every fiber of his being, Leth wants that attention. He doesn't want Evain to look at anyone else like this. He wants to be devoured.

Leth lacks a silver tongue for flirting, so instead of replying, he leans down and covers Evain's lips in his.

Evain's enthusiastic response proves he just might be a morning person after all. By the time they part, Leth is panting. Evain touches Leth's hair and says, "Perhaps I should have mentioned this earlier, but I prefer to top. Is that all right?"

"That's fine," Leth says, though *fine* is an inadequate word for the images seizing his mind.

"Wonderful." Evain pulls Leth down for another brief kiss before sitting up. "Don't move."

Leth leans back on his hands as Evain bends over by the packs. He doesn't need to rummage around—instead he directly opens a specific pocket and retrieves a gilded glass flask. By the size, Leth first assumes it's liquor, until Evain saunters back and sets the flask on the floor next to him.

"Do you bring that everywhere?" Leth asks.

Evain sinks to his knees and caresses Leth's neck. Twists one of Leth's braids around his finger. "Of course I bring lubrication everywhere." He tugs Leth's braid and kisses the corner of his mouth. "Do you expect me to use denseed oil, like I'm raiding Dansa's medicine cabinet?"

Then Leth is too distracted to think about Evain's forethought and preparation, because Evain's tugging at his clothes. Desire tingles along Leth's skin, and he helps discard his shirt quickly. He doesn't want space to think too much, because if he thinks too much, he'll ruin it for himself.

"You're nervous." Evain runs both hands over Leth's bare chest, exploring every curve of muscle and corner of bone. He lingers on a scar below Leth's ribs. "Have you done this before?"

Glaring, Leth unlaces his trousers. "I'm not nervous, and I'm not a virgin, if that's what you're asking." He's too annoyed to be nervous now—and even more annoyed because that's probably why Evain asked him. Evain can read him far too easily.

"Oh, good." Evain kisses Leth's collarbone, then moves lower, until his hair pools cold against Leth's stomach, and his breath gusts wet and warm over Leth's nipple. "I'm nervous enough for both of us."

Leth laughs. "There's no way you're—ngh."

His accusation is chased away by Evain's tongue digging a circle around his nipple. Every nerve in his body pulls to that one point of contact. Leth didn't know he could be that sensitive there.

"Of course I'm nervous," Evain says confidently. He replaces his tongue with his fingers, rolling the sensitive nub. "Why shouldn't I be, when I like you so much?"

He says it so naturally, like it's obvious. Leth wants to believe him. Then Evain tongues his nipple again, and Leth just wants to get fucked *now*.

After kicking his trousers away, Leth finally reaches for Evain's robe. The red silk has already fallen to bare his muscular left shoulder, and the dusky peak of his pierced nipple. Leth touches Evain's other shoulder through the feather-soft fabric, then touches the still-covered nipple, and Evain makes a low, pleased sound at the friction of Leth's fingertips through silk.

The robe is ankle-length, but so askew it barely covers Evain's groin, and Evain's erection is clear through the teasing drape of silk. He's large, but Leth isn't afraid of pain. He's only afraid of how much he wants this, when everything else he's ever wanted has been torn away from him.

All right, fine. He's nervous. He's not a virgin, but he's never fucked *Evain* before, and it's different. It matters.

"Can you really feel how much I want you?" Leth asks, as his fingers move to Evain's piercing. The gems are warm with Evain's body heat.

Evain's eyes flash red in the dim light. The hint of

demonic magic doesn't seem as disgusting as it used to. "I really can," Evain says, as Leth's hands fall to the sash of his robe.

The silk is easy to pull away. It slides from Evain's shoulder and pools on the bedroll, revealing the last expanse of Evain's body. His cock flushes darker than the rest of him, the head nearly purple where it rises from his foreskin, and his balls hang heavy between his muscular thighs.

Leth reaches out, unwilling to appear nervous or intimidated, but Evain catches his hand and brings it to his lips. He presses a kiss to Leth's knuckles, and the look in his eyes evaporates every last shred of doubt from Leth's heart.

Evain places his hands on Leth's chest and pushes him gently, until his back hits the floor. "I've thought a lot about how I'd like to fuck you," Evain says, kneeling between Leth's legs and reaching for the lube. "I don't trust any of the furniture here, so bending you over a table will have to wait. Would your feet even touch the ground?"

Leth's breath catches with the mental image. "Depends on the table."

Chuckling, Evain unscrews the bottle, and a faint floral scent fills the abandoned library. Anticipation twists just as sweet through Leth's stomach.

Evain's slick fingers delve between Leth's thighs, while Evain leans down to catch Leth in another kiss. Leth's grateful for the chance to wrap his arms around Evain's shoulders and close his eyes, to simply feel everything as Evain presses behind his balls and rubs oil over his hole. He doesn't enter, just massaging into tender flesh until Leth is desperate for more.

They've barely started, and a pathetic whimper escapes Leth's lips.

Evain kisses his jaw, his neck. "You're so gorgeous like this," he murmurs against Leth's pulse, and pushes two fingers in at once. "Apologies if I'm moving too fast."

Leth arches with the intrusion, overwhelmed but not enough, and snaps, "If you take much longer, I *will* stab you."

"Kinky." Evain laughs. He laughs a lot during sex, apparently, and every time, the warmth and joy vibrate through Leth's bones. Evain hooks his fingers upwards, massaging into Leth's prostate. "I wanted to tease you for hours, but you're too enticing. I can't last that long this time."

Pleasure consumes Leth's body. He doesn't think he'd survive hours of this.

Leth's mind almost clears when Evain's fingers withdraw from his body, and Evain sits back on his heels. There's a moment of air as Evain tips more oil into his hand, then slicks it over his cock.

His long hair spills over his shoulder, a waist-length curtain. He's so sensually beautiful, so perfectly sculpted, Leth finds it hard to believe he's human. In his current daze of lust, he wouldn't care either way.

Evain sets the glass bottle aside and takes Leth's thighs. Lifting his knees over Evain's shoulders is easy—he's flexible. Meeting the burning-hot intensity in Evain's gaze is far more difficult. But Leth refuses to look away. Refuses to deny himself the sight of Evain's face, twisting into pleasure as he enters Leth's body.

He doesn't need magic to feel Evain's desire after all.

EVAIN

Evain has spent two and a half centuries wandering the human realm. No part of his journeys prepared him for the feeling sweeping over him now. Something deeper and darker than desire. Something more all-consuming than obsession.

He doesn't know how he's survived this long without knowing how far the flush of exertion spreads down Leth's chest. Without knowing how Leth's eyes narrow, then widen with the force of penetration.

Without knowing that when he breathes, "Fuck, Leth, I could spend the next year inside you," Leth clenches down even tighter around his cock, igniting every drop of Evain's blood.

Leth's fingers are white-knuckled in the bedding. "You really don't shut up, do you?"

"There are several ways to shut me up." Evain rolls his hips, drawing an ego-boosting moan from Leth. "But right now, I don't think you can manage any of them, so I'll just have to tell you that your ass feels enchanting. Your every moan is like music. Your eyes…" He thrusts in harder, earning another exquisite tightening on his cock, and a punched-out breathy sound from Leth. Bending down, the angle forcing him even deeper into Leth's body, he says, "Your eyes say you want me dead, but the way you're clinging to my cock tells another story."

"You're insufferable," Leth hisses, hooking one hand into Evain's hair. He drags Evain down as if by a leash, and the sting in his scalp makes the kiss all the hotter.

Physical and magical pleasure build on each other. Evain has to pause when he's fully seated inside Leth, fingers reflexively digging into Leth's thighs, as a wave of magic surges through him. Only years of experience allow him to redirect the magic, channeling it safely into the core of his soul, without losing control.

He's no longer sure where he ends and Leth begins. He viscerally hates any remaining separation between them.

Next time he'll go slower—and he's certain there's going to be a next time. Because right now, he can't last for long. Quickening his pace, he reaches between them. Leth's cock fits perfectly in his hand, and Leth shudders with his touch. The wave of desire nearly sends Evain over the edge early, putting centuries of sexual practice to the test. It's all he can do to control his angle and keep up the rhythm on Leth's cock.

Making Leth come first is a point of pride. Evain braces on one hand as Leth's cock jumps in his grip, so he can see the moment Leth's eyes roll back. Leth goes rigid beneath him, too trapped beneath Evain's weight to arch up, and spills onto his own stomach.

Leth's choked-out moan hooks deep into Evain's subconscious. He's going to remember that sound forever.

Evain wants to say something, but every language he's ever known departs him. All he can do is drive one last time into Leth's tight body and come with a breathless moan of his own.

Afterwards, Evain withdraws reluctantly and sprawls out on the bedroll beside Leth. Sweat cools on his skin. His breath steadies, and the magic settles slowly inside him, incorporating into his core.

When Leth sits up, Evain grabs his wrist without thinking. "Five minutes? Cuddle with me for five minutes, and I'll be happy."

Leth tenses under his grip, then relaxes. He lies back down and pillows his head on Evain's shoulder. "Three minutes."

"Your generosity astounds me." Evain's fingers wander into Leth's hair, while his thoughts wander towards the future.

He was a fool for ever thinking this could be temporary. That after having Leth once or twice, he could move onto the next conquest. Instead, every taste only deepens his obsession. Evain has been trapped in arrays before, and it feels a little like this: if he steps beyond the lines, he'll die. But he can break free of array traps given enough time and power. No magic exists to break his heart free from Leth.

Leth's breath tickles across Evain's chest, and his hand slowly relaxes against Evain's stomach. Evain wants a hundred years of this—but that means telling Leth what he really is.

Sooner or later, Evain will have to choose between telling the truth or running away. There's always a new name, a new country, a new life to explore. Sooner or later, Leth will notice Evain doesn't age, or that he never summons the demon from his contract. Evain will make a mistake, and Leth will see through the deception.

Probably sooner. Leth is clever.

When we return to civilization and reunite with the paladins, Evain decides, looping a loose strand of Leth's hair around his finger. *When he's not trapped with me in wilderness and ruins. I'll explain when he's not dependent on me. It's too dangerous here.*

Twenty minutes later, Leth moves. Evain is deeply proud of how unsteadily he rises to his feet. "We should look around this place," Leth says, not meeting Evain's eyes.

Evain would really like to continue cuddling, but he isn't offended by the slight retreat. He stretches out on the bedroll, and sure enough, Leth glances over at the spread of muscle and skin. Leth's definitely still interested in Evain, but one incredible fuck isn't going to resolve all his control issues.

Maybe two incredible fucks. Or three, or a dozen… Evain drags his imagination back to the present and rises to his own feet. "I'll check on Daisy."

AFTER CONFIRMING DAZIROTH is doing just fine—and surreptitiously wiping blood from the horse's chin—Evain returns to the library, where Leth is sorting through a pile of dusty leather and paper. He's righted one of the tables to work at and put more wood on the fire, but shadows still waver deep in the corners.

Evain sends a light mote overhead to brighten the room further. He has plenty of stored magic to burn.

Keeping his head bowed, Leth asks, "How's Daisy? Do we need to go out and find forage for him?"

"He's fine. There's some grass growing in one of the other chambers." Evain isn't about to explain that his horse hunts and kills rats—but he feels another pang of guilt at the deception.

He's hidden his nature ever since he arrived in the human realm, and never felt guilty for it. But deceiving Leth feels different. Leth barely accepts his demonic powers when Evain pretends they're from a contract. If he knew Evain was actually an unbound demon?

Well. That's a problem for another day.

Evain sets a chair upright and tests it. The chair creaks in protest, so Evain abandons it to lounge against the dusty stone wall instead. "Find anything interesting?"

"It's all interesting." Leth holds a palm-sized piece of paper up to the light. "But not particularly informative. I can't read Lyrisenian."

Evain calls the light mote closer to him. "Let me see."

Their fingers brush when Leth hands over the fragment, and arousal sparks through Evain. The ink is faded and the sentences incomplete, but he can make out a few words. "I'll tell you what it says in exchange for a kiss."

He gave Leth at least fifteen minutes of space already. His resistance has limits.

Leth glares. "It's nothing important, is it?" But he rises on his toes and pulls Evain down by the neck for a feather-light kiss. Barely there, and it sears Evain to his core.

Moon Mother's tits. He thought he would be *more* chill after fucking Leth, not less.

Evain licks his lips and replies, "I'm sure it was very important to whoever wrote it. But yes, it's part of a soup recipe." He returns the scrap to Leth, who doesn't seem disappointed.

"My guess is whoever ran this chapel took any important books away before they abandoned the place." Leth returns the soup recipe to the pile of crumbled pages on the table. "There aren't enough book fragments here, compared to the number of shelves."

"That makes sense." Evain hesitates, torn between the urge to hide his knowledge, and the urge to show off. Showing off wins. "After looking around in better light, I believe this used to be a summoning chapel. The carvings have all been destroyed, but I recognize some rune fragments."

A brief frown crosses Leth's face. "Summoning chapels are forbidden in Charain. It's too dangerous to summon demons to the same place over and over."

"Far easier, though," Evain says.

"Like I said. Easy's the same thing as dangerous, when it comes to demons." Leth moves to the door, pausing to glance over his shoulder. "I'm going to look at the carvings."

It's the closest thing to an invitation he's going to extend. Evain follows after him. "What a coincidence, so am I."

Repeated spellcasting changes a place. Wards are easier to set where they've been set before; healing potions easier to brew where they've been brewed before. Lesser demons can be summoned anywhere, but more powerful demons are more complicated. Great power or an amenable place are helpful.

The main chamber is colder and brighter than the library. High windows without glass allow in ribbons of sunlight, and thin patches of snow drift across the floor. Evain silently accompanies Leth around the summoning chapel, thinking about what he said the night before. *I wish I could share my power with you, so you could feel in your soul exactly how much I want you too.*

The trouble is, it's not impossible.

If Evain revealed his true name and bound himself in a contract with Leth, he could share that power and more. Walking the broken flagstones, Evain can't help thinking about all the demons bound here, temporary or permanent, willing or not. What would it be like to tie himself to Leth? They could share power and pleasure alike. With a willing contract, Evain could even share his lifespan, and Leth could accompany him through the centuries to enjoy all the wonders of the human world.

It's a foolish fantasy. Leth would never agree.

The chapel is inert now, even to Evain's inhuman senses. The Lyrisenian mages and their demons are long gone. Evain only cares about Leth's slight figure moving from carving to carving, lips slightly moving as he deciphers the runes.

Leth tucks his hands under his arms as he reads. His breath clouds in the air, and Evain considers returning to the library to fetch Leth's coat. The red scarf that looks so good on him. Instead, he shrugs off his own coat.

"Can you tell what this rune is?" Leth asks as Evain approaches. "The lower half is gone."

"I can't." Evain drapes his coat over Leth's shoulders, then holds him firmly in place, in case he tries to shrug the garment away. "It could be dispel, north, or shoelace."

Leth pulls Evain's coat tighter around his shoulders and leans in when Evain wraps his arms around him. He doesn't relax, but he doesn't pull away either. "Probably not shoelace. Though I wouldn't want to assume."

"They could have summoned a demon to work as a cobbler. Anything's possible."

"Did you…" Leth touches the rune. "Do you think Haldis and Marta and the rest are all right?"

Evain lets go when Leth moves. He doesn't think that's the question Leth meant to ask at first. "I'm sure they're fine. And one of their gods will be able to tell them we're not dead, so it shouldn't be too much of a fuss."

"We should try praying," Leth says. "Maybe Radiant Vara or Mother Sephine can tell their paladins to meet us at the nearest village."

"I don't know how free they are with their answers these days, but maybe they can tell us where the nearest village is too. My sources are a bit out of date." By a couple of centuries.

"No need." Leth slides his hands into the coat pockets. "I know a finding spell."

Fuck. Evain can't concentrate on gods and villages anymore. That coat looks even better on Leth than the red scarf. It's far too big on him, and every hang and fold make it clear that it's Evain's coat. Evain's warmth and scent surrounding Leth. Evain likes that a lot.

He likes it so much that he can't help stepping closer and pushing Leth to the wall. After the slightest instinctive resistance, the way Leth allows him makes Evain's cock stir. He tilts Leth's face up with two fingers under his chin. "Hey, there."

Leth swallows, his throat moving under Evain's fingers, and doesn't say anything. His eyes are bright compared to the dead, charred runes.

This is too quick, especially when there's so much Evain can't tell Leth yet—but self-restraint is a human trick he's never been good at. Not when he really wants something. "I wanted to let you know that we're dating, by the way."

Leth blinks. "We're what?"

"Sorry. I shouldn't make assumptions." Evain slides his hand behind Leth's neck, savoring the softness of his skin and hair. Logically, he should stop talking. Stop rushing this. Leth just drives him a little crazy. "But *I'm* definitely dating you. Exclusively. I don't want anyone else."

Leth's throat jumps again under Evain's hand. "That's easy to say when we're alone in the wilderness."

"It's very easy to say, wherever we are." Evain nuzzles the top of Leth's head. He's pretty sure most human hair doesn't smell this good. "You're really attractive and smart, and you smell amazing, and I like the way you look in my clothes almost as much as I like the way you look out of them."

Pressing a hand to Evain's chest, Leth doesn't shove him back. Just puts an inch of space between them. "What if I don't want to date you?"

That's easy. "I'll have to seduce you."

"What if I don't want to be exclusive?" Leth asks next.

Evain's eyes narrow. He can't read whether Leth is serious or not, and the idea of Leth seeing other people—kissing other people—feels like his bones are strung with too-tight string. Either the string will snap, or he will.

Evain stays silent while he thinks, because every answer he bites back would make him sound insane. His silence is damning enough.

"Fuck, you're such a hypocrite." Leth's fingers tense against Evain's chest. "Evain Marha, who flirts with everything that moves."

"I won't deny it." Evain adjusts his coat on Leth's shoulders. "I'm a hypocrite. You're free to flirt with whoever you like, and I'm free to fume unreasonably about it."

He meets Leth's hazel eyes until Leth's face reddens. Ducking his head, Leth plays with a strand of Evain's hair. "I guess I don't mind that," he says, and satisfaction flushes through every nerve in Evain's body.

"I appreciate your generous understanding."

Evain steps back, and his hair slides from Leth's fingers. Leth gives a hint of a smile. Tugging the too-long red coat closer, he moves to look at the next set of carvings.

"A lot has changed for me this year," Leth says, looking at the runes and not Evain. "I'll be honest, I'm not really sure who I am anymore. I don't want to commit to anything right now, besides the job you hired me for." His fingertips touch the wall, brushing past the half-melted rune for *protect*. "But while we're figuring this out, I won't see anyone else."

That deep, dark feeling crashes over Evain again. Better and worse than obsession. After two and a half centuries in the mortal world, he's fallen in love.

LETH

What follows is one of the most restful weeks in Leth's life. No traveling, no rushing to the next task. No looming threat. Once they determine there's enough game to hunt nearby, there's little to do but wait until their strength recovers and the weather subsides enough to travel. Leth prays to Radiant Vara and Mother Sephine, asking them to direct Arthur and Freya or Haldis and Marta to meet them. The gods don't answer directly, but Leth has a feeling they hear him.

In other respects, though, it's one of the *least* restful weeks in Leth's life. Muscles hurt that he didn't even know he had, and he now fully understands why Dravan teachings discourage excessive lust. It would be so easy to forget all his other responsibilities in the ecstasy of Evain's touch.

When the weather clears a week later, Evain is the one who says they should set out. Leth thinks Evain is being responsible, until Evain adds, "We're almost out of lube."

They agree to leave the chapel before activating the location spell. While the disused chapel is safe enough, the runes and shadows still put Leth on edge. He worries his spell will find something far more sinister than the nearest village if he casts it in the chapel.

At the edge of the ruined village, the snow-blanketed forest sweeps up the mountainside ahead of them. Daziroth carries their supplies—what little they came with, and more food they've hunted and gathered over the past week.

"I can cast it, if you want," Evain says. "Save your strength."

That's the only thing that's been annoying Leth this week—Evain constantly offering to cast spells for him. Leth gets it. With the way Evain's magic works, the past week has given him power to spare. Evain even insisted on setting their wards each night.

Granted, he was right that Leth was too fucked-out and tired to stand up again yesterday. But Leth has always hated feeling useless. "I already prepared the spell. I just need to activate it."

"All right." Evain bends to kiss Leth's cheek before stepping back.

Leth may never get used to the full force of Evain's attention. He just knows he likes Evain's flirting much more when it's directed at him instead of other people. It's a little embarrassing to realize how much of his distaste for Evain may have been jealousy the entire time.

Shaking his head to clear it, Leth smooths out a patch of snow-softened dirt with his boot. He kneels to trace an array with a gloved finger. Locating magic isn't one of his specializations, so he can't cast this on reflex like his combat spells. And he's not Karis Cooper, or any god-bound mage—he can't locate a specific person or scry on anything. But all he and Evain need is a rough direction.

"Find for me," Leth says. The circle of runes flashes silver, mirrored by the flash of the prepared spell bead at the edge of his vision. The light coalesces into a single mote and streaks away before vanishing.

"Southeast it is," Evain says, holding out a hand. Leth allows himself to be pulled back to his feet.

His thoughts linger on the ruins as they leave them behind. People lived there once, and now they don't. Lyrisenia was an empire once, and now it isn't. "You'd think we would have a better idea of what happened to Lyrisenia. It only fell a couple centuries ago."

Evain glances over his shoulder. He's walking a little ahead of Leth, and Daziroth blazes the trail ahead of them both. The massive black stallion occasionally pauses to snort at the snow, tail flagging with excitement.

"Some people would call three hundred years a long time," Evain says. His long hair hangs in a plait down his back.

Leth recalls the feel of it sliding through his fingers. "My family history goes back further than that. I suppose much of it is more legend than history, but there should still be more records from Lyrisenia. Stories should have been passed down, and enough Lyrisenians moved south to Charain and Praia."

"The ones who knew the most died." Evain's head lifts towards the ice-blue sky. The line of his neck disappears into his coat. There's a scratch mark under his ear, left by Leth the night before. "The three biggest mage universities were in Lyra."

Leth shudders. Much of Lyrisenia's disintegration was slow. People had time to move or adapt. But whatever caused the Lyralan Crater happened in an instant.

"One theory is that the mages were meddling with powers beyond their reach," Evain continues. "Back then, Lyrisenians didn't like being dependent on gods. Demonic contracts were considered easier to control. But demonic summoning on that scale may have unforeseen consequences, and Lyra's universities were known for experimenting. One of the few facts I'm aware of is that a month before the Lyralan explosion, the empire disbanded the universities. And immediately after the explosion, the remaining government attempted to ban all demonic magic."

They stop behind Daziroth, who wants to inspect another lump in the snow. The trail rises above them, but not too steep and not too high. Leth suspects this was once a road, carved for easy traveling through the mountains.

"Do you think the universities caused the disaster?" Morbid topic aside, Leth enjoys this. Talking theory and history with Evain. Connecting on a level beyond pure lust—though he can't help watching Evain's hands and remembering how they felt on his skin. Each gesture is elegant, even through the winter gloves.

"Maybe they did," Evain says. "Or maybe they didn't. It could be the universities were trying to prevent the disaster, and the disbandment ruined their efforts. The thing about humans is that however keen they are on destruction, they're even more dedicated to progress. To fixing things."

"Like Ronan and Dansa founding the Locksmiths."

"You too." Evain nudges his shoulder. "You helped unbind the gods too."

For a moment, there's no sound but their footsteps crunching through broken snow. "I did that for selfish reasons. And it didn't get me what I wanted."

"Do you regret it?"

Leth didn't hesitate defending his choices to Anton or Captain Gannet. But when Evain asks, Leth pauses. Evain was in the Locksmiths too. He helped Leth steal the Dravansword and used his dark-burning magic to hold off the Dravan soldiers while they escaped Fort Tarhaeg. Leth owes Evain a complete answer. He owes himself one too.

"I prayed in my family's chapel the night after the Unbinding," Leth says eventually. "I asked for power, and Ka Dravos appeared before me. He refused to grant me a contract. He refused to grant *anyone* a contract. Had I known in advance that I wouldn't receive Ka Dravos's blessing, I wouldn't have betrayed my family." Despite the cold around him, Leth is warm with movement and Evain's presence beside him. "But I don't regret it now. I'm glad I didn't know what would happen, and that my false hope led me down that path."

Silence falls between them. The trail crests under their feet, and dark pines blanket the valley before them. A frozen river winds like a diamond ribbon through the trees.

As their path turns downhill, Evain says, "I'm glad you joined too." And Leth knows exactly where the conversation is heading even before Evain continues, "If you hadn't, I never would have known what an incredible ass I was missing…"

"Starting to regret it now," Leth says, but his heart lightens, and he can't help grinning in return.

That lightness vanishes when they descend into the valley and reach a campsite tucked in a bend of the frozen river. Only a day's worth of snow layers over the cleared earth, compared to the higher drifts banked around the area. There's a latrine dug downwind, and four fire pits dug in the cardinal directions.

Leth's blood runs as cold as the river. He casts a basic detection charm for confirmation he doesn't need, because he wants to be wrong. But traces of familiar wards linger around the perimeter.

"What's the problem?" Evain asks. Daziroth nibbles his sleeve.

"This is a Dravan campsite." Leth tries not to let his shoulders knot up with tension. "They came from the southeast, and headed west after leaving here."

Evain shoves Daziroth's head away. "Your brother's troop?"

Given the size of the campsite, plus Anton's passing through Lanwatch, Leth has to assume so. "I don't know why he would be here. This is farther north than he should be if he's just hunting vaidkos near the border."

"There are only two reasons foreigners visit Lyrisenia these days," Evain says. "They're running from something, or they're looking for something."

Anton doesn't run. He's not like me.

Shoving Daziroth's head away again, Evain moves to inspect the campsite. Daziroth turns his attention to nuzzling Leth's pockets instead. Watching Evain and absently petting the horse's massive neck, Leth tries to remember the details of the last day he saw Anton. What cabinet was Anton closing when Leth walked in? What book did he carry out? Was it even related to this trip? But all Leth remembers clearly is the impact of his brother's hand against his cheek.

"They must have stopped at the same village we're heading towards." Leth's eye aches with the echo of a bruise. "We should keep going and ask questions when we get there."

It's a weak excuse. The truth is he just doesn't want to see Anton.

The tense, prickly feeling doesn't ease from his skin until the camp lies miles behind them.

)O(

"SOMETHING'S WRONG," EVAIN says suddenly the next day. There's a sharp edge to his voice that Leth hasn't heard often before.

Leaving off from subtly pressing the bruises on his neck, Leth pulls his scarf up over his chin. Their surroundings seem the same as before—yet more snow-frosted forest clinging to crags of stone. But he trusts Evain's instincts and Daziroth's animal sensitivity. The stallion's ears prick forward, focused intently on the crags north of the road.

"Is it another rift?" Leth asks.

"I don't think so. It's demonic in nature, but not a rift." Red light flickers around Evain's hands. "Wait here with Daziroth. I'll take a little look."

Leth's annoyance flares as bright as Evain's magic. "You can wait," he says with forced calm, and sets off away from the path.

Behind him, Evain swears and orders Daziroth to stay put, like he's talking to a dog instead of a horse. He follows Leth off the path, and as the trees close around them, he says, "You're annoyed at me."

"I am not." Leth tries to count his breaths, but it doesn't help. Nothing really helps him control himself when it comes to Evain. His shoulders tense, and he can't stop himself from saying too much. "I just want you to stop treating me like I'm weak. Just because I have less magic than you and Marta and the rest with your contracts. I don't need to be left behind like a child."

Evain touches his shoulder, and Leth lashes out on instinct. He knocks Evain's hand away, shoves—and Evain doesn't resist. The next moment, Evain's back is against a tree, and Leth's hand is on Evain's throat. Snow and pine needles shower down around them. Leth feels Evain's pulse even through layers of glove and coat, and Evain's dark eyes soften with something more dangerous than desire.

Leth's anger vanishes in a surge of want.

His hand loosens, and his eyes close as Evain leans down. Leth opens to the kiss. Like a rune of binding flame, Evain's tongue paints heat into his mouth. Every breath evaporates between their lips, and Leth's blood rushes downwards. Evain is just as hard against him.

Reluctantly, Leth breaks the kiss and presses his forehead to Evain's chest. Unknown danger lurks in the forest, but Leth just wants to rest here a moment longer with Evain's hands sliding down his back. Tightening around his waist.

He feels better after letting himself be angry. And he feels safer being angry or sad or upset with Evain than he ever has with anyone else.

"I used to think you were annoying," Evain says, his voice light. "I thought you were an uptight prude with no sense of humor. Hardly worth the effort of riling up. Overly rigid and blind to the value of other experiences." He chuckles. "I thought it was a waste for such an attractive man to be so fucking joyless."

Leth laughs. "Your sweet-talking needs work." But for some reason, the litany of insults is comforting. Maybe it's the clear, overwhelming fondness in Evain's voice. Leth wants to say more, but his throat feels blocked.

"I've seen plenty of faults in you," Evain says, "but never weakness."

Maybe the stinging in Leth's eyes isn't weakness. He still waits until the urge to cry passes before extricating himself from Evain's embrace. "We should keep moving."

"Clever, though," Evain says brightly. "I always knew you were clever."

They continue side by side until the grove of trees gives way to a rocky hillside, gaping open in a deep-shadowed cave. The forest around them is far too quiet, and Evain's face is paler than Leth's ever seen it.

More red magic flickers around Evain's hands. "I only sense remnants. Whatever was here should be gone already."

"I guess we'll see." Leth draws his sword and points to the traces of footsteps angling from another direction of the forest, heading into the cave. Light snow obscures the number and details, but the signs of disturbance remain.

A mote of red light spins into being above Evain's head. The shadows at his heels seem to deepen, ready to coalesce into sharp edges at a moment's notice. Evain gestures, and Leth leads the way to the entrance of the cave. The red light illuminates the dark stone around him.

As he reaches the threshold, the smell hits him first. It's an assault on his senses, triggering a deep, instinctive revulsion. All Leth's willpower keeps him moving forward, instead of folding in half and emptying his stomach.

Then the shadows clear from the cave, and the sight is worse than the smell.

"Radiant fucking shit." Evain's voice echoes against the cold stone. There's no point in keeping quiet; the only person in the cave can't hear them anymore.

Remnants of a man scatter like broken pottery across the stone floor. White bone pierces through bruised and frozen skin. Shock rattles Leth, and he can't decide whether it's better or worse that the dead man's face is pulped beyond recognition.

Blood spills across the floor in a deliberate pattern. Even through his shock, even though portions are smeared and uneven, Leth recognizes a mage's array.

EVAIN

The mote of light wavers.

Evain lacks the instinctive human response to death. While he likes humans—he likes some of them impossibly much—without a personal connection, the broken corpse doesn't fill him with nausea or horror. But the bloody array slices deep into his every fear.

Very few demons require blood sacrifice to summon. Evain doesn't want to run into *any* of them.

"It's a summoning array," Leth says, with the iron calm that means he's locking his distress deep inside. Hand still tight on his sword, he takes a shallow breath and steps forward to inspect the array. "Sacrifice, trade, runes of binding. Someone wanted a contract."

"Don't touch it," Evain snaps.

Leth covers his nose. "I wasn't going to touch it."

"The summoning failed. Either the runes were wrong, or the power was insufficient." Evain swallows hard, tasting the frozen blood scent at the back of his throat. "Or the sacrifice was insufficient."

"How can we be sure it failed?" Leth pivots to watch the entrance to the cave.

Evain laughs darkly. "We would know if it succeeded." The mote of light shivers again, but Evain can still make out some of the runes. Hunger. Ravenous hunger. "The bones would be gnawed clean of flesh."

Leth looks up at him finally, lips pressed thin together. "Do you know what demon this was for?"

"Not by name," Evain says. "It's a hunger demon. Let's just say there's a reason they're rarely summoned."

Even in the dark winds of the demonic realm, devourers are monsters. Their hunger is boundless. Insatiable. If properly harnessed, they're a powerful tool. If improperly harnessed… Evain can't imagine a lasting contract that wouldn't twist the mage beyond recognition. He takes a deep breath, trying to mimic Leth's habit for calming down. It doesn't work. The bloody array keeps his attention. "We need to go."

Leth shakes his head and sheathes his sword. "I want to lay him to rest."

"*No.*"

Evain only realizes he's grabbed Leth's shoulder when Leth tries to pull away—and Evain's hand tightens instinctively. Leth's eyes widen in the wavering red light, and he's tense under Evain's touch.

But even like this, desire flares from Leth's heart to his.

Evain closes his eyes. Breathes. Unlocks his fingers from Leth's shoulder. "Outside. I can't think in here."

Leth touches his own shoulder. He takes one last look at the shattered corpse before heading for the entrance. Outside, in daylight clear and sharp as ice, he asks, "What's wrong?"

Fear still claws into Evain, but he can talk through it now without snapping at Leth. "This is beyond both of us. We need to rejoin the others. Any of the paladins. This demon isn't something you and I can handle on our own."

Leth's lips thin out. "Even with your contract?"

Evain laughs. Fuck. If he had a contract, yes, he could face ten hunger demons at once. If he was bound to Leth and could use both their powers combined—if he didn't have to use his own power simply to stay in the human realm—

"Trust me on this, all right?" Evain feels the darkness of the cave looming behind him. He feels safer standing between it and Leth. "I need you to stay by my side until we have backup. This isn't about weakness or coddling you or even how much I just enjoy taking care of you, all right? This is very serious."

Leth stares, cold-faced. Then, to Evain's relief, he nods. "I understand," he says, which is exactly what Evain wants to hear, and reaches out. He squeezes Evain's gloved hand in his. "And I do trust you," he adds, which cuts to the bone.

)O(

THEY RETRIEVE DAZIROTH and take the trail again. The plan is to reach the nearest village, as established previously. Most Lyrisenian settlements keep fairly close watch on their surroundings, for safety's sake. If the attempted summoning is part of a pattern, someone there—a hedgewitch or a village elder or a hunting chief—will know.

Plus, if Leth's prayers went through, they'll have backup on the way.

Evain has never liked relying on divine intervention. Guarantees come with strings attached. But asking for a favor now and again is fine by him.

One thing continues to bother him as they trudge through the snowy forest, a thought that's colder than the ground underfoot. Evain doesn't believe in coincidences. He's hesitant to bring it up, because Leth has been moodier and more volatile since they passed the Dravan campsite yesterday. But as wood smoke rises ahead, and the road changes to stone instead of dirt under the snow, Evain decides he should say something. Leth's right about one thing—he isn't a child, and treating him like glass isn't doing him any favors.

"I've been thinking about the Dravan camp," Evain says, watching Leth.

"You think my brother might be responsible for the murder." Leth's calm expression doesn't change, and he sounds like he's talking about the weather. Like he's retreating from his emotions again.

Evain would really love a chance to wring Anton ka Tariel's neck, one of these days. "Like you said, there's no good reason for him to be here." He clicks his tongue, and Daziroth stops trying to eat a tree. "And I know how deep your precious Tariel library runs.

Would that library happen to have, for instance, a map of ancient Lyrisenian summoning chapels?"

"We had a few books on Lyrisenia, but it's been at least ten years since I read them." Leth fiddles with the end of his red scarf, and Evain wishes those gloved fingers were playing with his hair instead. "I don't think it's a coincidence either. But Anton isn't the one summoning demons."

"How certain are you?"

Leth glances up at him. "Anton looks down on any mage without a divine contract, whether they're plain witches like me or demon-bound like you. According to his worldview, I'm worthless, and you're scum. Worse than worthless."

Evain is far more bothered by the idea of Leth being called worthless than by himself being called scum. Strangling might be too good for Anton. "Though I'll admit it's useful, raw power isn't everything."

"I know that." Leth glances up again, and there's a hint of pink in his cheeks. A flicker of desire. "And it took me a while to figure out, but not all demon-bound mages are scum."

"Really?" Evain drawls. He's far happier to follow this line of conversation. "Have you met any decent ones, recently?" He tugs one of Leth's braids.

"I don't know," Leth says, with a slight, teasing smile. "Shae Nightven is pretty nice."

"Who's that? I don't remember him at all." Evain tugs another of Leth's braids. "Forget about other mages. When we get to town, I'm getting us a proper bed for the night, and then I'll show you *nice*."

Leth's smile deepens. "I'll look forward to that."

Evain is far too focused on the light reflecting in Leth's eyes. He doesn't see what happens ahead, before Daziroth suddenly screeches and shies to the side of the road.

Everything happens at once. Leth draws his sword, a spell bead flashing in his hair, and Evain summons red shadows to his fingertips. He throws himself in front of Leth—

And the binding magic chokes him.

The shadows evaporate from Evain's hands, forcibly dispelled. Stomach flipping with nausea, he looks down. Where his skidding steps have wiped away the snow, patches of stone show beneath his feet, carved with the unmistakable lines of a demon-binding array.

Lyrisenia's humans haven't survived this long without taking precautions. Cut deep into the stone, concealed by snow, the simple trap keeps vaidkos and lesser demons from wandering into town. It shouldn't be able to impede a greater demon like Evain. If he had been more careful, more alert, less distracted by his foolhardy impulse to protect Leth, he would have noticed the array.

The binding isn't strong. Given a few hours and his accumulated power, Evain can break out.

But he doesn't have hours.

Daziroth stands across the road, staring at Evain and trembling with alarm. He sensed the array first, and if Evain had been paying proper attention, he would have realized that.

"I don't see anything," Leth says, poised just a few feet away. He's scanning their surroundings for danger, still not realizing the danger has been walking beside him this entire time. "Daziroth probably just spooked at something. We should still be—what's wrong?"

Shuddering, Evain fights for control. The binding array doesn't just prevent him from using his combat magic. His concealment spells are fraying by the moment too. The magic that hides his claws and the true crimson of his eyes.

He wanted to tell Leth, but not like this. Not yet. When they got to town, or a year from now. Five years. When he was ready.

"Nothing's wrong," Evain lies, for as long as he can. He's not a praying man, but he prays that it's enough.

Frowning in concern, Leth sheathes his sword. "You look sick."

"Leth." Evain steps forward, hand reaching on reflex—and his fingertips hit the bounds of the array with a visible ripple. Pain shudders through him. It's worse when he fights it. "Take Daziroth into town. I'll look around here and make sure nothing is amiss. But you should head in. See if you can find us a room. I'll just be a few minutes."

Nausea rolls through him with agonizing force. His concealment is almost gone.

"Evain, what's going on?" Leth's frown deepens. "Don't fuck with me. Just a minute ago, you were forbidding me from leaving your side. Now you want me to ride into town alone?" His foot touches the edge of the array, but it doesn't affect him. He's human.

Evain takes a step back, then another, until the air shivers around him again. His entire world is reduced to a five-foot diameter circle of space, and he can't run from this revelation anymore.

He doesn't feel his concealments end. He only sees the moment Leth's eyes widen in shock.

Red eyes aren't damning on their own. They could still be the result of a contract. But Leth looks down next at the array lines beneath their feet. For the first time, Evain hates Leth's intelligence and expertise. Of course he recognizes the runes immediately.

Silence hangs between them, as choking as the binding magic. Evain longs to break it but has nothing left to say.

Leth steps back. The spell beads in his hair click together with his trembling. Another step back takes him outside the array. Seven feet from Evain, and it feels like miles. "Walk to me."

"You should go to town," Evain says quietly. "I'll join you when I can."

"Evain, *walk to me*," Leth repeats. He touches his sword, then balls both hands into fists. There's no desire left in his eyes, only horror. "Why aren't you moving?"

His heart the coldest it's ever been, Evain answers, "Because I'm a demon."

LETH

Leth shatters with the words. Like he isn't human anymore either, just shards of winter stitched together with skin and fear. Denial chokes in his throat. He doesn't want to believe it, but he has to.

Every spell has a purpose. This spell's purpose is to bind demons.

"I've hidden nothing else." The worst part is that Evain's voice is the same as ever. The same tender voice that's whispered sweetness and filth into Leth's ear every night and day for the past week. "I'm still the same person who annoyed you to death in the Locksmiths. I'm still the same person who dragged you out of Ostaris, and still the same—for all the rest."

All the rest.

The marks on Leth's neck. The gloves on his hands. The coat on his back. Rough fingers in his hair and soft lips at the corner of his mouth. The hand covering his eyes, an invitation to lose control. Evain's influence is bruised into every part of him, inside and out, and Leth welcomed the hurt at every turn.

He lost control of everything, step by willing step, from the moment he left Ostaris.

Leth can't face that, and he falls back on old training to get through his panic. He has to focus on strategic concerns, instead of the ice fracturing in his heart. "What's your real purpose here? Why are you really sealing the rifts—if that's even what you're doing?"

"That was all true," Evain says. "I like humanity, and the rifts are getting worse. I don't want to see the entire continent ravaged by demons."

"You said Lyrisenia was your homeland."

"I changed some details. The important parts are true." Evain raises his hand, then lowers it. "You can have the Varans truth spell me, if you—"

"This isn't a detail," Leth snaps. "What about the sacrifice in the cave? What do you really know about that?" His lungs hurt. Breathing is too hard. Stumbling back, Leth unpins and unwinds the red scarf as if the cold air on his neck will help. Ludicrous rage fills him, directed at Evain or himself, he isn't sure. "Should I even be angry at you? Of course you deceived me. It's in your nature."

Evain's red eyes are unreadable. "I intended to tell you the truth."

"When?" Leth snaps. "Before or after you fucked me? Before or after I…" He can't say what he was about to say. Can't admit that Evain stole away his heart as well.

"I won't ask you to trust me now." Evain looks paler than Leth has ever seen him. A nice approximation of human emotion. "I'll let you bind me to your will. You'll have complete control. No trust necessary."

A binding. Walking around Lyrisenia with a pet demon on a leash. That's not the kind of contract Leth dreamed of as a child.

"And give you the opportunity to talk me around?" Leth's own weakness galls him. A year ago, he wouldn't be standing around with his sword still in its scabbard. "I shouldn't be talking to you now. I should kill you here."

Evain spreads his arms. "Bind me, banish me, kill me. Whatever you want, I'll make it easy for you. My true name is Aevendaris."

The syllables strike the breath from Leth's lungs, burning away his anger. The red scarf falls from his slack grip.

A true name is a demon's greatest weakness. As if Evain ripped out his own heart and placed it still beating in Leth's trembling hands. No. It's a far more complete surrender than simply giving up a heart.

"Use that name to bind me," Evain says. "Create a contract entirely on your terms. My life and all my power are yours."

Stumbling back again, Leth breaks his gaze away from Evain's tense face.

He can't deal with this.

Evain calls his name, but Leth doesn't turn back. He strides across the snow-covered road to where Daziroth still stands warily. The horse nuzzles Leth's ear when he takes the reins, and Leth barely feels his soft nose or the heat of his breath. There's a disconnection between Leth's mind and body.

His limbs cooperate enough that he manages to swing up into the saddle. As soon as he's up, Daziroth moves a few steps towards Evain, but he stops when Leth tugs the reins.

Leth finally looks down at Evain again. Even from his height on Daziroth's back, Evain's presence still feels too huge and overwhelming. The desperation in his red eyes looks so deceptively human.

"If you have to leave, go into town," Evain says. "It's safer there. I won't follow."

"Aevendaris." The name feels sharp on Leth's tongue. He swallows the shards of his pride, and asks the only question he really cares about, even though he can't trust the demon's answer. "If you're not bound to a desire demon, then you *are* the desire demon. Tell me the truth, Aevendaris. Did you bespell me?"

Evain flinches as if struck, then laughs, low and bitter. "I didn't need to."

The answer is painful enough that Leth thinks it's true. He tears his gaze away. "If I see you again, I'll kill you."

Leth pulls Daziroth around to the west and kicks him into a trot, then a gallop. The pace is reckless through the snow-strewn forest, but the horse's stride is far steadier than Leth. Wind whips past him, stinging his face, as he rides away from the town and the demon and the shattered remains of his heart.

EVAIN

By the time Evain breaks free, the sun is sinking and the shadows rising. His exerted magic has melted a wide circle of snow away. When he stumbles out of the array and falls to his knees, the stone jars painfully through his bones.

Leth's red scarf lies limp a few feet away.

Evain spent his first hour in the array fantasizing about chasing Leth down. Entrapping him, forcing him to listen, forcing him to understand that Evain is *different* from other demons. But he wouldn't be different at all if he caught Leth that way. Escaping the array takes enough time for Evain's reason to reluctantly take charge.

Besides, his magic is nearly spent, Leth has a horse and a head start, and Evain has a feeling that Leth wasn't joking about killing him.

Frustration pushes Evain to his feet again. Blood boiling with unfamiliar helplessness, he glares up at the setting sun. "Hey! Radiant Fucking Vara! You can tell Karis this is all Ronan's fault!"

The sun doesn't answer.

Snarling, Evain claws at his hair and tries to concentrate. His disguises shudder back into place, each spell sluggish and slow. He can't see his eyes darkening, but the sharp claws against his scalp blunt into ordinary human fingernails. Running his tongue over his teeth proves they aren't as sharp either.

There. Now he looks like an ordinary human, with horribly fucked-up hair. He shakes out the mangled braid and ties it back in a simple tail, muttering as he works. "Take Leth to Lyrisenia, Ronan said. It'll be fine, Ronan said." Evain shakes his finger angrily at the sun. "Well, it's not fucking fine, all right?"

The snowy woods swallow up his snarl, leaving not even an echo.

Fuming, with a cold in his bones that has nothing to do with Lyrisenia's winter, Evain bends over and picks the red scarf up from the ground. He shoves it in his pocket and trudges towards town.

☽○☾

THE TOWN PROVES to be a community of about two hundred living in a cluster of stout homes. When Evain doesn't find anything that looks like a tavern, he knocks on a door at random. A plump woman with a hunter's belt answers the door, and her wariness subsides when Evain introduces himself in Lyrisenian. She gives him directions and information, including that the town is named quite simply Snowtown, and what passes for a tavern is Old Sarah's house down the street. But Old Sarah doesn't take guests, so Evain should try Birchven down the street for a spare room.

The hunter is friendly, but when a plump little boy peeks in from the other room, she tells him sternly to go back until the guest is gone. After giving directions to Birchven's house, she closes the door firmly in Evain's face.

An hour later, the man called Birchven is several gold richer, and Evain has shelter from the cold. The house is one of the larger places in Snowtown, given that Birchven apparently lives alone, and the promised spare room is an actual second bedroom, not the closet Evain expected. A hefty fireplace squats in the wall between the sitting room and kitchen.

Evain sits at the kitchen table, sipping a tankard of Old Sarah's brew while Birchven readies the room. He barely tastes the rich stout, but it's something to do as he tries not to think about Leth.

"The room's ready." Birchven emerges into the kitchen. Somewhere in his forties, he's a few inches shorter than Evain. Soft around the edges, with a pleasant smile and nice calluses on his hands. Sitting across from Evain, he pulls out a pipe. "Do you mind?"

Evain waves his hand, and soon the little kitchen fills with faintly spiced smoke. There's a hint of sweetness unique to Lyrisenian pipe blends. The scent knocks Evain's memories back a few centuries, when the pleasures of the human world were pure novelties. When things hurt less, because he cared less.

"Any paladins in town recently?" Evain runs his fingers over the lip of his tankard. "Varans or Sephinians?"

Birchven's eyes follow Evain's fingers. Slow, easy attraction fills the room, as sweet as the smoke. "Forget recently. I don't think we've ever had paladins in Snowtown." Birchven tilts his head up and puffs out a wobbly ring. "Not that I'd recognize them if I saw them."

"You may get your chance soon," Evain says. "Most of them are fairly dull, though."

"Nothing new is dull in winter." Birchven chuckles. "Are those your friends you said you'd split from?"

"Don't tell them I called them dull," Evain says with a habitual smile.

Evain has already arranged to stay for a week, though he isn't sure he will. The plan was originally to wait and see if Leth's prayer had any effect, and whether any of their friends showed up per divine guidance. But Evain doesn't know what to do now. He doesn't want to leave, but he doesn't want to stay. His mind is too blank and hazy to latch onto strategy. How can he just go back to sealing rifts, like nothing happened?

Whatever he does, he has to stay at least one night in Snowtown to recover from breaking the array. Maybe he'll be able to think again in the morning.

"Can I get you another?" Birchven points his pipe at Evain's cup.

Magic simmers under Evain's skin. Not nearly as heady a rush as he's used to now, nothing like Leth's addictive lust. But Evain could intensify Birchven's desires if he wanted. He just needs to unbutton his shirt. Roll up his sleeves. Lean forward a little. He probably should if he wants to recover more quickly. Part of him doesn't really want to recover, though. He wants to wallow in weakness, like a penance.

"Still working on this one." Evain slouches back in his chair and takes a sip. "I saw a few big campsites out in the woods. Did any other strangers pass by recently?"

Birchven squints. "A pack of foreigners camped outside town last week, aye. If you're looking for weird folk, I can't help you, but I can point out the hedge-witch's house in the morning. A few of the Charaini visited her."

"You're magnificently kind." Evain's getting a good sense for the people of Snowtown already. Kind but careful. Welcoming but cautious. Evain won't infringe on Birchven's hospitality by querying further. "What's Snowtown like in summer, anyway?"

Birchven cocks his head but takes to the change of topic easily. He talks a lot, and Evain mostly listens. When Birchven asks about Evain's travels, Evain turns the conversation to the waterfalls of Ellaroc. Clear cascades over purple stone, breathtaking green and sky-blue flowers clinging to every damp surface. Sweating heat lingering through toothless winters. Stories Evain has told dozens of times before, that have nothing to do with ruins and bruises and Leth.

Evain thinks he's making a pretty good show of it, until Birchven sets aside his pipe and says, "You know, if you've gotten used to southern winters, the nights here are warmer with two to a bed."

Suddenly Evain can't ignore the yawning emptiness inside him anymore. The overwhelming feeling he can't quite name. However much he talks, however much power he takes in, he can't fix himself. Bedding

Birchven would be simple, but Evain doesn't want simple. He only wants Leth.

Besides. Birchven wouldn't want to bed him either, if he knew Evain's true nature.

A shadow must cross Evain's face, because Birchven picks up his pipe again. "Sorry, sorry. Don't mind me."

Evain shakes himself and paints on another smile. Not as bright as usual. "No need to apologize. I know it sounds like an excuse, but I'm committed elsewhere already."

Birchven considers, then laughs off his embarrassment. "No surprise there, a face like yours. Let me know if you need an extra quilt, then."

"Thank you," Evain says, then falls silent. He can't think of anything witty to add, or any more stories to tell.

)O(

STILL MOSTLY DRESSED, Evain sprawls out on Birchven's comfortable spare bed and stares up at the rafters. His red silk robe is still packed on Daziroth, unless Leth has dumped it out somewhere in the forest. Evain's chest aches. Not about the robe—he's ruined hundreds of silk robes over the centuries. But imagining Leth's face as he spills out the saddle bags. Twisted into anger? Would he shout? Or would he stand silently, blank and cold?

Evain's fingers twist in soft red wool. Is Leth warm enough without the scarf?

This never would have worked. None of his options would have worked. Keeping his secret from Leth until they tired of each other and moved on with their lives? Evain's obsession runs far too deep, burns far too tenderly in unused and unarmored corners of his heart. He can't fathom tiring of Leth.

He already knew keeping the secret forever wasn't an option. Eventually Leth would realize Evain never ages. Eventually Evain's guilt would grow too great. But his plan to tell Leth as soon as they reached safety—as soon as it was the right time—when would Evain feel safe enough? When would the time be right?

From one excuse to the next, he deceived himself as well as Leth.

Next week or next month, five years from now or ten, the result would have been the same. Betrayal lancing through Leth's voice, furious pain in his eyes. Perhaps it's better that it ended now, before Evain piled on more painful days or years of deception.

Perhaps he shouldn't have courted Leth in the first place. But he can't bring himself to wish for that.

Evain brings the scarf to his nose. Inhales, and breathes in only wool and snow. No trace of Leth. Darkness wavers in his vision. Maybe the next time he stumbles across a rift, he should just let the wild magic carry him home. However much he loves this world, he doesn't belong.

As a demon, there are emotions Evain rarely feels. Perhaps that's why he takes so long to put a name to the abyss in his heart. Perhaps it's simply that his thoughts circle so slowly now, pushed and pulled by the tidal emptiness. When his anger and frustration fade, what remains is only profound sadness, etched like binding runes into his bones.

He doesn't know how humans stand it.

LETH

Daziroth resists Leth at first, reluctant to move forward. His bridle lacks a bit, and wrestling his head around takes all Leth's strength. "Will you stop fighting me?" Leth snaps once. His eyes hurt from the cold, surely, not because he's about to cry. Digging his heels into Daziroth's sides, he coaxes, "When we get to the camp, you can eat anything you want."

Miraculously, the stallion settles down after that, and moves into a steady trot through the snow. His gait is smooth, barely jarring Leth in the saddle. Leth welcomes the wind cutting against his neck, streaming through his hair. As if the cold can erase the demon's touch from his body and soul.

Leth's route isn't a conscious decision. It's an inevitability. After all his foolish thoughts of freedom and rebirth, he falls back on the oldest pattern of his life and rides towards his brother's camp.

Anton is often difficult and sometimes cruel, but he's Leth's brother. And he's not a demon.

Exhaustion eventually dulls the knife in Leth's heart. He doesn't know how long he's been riding. The river of stars runs clear overhead, but Leth's mind is too dazed to track the progress of the moon. Every so often, he tugs Daziroth to a walk, unwilling to exhaust him, but the indefatigable stallion is always ready to trot again.

They reach the previous abandoned camp, and following the Dravans from there is easy. A troop of thirty is hard to hide. Leth urges Daziroth along the path, and as the sky lightens to a delicate gray, a smudge of smoke rises above the trees ahead. Canvas tents show through the gaps in the trees, but Leth knows better than to ride in unannounced.

He reins Daziroth in and whistles. Two sharp notes and two long. The thin sound sinks into the trees. After a moment of quiet, a figure in gray steps out from behind a tree.

"State your business," the soldier calls out. One hand is on her sword, and the other in the pocket of her winter uniform.

Leth lifts his hands away from his weapons. "No need for the alarm talisman. Just take me to Anton."

Her eyes widen in recognition, before narrowing again in renewed suspicion. Two months ago, that would have stung. Now, Leth's tired enough that he doesn't have to feign his blank expression. He's too tired to care about anything right now.

The exhaustion is a relief.

"Wait here," the soldier says eventually, and retreats through the trees.

Leth dismounts and shakes out his legs. Dizziness sweeps over him, black spots blurring over the snowy landscape. Leaning against Daziroth's shoulder, he tries not to wish he had someone else to lean on instead. Deep, counted breaths restore his balance by the time the soldier returns with company.

Anton stands taller than the rest, and he outpaces them striding through the snow, his gray-furred mantle sweeping behind him. Stopping a few feet from Leth, his stern features draw into a familiar scowl—until, to Leth's shock, he laughs.

"What in Valor's name are you doing here?" Anton lifts a hand before Leth can answer. "Nevermind, tell me at camp."

"I just need to resupply," Leth starts, then flinches as Anton clasps a heavy hand over his shoulder. The rest of what he was going to say vanishes.

"Tell me at camp," Anton repeats. "You're frozen solid, little brother."

There's a warmth in his voice, a friendliness, that Leth hasn't heard from Anton in well over a decade. His throat clenches, and he can't say anything else. He can only nod, lowering his gaze, as Anton orders his people to take care of Leth's horse.

Like a clockwork doll, Leth follows Anton into camp. Whether or not anyone stares at him, he doesn't know; he doesn't look up until he's in Anton's tent. The difference in temperature is startling, thanks to the heat charms stitched inside the reinforced canvas. The tent is large enough for four men, but there's only one unmade bedroll. The rest of the space is taken up with a low table, a pile of saddlebags, and a wooden trunk. A yellow-white mage-lamp hangs from the center of the tent. There must be a few Dravans with inherent magic in the troop, who can still practice witchcraft after losing their divine contracts.

"I'll be back in a minute," Anton says. "Take your coat off and warm up." He squeezes Leth's shoulder again, then ducks out of the tent.

Leth stands frozen for another moment, then mechanically pulls off his gloves and shoves them in the coat pocket. His joints feel like hinges in need of oil. He shrugs out of his coat and folds it neatly. Running his fingers over the stitching, the red lining, he lets a breath of a laugh escape his lips.

How eager he was to weaken himself for Evain. A child lured by pretty gifts.

The tent flap opens, and Leth turns, still holding the coat. His fingers tighten in the garment as Javius and another soldier step in. The other soldier sets a tray of food down on the low table, then exits, leaving Leth and Javius alone.

"You shouldn't be here," Javius says.

Leth has to look up at him. He has to look up at a lot of people, but it's rarely this galling. "If I want your opinion, I'll ask for it. But don't hold your breath." He's too tired to be polite.

Javius looks thinner than when Leth last saw him at Fort Tarhaeg, not two months ago. Haggard. The northern weather must not agree with him. "I know you don't like me, Leth." Javius glances behind himself. "Find me later, all right? I need to tell you something."

"You can tell me now." Leth's skin crawls. The last thing he wants to do is follow Javius somewhere alone. This is bad enough already, even knowing his brother and thirty other Dravans are just on the other side of the canvas.

Javius's face twists in a deeper scowl. He steps forward, and says, "Listen."

But the tent flap opens again. Leth's hand falls from his sword hilt as Anton ducks inside. "Javius, the scouts are back. Take their report for me."

"Yes, sir." With a last scowl at Leth, he leaves the tent.

Anton unfastens his furred mantle and drops it on his bedroll. He's too big for the space, like a caged wolf. Dropping to his knees beside the table, he gestures to Leth. "Sit down. We can eat and talk."

Leth has to forcibly unlock his grip from the coat. He unhooks his sword from his belt and sets it down with the coat, then kneels across the table from Anton. The fact that he only wobbles slightly is a victory; his every muscle aches from riding all night without sleep.

Even through his exhaustion, he braces himself for confrontation—that never comes. Anton takes a portion of fruitbread and rabbit and pushes the rest to Leth. "Coffee?"

"Thanks," Leth says. He barely tastes the food.

Anton doesn't eat much. He sips his own coffee and asks, "What are you doing here, Leth?"

That's a big question. Leth can answer the edges of it. "I've been working with a group of paladins to seal wild magic rifts." That isn't a secret. Hopefully mages throughout Lyrisenia and Charain will know how to seal rifts by spring. If any of what Evain said was true.

"I was separated from my party in a storm, and I ran across one of your camps. I followed your trail here."

"Sealing rifts?" Anton's eyebrows lift. "I didn't know that was possible."

"I've sealed one myself," Leth says, then looks down. He recognizes the tone in his own voice—that faint, hopeful boasting, as if this time he can finally make Anton acknowledge him. Old habits die hard. He had thought Anton finally struck that out of him last time in Fort Tarhaeg.

But instead of jeering, Anton gives a low whistle. "That's damned impressive."

Leth twists the mug in his hands. "If you have any mages in the troop, I can teach them how to do it too." He's not sure how to handle the praise. It doesn't feel as good as he would have thought. "What are *you* doing in Lyrisenia?"

Again, Anton doesn't snap. "Hunting demons," he says easily. "The crown ordered us up here."

Of course it's an easy answer. Leth's stomach twists in shame. Ka Tariels are supposed to hunt demons. Not work with them. Not fuck them. Not *like* them. Even if Evain seems different. Even if Evain seems kind. That just makes him even more dangerous than the rest.

Dangerous. But Leth still doesn't want to mention Evain to Anton.

"Which order are you working with?" Anton asks. "Where are they?"

"The Varans and Sephinians are both involved. I don't know where the closest group is." Leth swallows another tasteless bite of rabbit. "I won't bother you for long. If I can buy some supplies off you, I can head out for Lanwatch tomorrow."

"Hey." Anton reaches across the table and grabs Leth's shoulder again. His smile is reassuring, if a little strained. "Stay here longer than that, all right? We have a spare tent you can use. I'm sending a party back to Lanwatch in a week, and you can ride with them. It's too far to go by yourself."

Leth can't bring himself to care either way. He doesn't feel anything when Anton claps his shoulder, or when he lets go. "All right."

"Good." Anton sits back on his heels and downs the rest of his coffee. "We're family, you know. That still means something."

Leth just bows his head and finishes his meal in silence.

EVAIN

Birchven knocks on the guest room's door around noon. Rubbing his eyes, Evain drags himself from bed and to the door. Staring at the rafters all night wasn't particularly restful.

"What is it?" he says, the Lyrisenian words rusty between his teeth.

Birchven's gaze flicks down to Evain's barely buttoned shirt. The shot of power is more effective than coffee. "Three more strangers rode into town this morning. I don't know if any of them are paladins, mind you, but they're talking to Old Sarah now."

"Thanks." Evain runs his hand through his hair, then smiles intentionally. He needs another flare of Birchven's attention, to wake him up enough. "I need a moment to dress, but after that, would you be so kind as to point me to Old Sarah's place?"

"Of course." Birchven swallows. "I'll be in the kitchen."

Unhappy but awake, Evain closes the door and slips back into his coat and boots. Then he combs his hair out with his fingers and plaits it neatly. When he looks perfect enough, he stalks back to the door, then hesitates.

He wraps the red scarf around his neck before leaving the room.

)O(

SNOWTOWN IS MORE alive in daylight. There are more people out to gawk at Evain, at least, as he follows Birchven to the largest house on the street. Three familiar horses are tethered to the post outside—Arthur's massive chestnut, Shae's little dark pony, and Freya's sturdy bay.

"That's the place," Birchven says. "Are you good? I need to head out and check my traps."

"I think I can find it." Evain struggles to drag one of his usual niceties out from the cobwebs in his head. "Thanks for the room."

"Safe winter and strong wards." An old Lyrisenian platitude.

"Safe winter." Evain manages not to grimace until Birchven turns away down the snowy street. Strong wards—to keep demons out. Evain has no need of those.

He's still staring off into the distance, breath frosting in the air, when Old Sarah's door swings open. Arthur, Shae, and Freya emerge onto the street and spot Evain at once. Shae pauses at the doorstep, pulling a ring off his right hand as the others move forward.

"Evain!" Freya waves her arm. If she's wearing her sun-emblazoned tunic, it's hidden under her fur-trimmed coat.

"There you are." Evain moves towards the horses. "Took you long enough." It's meant to be a jest, but his voice falls flat and harsh. He can't handle the switch from Lyrisenian to Charaini as well as he usually can.

"Long enough?" Freya laughs. "We headed here as soon as Radiant Vara spoke to us. Which, for the record, I'm still not used to. Did you know Mother Sephine speaks to Haldis and Marta in gentle dreams?"

"I didn't," Evain says. "Let me guess, your Vara does things differently."

"Sudden visions in broad daylight," Arthur chimes in. He gestures. "Boom. Very startling. But I still like it better than the vague feelings we used to get."

"I never even got that," Freya says with a sigh.

Shae joins them, frowning. "Where's Leth?"

Evain freezes.

He really must be off his game. He hasn't prepared an explanation at *all*.

Arthur's smile fades, and his eyes narrow. He's better at reading people than Evain would prefer. "Is everything all right?"

"No," Evain says shortly. There's no reason to pretend. "Leth's all right—he has Daziroth. But we argued, and he left."

"Radiance," Arthur swears.

Freya swings around to look Evain in the eyes. "He just left? In the middle of fucking nowhere? What the fuck could you have fought about that badly? It's not like he liked you to begin with."

"That's none of your concern." Helplessness feels a lot like rage, simmering under Evain's skin. Shae steps back, touching one of his rings, and a hint of dark power edges the air. Evain takes a deep breath, trying to pull himself together. "Leth doesn't want to see me. Now that you're here, I want you to find him. I'll show you where we split off, then I'll…"

He doesn't know what he'll do next. He has all these pieces in front of him, but he can't sort them into a coherent plan.

"Then you'll what?" Arthur prompts.

"I don't know," Evain says. The words hang in the air between everyone.

After a moment, Arthur rubs his face. "I'm going to pray." He stalks away into a brighter patch of sunlight.

Freya watches him go, fiddling with her pendant, then turns back to Evain. "Seriously, what the fuck did you fight over?"

"None of your concern," Evain repeats sharply.

Then Shae says, in fluid Lyrisenian: "Did he find out you're a demon?"

Alarm hits Evain like an avalanche. He whirls to face the necromancer, bracing for an attack. Shae knows. Evain doesn't know *how* Shae knows, but his limited reserves of magic coil inside him, ready to burst out into blades of shadow.

But instead of striking, Shae raises his hands slowly, palms out to show he's unarmed. His pale face is utterly calm, and no magic flares around him.

Evain holds his own magic in reserve, poised and wary.

"What did you say?" Freya asks. When Shae doesn't answer, she asks Evain, "What did he say? Fuck! This isn't fair, you know I don't speak Lyrisenian. All right, Arthur, what did *Vara* say?"

Sunlight brightens, then dims around Arthur. Touching his chest in reverence, he tells them, "Radiant Vara said to go ahead and talk to the hedgewitch. We only wanted to talk to her to ask about you two, so I'm not sure why. But I trust him."

The hedgewitch. Evain wanted to talk to the hedgewitch too—about a man's broken body in a bloody circle. He needs to drag himself out of this unhappy haze. The wilds of Lyrisenia haven't become any safer since his heart broke.

"You two go ahead." Shae grabs Arthur's wrist, his bare fingers disappearing in the gap between Arthur's glove and sleeve. "I'm going to talk to Evain."

Arthur and Freya lead the horses away. Only when they're out of earshot does Shae say, "Let's move. The townsfolk are starting to stare."

Evain's joints unlock. Sure enough, the townsfolk are staring—not at Evain, but at Shae's silver rings. Some humans think necromancers are monsters as bad as demons, but unlike Evain, Shae has never hidden what he is. He suffers the scorn without pretense.

They follow Arthur and Freya at a distance to a narrow, well-shoveled path leading off the main road and into the woods. The witch's cottage squats at the end of the path. Shae stops midway, at the point where they're farthest away from other people in both directions. Dark evergreen trees twist into the sky around them, and stubborn red flowers bloom through the traces of snow on the ground.

Mahr. They die with the frost and bloom as it melts, living a hundred life cycles every winter. Blood in the snow, Lyrisenians call them. Beautiful, fragile yet persistent. Poisonous. Evain took the name Marha from them.

"When did you realize?" Evain asks in Lyrisenian.

"The day we met outside Ostaris." Shae pulls a ring from his pocket and holds it up to the light. "This spell detects demons. I have to take the ring off every time you're nearby, or it feels like my hand will freeze off."

"I see," Evain says faintly.

"You have great control over your aura, though," Shae says, in what might be intended as comforting but comes out as rather condescending. "I'm very sensitive to auras, but I wouldn't have guessed if not for my enchantment."

Evain honestly doesn't remember much about his first conversation with Shae. He just remembers being preoccupied with whether Leth would show up or not.

The important thing is that Shae has known he was a demon the entire time—but hasn't tried to kill or banish him. Evain crosses his arms, willing his magic to settle inside him instead of crawling like mahr from beneath his skin. "Who else knows?"

"I told Arthur, of course, but no one else." Shae shrugs. "We were ready to deal with you if you proved dangerous, but since Vara approved of Arthur taking this quest, we figured you couldn't be that bad."

"You're unusually calm about this."

"I've met demons before." Shae glances away. "They weren't like you."

"Most aren't." Evain watches the mahr growing up from the snow. Dark needles rustling in the wind. The path before him and the path behind him look just the same. "Anyway, you're right. Leth found out I'm a demon. There's an additional complication in that I succeeded in courting him before he realized. He's very reasonably upset. What do you think I should do now?"

Shae chokes, his calm facade finally fracturing. "You're asking me?"

"Who better?" Evain sighs and reaches down to pluck a mahr blossom from the edge of the path. It's bright against his dark leather gloves. "You know demons, and you know humans. You know relationships. Should I let Leth go, or try to persuade him back?"

Shae sets his hands on his hips. "I killed the last demon I met. Most humans hate me. And I only landed a relationship because Arthur is the sort of ridiculous man who bought an engagement ring before we even kissed."

Sarcasm sounds particularly melodic in Lyrisenian. Evain rolls the flower stem between his fingertips, and listens.

"But fine. I'm not qualified, but I guess I'm the only one here." Shae sighs. "You're upset enough that I guess Arthur was right. You're in love with him. But that won't help you, because loving him isn't enough."

Evain's grip on the flower tightens. "That's not very encouraging."

"Did you want encouragement?" Shae asks sharply. He steps closer, his gray eyes bright and stern as steel. "You came to the wrong necromancer for that. You're a demon, and he's a human. Maybe it's best you never see him again."

Refusal surges hot through Evain's veins, driving him forward. Fists clenched, he checks himself.

Shae points one ringed finger at Evain's face. "There. That look in your eyes. Whatever you felt when I said that?" His hand falls, and he turns away down the path. "There's your answer."

The fragile mahr falls to the snow. Evain knows in that moment he can't give up. Hunting Leth down won't work—but while he gives Leth time to cool down, he can prove that he's the same as he ever was. That he's *better* than he ever was. He'll seal rifts and fight vaidkos and rip invading demons to shreds with tooth and claw if he has to.

And the first item on the list is whatever asshole is summoning that hunger demon.

☽○☾

SNOWTOWN'S WITCH IS a tiny elderly woman, hunched over until she stands no taller than Evain's waist. Her white hair hangs in two thick plaits over a gray fur coat that must weigh as much as she does. The picket fence around her cottage shows signs of frequent repair, half the stakes made of different kinds and ages of wood. The witch stands on one side of her low gate, firmly shut with Arthur and Freya on the outside.

Arthur turns around as Evain and Shae approach. "Thank Vara. She doesn't speak Charaini, and I barely know any Lyrisenian."

"It's been awkward," Freya adds.

The witch's dark eyes narrow. "Can you two speak properly?" she addresses Evain and Shae in Lyrisenian. "Tell these southerners to leave us be. There are enough of you meddling around here already."

"My deepest apologies," Evain answers in the same language. He sweeps a bow and comes up with a practiced grin. "They're too clumsy and foolish to pay proper respects to the great witch of Snowtown. May I have the honor of learning your name?"

Shae snorts next to him, and Freya whispers, "He's insulting us, isn't he?"

"My name is Nia, but don't flatter me, boy," the old woman says, though her eyes light up, and she looks at Evain with palpable appreciation.

Evain's not really in the mood, but he needs to store power when he can, if he's going to be of any use moving forward. "It's only the truth, great and powerful beauty. I'm Evain Marha, and this is Shaesarenna Nightven. The others are our doltish servants." Shae stifles another laugh. "We want to know about the other southerners you met recently. Did they wear a lot of gray, with bronze wolf pins? And a bad attitude?"

"Acolytes of the war god," Nia says. "Yes."

There's only two reasons foreigners come to Lyrisenia these days. Evain asks, "What were they looking for?"

"I refused to tell them anything." Nia's wrinkled face grows fierce. "And I won't tell you where the old summoning chapel is either."

Evain's blood runs cold. "No need to tell me. I already know."

LETH

"Drink?" a soldier asks, offering her flask.

Leth glances at Javius, who sits across the fire with a dour look on his face. It would be paranoid to think Javius might somehow have tampered with the soldier's flask. She already drank from it before offering. "No thanks," Leth says anyway. He isn't in the mood.

"Go on," Anton says to his right. "You're hardly on duty."

"I'm fine." Leth's tired enough he feels half-drunk already. He still hasn't slept, and alcohol won't ease the tension building behind his eyes. After breakfast, he spent the day riding north with the Dravans—on an unfamiliar horse. Daziroth broke free from Anton's soldiers, and by the time Leth found out, the horse was long gone. Leth could only take a spare horse from Anton and move on.

At least the Dravans move more slowly than Leth's flight the night before, and his new horse easily follows the group. Leth doesn't have to focus on anything besides staying in the saddle. Wherever they're heading, the Dravans take a longer route than Leth and Evain would have; their supply wagon-sleds can't cut through the trees.

Now, they've camped in a broad pass between two mountains. Old mile markers stick up through the snow at either side of the pass—once a wide road, now a rough field. Two mages in the troop cleared the snow from around the fires, and everyone sits on the ground. Even Anton, though his show of bonding with his troops falls a little flat with the way everyone still calls him *sir* and laughs too hard at his slightest jest.

The general's fire is also set away from the rest, with only Leth, Javius, and two other soldiers gathered with Anton. Six years ago, Leth would have been thrilled to be set apart with his brother. Now, whether it's exhaustion, heartache, or just the slow erosion of all the years in between, Leth just feels numb.

"You never change, do you?" Anton takes a swig from his own flask. "Don't waste the stew, at least."

Leth scrapes his wooden spoon into the bowl. The broth tastes sour, and he misses Evain's cooking. The man had a knack for it, unlike Leth, who was banned from the Locksmiths' kitchen after a week.

Leth would probably be a better cook too, if he had centuries to practice.

Aevendaris. Leth has to remember the demon's true nature, not his cooking. Not his wicked smile and magic kisses, not the feel of his breath on Leth's neck and firm hands on Leth's waist.

Running away was the right decision. If he sees Evain again, Leth doesn't know if he'll have the willpower to kill or banish him. Evain was right too. He didn't need to bespell Leth at all.

Better to make a clean break, Leth tells himself for the hundredth time that day, while Anton jokes with the soldiers across the fire. Only Javius is as silent as Leth tonight, a frown on his haggard face. His gaze keeps drifting towards Leth, and Leth's too tired to figure out why.

At least Javius wouldn't dare do anything in front of Anton.

Leth finishes his stew quickly, forcing down the unpleasant taste. After setting the bowl aside, he wraps his arms around his knees. He doesn't want to socialize, but he doesn't want to head to his empty tent yet either. His maudlin thoughts are bad enough by firelight, surrounded by people. They'll only get louder when he's alone, and despite his exhaustion, Leth doesn't know if he'll be able to sleep.

Except a sudden lethargy wells up inside him. An unnatural fog unravels his thoughts and weighs down his limbs. The campfire swims black before his eyes.

Something's wrong, but Leth is too dazed and tired to do anything about it. As unconsciousness envelops him, the last thing he hears is his brother chuckling.

"Looks like it's kicking in."

MOVEMENT TUGS LETH into awareness. Steady, gentle pulling in his hair. For a dazed moment, happiness bubbles inside him, with the memory of Evain stroking his head. But it can't be Evain. He left Evain. A dim light swings overhead, appearing and disappearing like the moon behind clouds. Except it's not swinging—that's just his head spinning and spinning. His shoulders ache, and his eyelids are so heavy, it's hard to keep them open.

He recognizes the lamp. He's in Anton's tent.

The light disappears again as Anton leans over. His fingers rub against Leth's scalp, and for a dazed insane moment, Leth thinks his brother is brushing his hair. Then Anton sets something down on the table, with the barely audible click of onyx on wood.

Anton is unbraiding the spell beads from his hair.

"Stop," Leth tries to say, but the sound halts in his throat, muffled by the cloth gag between his teeth.

Ignoring his whimper, Anton continues unbraiding Leth's hair. With deceptively gentle movements, he slowly and surely strips away each of Leth's defenses.

The tent darkens. Leth tries to open his eyes again, but they're too heavy. His head is too heavy. He needs to fight back. Needs to mobilize his cotton-soft limbs, activate any spells remaining to him.

But he's too weak from whatever Anton drugged him with. As Anton takes away another onyx bead, Leth passes out again.

☽○☾

WHEN LETH WAKES again, the tent is lighter, and his head is clearer. However long he's been asleep, it's long enough for day to ascend and most of the drug to leave his system. Leth forces himself to relax and feign sleep as he assesses his predicament. He's on his side, with his wrists bound behind his back. The strain on his shoulders is a dull, steady ache. Smaller aches radiate throughout his body, like he's been tossed in a sack of rocks.

Something shifts nearby. He isn't alone.

Cracking open his eyes, Leth finds himself in Anton's tent again. Daylight through the canvas illuminates the figure crouched beside him, too thin and gangly to be Leth's brother.

"You awake?" Javius whispers.

Leth doesn't try to answer. The gag's still between his teeth, drying out his mouth.

Javius swears. "Don't scream when I take this out, all right?"

It's all Leth can do not to bite Javius's fingers when the man pulls the gag from his mouth. He tries to sit up, but his muscles are still too weak from the drug, and he slumps back to the bedroll.

"Don't bother." Javius sits back on his heels and rubs his chin. "Never liked you much, but I don't feel right about this."

Leth watches Javius warily. There's more rope around his ankles—tied over his boots, which isn't very secure. That might be the easiest binding to wriggle out of first, if he can muster the strength.

"Anton hasn't been himself since the Unbinding," Javius continues. "Or maybe he's been more himself than ever, fuck. He misses having Valor. We all do, but the rest of us are starting to get over it, you know? I thought he'd settle down too. But he hasn't."

Javius's eyes are bloodshot, and there's something frightening in his voice. A fearful tone that forces Leth out of his desperate, wary pragmatism. The full knowledge that his brother is the one who drugged and bound him drags Leth under like an avalanche, burying him in ice. Crushing his lungs beneath his ribs.

"I never liked you, but Anton *hates* you. Do you know why?"

Leth struggles to follow Javius's line of thought. He can't quite grasp the thread of logic.

Javius doesn't wait for an answer. "Years ago. He was eighteen, so you must have been twelve? The two of you sparred, and you knocked him on his ass."

Leth has sparred with hundreds of people, thousands of times. He doesn't remember the first time he held a padded stick and stumbled through a routine against a training dummy. But he remembers the fight Javius is talking about—a bright summer day in the courtyard of Fort Tarhaeg.

"That was the last time we ever sparred," Leth says.

"You beat him, and he couldn't stand it." Javius rubs his chin again and jerks his head back to look at the sealed tent flap. "Anton's hated you ever since. You remember that time we went drinking, the night before your initiation ceremony?"

"I remember you spiked my drink."

"That's right," Javius says. "Because Anton ordered me to."

"No," Leth whispers, tensing against his bindings. He listens rapt with horror as Javius continues.

"He gave me the drug himself. I'm not saying I'm a good person, here. Maybe I went a bit too far teasing you. Anton wasn't happy about that." Javius waves his hand, as if dismissing his past self. "But Anton's the one who wanted you to miss the ceremony. He planned to keep you out of the military because that was the only area where he was still superior. You were better with a sword, and you had innate magic. All he had was Valor."

Leth shudders. He doesn't want to believe it, but it makes sickening sense. Would Javius dare touch him, if Anton didn't approve? Anton wasn't harsh but fair, upholding protocol when Leth missed the ceremony. The game was rigged against Leth from the start.

"That's who Anton is," Javius says. "He can't stand not being in control. Not having power. Now that Ka Dravos has abandoned us, Anton needs new magic."

Leth's stomach sinks yet again. "What's my brother really doing in Lyrisenia?"

"I told him to pray to other gods. Vara or Sephine. He told me he was done with gods. He wants magic he can control."

Leth still can't remember what section of the library Anton was looking through, but he remembers his own naive denial when Evain asked if Anton could be responsible. "I saw the array in the cave. Drawn in blood, with a man's life spilled everywhere."

Javius's breathing is ragged. He rubs his hand through his beard. "It wasn't enough. The demon he's summoning is too powerful. The place wasn't right, and the sacrifice wasn't enough because Anton didn't care about him. Anton needs to offer something more important—and then you walked up out of nowhere, like Ka Dravos himself sent you."

We're family, you know. That still means something.

"He wants to sacrifice me," Leth says, barely hearing himself. The words feel unreal.

Javius's head jerks in a nod.

Straining and twisting, Leth manages to lever himself up onto his ass. The effort sends the tent spinning around him. He wants to deny Javius's words, but he can't. The evidence is all around him, in the rope around his wrists, the weakness coursing through his veins, the betrayal clawing through his heart.

When he found out Evain was a demon, when he jumped onto Daziroth to ride away, Evain told him to ride into town, where it was safer. Because despite the lies, despite the secrets, despite the pure mundane annoyance, Evain always acted to protect him.

What people do matters much more than what they are. And by running away from a demon, Leth threw himself into the clutches of a monster.

A voice sounds from outside the tent. A soldier reporting back from watch. Javius flinches, then runs his hand over his face again. Sweat gleams at his temples.

"Why are you telling me this?" Leth is under no illusion that Javius is a friend or ally.

Javius grimaces. "Maybe I just need to tell someone. Most of the soldiers here don't really know what's going on. Fucking Valor. I don't know how it got like this."

"Of course you know," Leth snaps, then takes a deep breath. Fuck. He can't argue now, and he has no interest in Javius's despicable self-justification. He needs more information. "Where's Anton now? Where are we?"

"We're camped outside the chapel he's been looking for," Javius says. "He's setting up the array now."

Another voice outside. Leth can't make out the words. Javius stands and moves to the door of the tent, listening. As silently as he can, Leth tries to shift his legs underneath him. His eyes fix on the knife at Javius's belt.

"Javius," Leth hisses. "Untie me. I have friends nearby. We can stop him."

Javius shakes his head. "It's too late."

"Anton can't control a demon like this," Leth says. "You know he can't. I saw the array. The sacrifice wasn't the only problem. His lines were wrong, and he's never practiced this kind of magic."

Javius's eyes are unreadable, his lips tight behind his scraggly beard. "You're going to get me killed," he finally says.

"You're dead anyway." Leth holds his gaze. "When Anton loses control, he's not just feeding me to the demon. Every soldier in this camp is dead, unless you help me now."

He knows by the slump in Javius's shoulders that he's won. The victory tastes sour.

Swearing, Javius crouches next to the bedroll again. He pulls a bottle from his pocket and as Leth watches, pours a portion of it onto the canvas floor. "There. I've dosed you up again, just like I'm supposed to." He hesitates, then unsheathes his knife and sets it next to Leth. "And you grabbed my knife, without me looking."

"How long do I have?" Leth asks.

"Anton should be back in an hour." Javius stands up and pauses at the tent flap. "You don't know what it's like having a friend like Anton. He'll chew you up, but he won't spit you out. He just keeps fucking chewing." For a moment, pale gray sky outlines his haggard figure. Then he closes the tent flap behind him.

As soon as the flap closes, Leth twists around to grasp the hilt of the knife between his bound hands. Flipping the blade around is tricky, and between the angle and restraints, he can't move his hands much. Sawing through the rope is a long, arduous process.

It's something to concentrate on, at least, instead of dwelling on how blind he's been his entire life. Leth thought he had already lost all his illusions. When Anton gave Javius a slap on the wrist for the incident six years ago. When Ronan explained the Binding, and he learned Ka Dravos had never heard his prayers. When Ka Dravos rejected his plea for power after the Unbinding.

When he realized Evain was a demon.

The blade slips, and pain slices into the meat of his hand. As warm blood wets his fingers, Leth counts his breaths, adjusts the knife, and resumes scraping the blade against the rope. A breathless, broken laugh wracks his lungs.

He misses Evain.

More than anything, Leth wants to break down and cry, but he can't do that by himself. He can't allow himself to falter when there's nobody to catch him.

A strand of rope snaps. The knife cuts sharp into his arm again as the bindings loosen around his wrists. Ignoring the pain, Leth yanks his battered hands free. His shoulders scream with the release, and he hunches over, gritting his teeth, until the agony recedes.

He wipes his bloody palms on his trousers and picks up the knife again. Cutting the bindings around his ankles goes more quickly. He stands up after several failed attempts, limbs shaky and blood circulating painfully through his arms and legs.

Clutching the knife, he takes a step towards the tent flap and realizes he doesn't know what to do next. An elaborate plan sketches through his mind—first, slice through the back of the tent. Confirm the camp layout is the Dravans' usual, then set a deliberate trail in one direction before doubling back and stealing a horse. He'll need to steal a coat, too, if he doesn't want to freeze to death. If they're really at the chapel already, he knows the route to the nearest town. It'll be a long, cold ride alone, but he can make it.

But Leth doesn't want to make it alone, anymore.

He used to rely on prayer when he was scared. Tradition when he was uncertain. He used to rely on his own strength and conviction when he felt helpless. Now, bleeding and trembling, Leth kicks the bedroll away for space and kneels on the ground. He digs the blade into the back of his left arm until blood spills like a river, then drops the knife. Dipping his fingers into the blood, he starts painting a circle on the rough canvas floor.

No sane array ever looked like this. Leth draws no runes for binding, no runes for control. He demands no shield and no protection. Each stark line is an act of reckless trust.

He wants power. He wants comfort. He wants Evain. He wants.

"Aevendaris," Leth says. His need surges from him and sets the bloody lines ablaze.

EVAIN

“He didn't see what hit him.” Shae lets go of the canvas bundle and rises to his feet. He leans against Arthur, and the paladin's divine aura shimmers around them both. “All he could tell me was that he was a Dravan before he died, and there's a woman in Ostaris who should know that he loved her.”

Evain waits with Freya at the entrance of the cave, standing guard as Shae and Arthur inspect the sacrificial corpse. Freya mostly watches the tree line, even though the most disturbing part is over: Shae using his necromancy to gather fragments of flesh and bone into a canvas tarp. The shape on the ground is far too soft and undefined.

At least the smell has dissipated into winter's chill.

"Let's go, then." Waiting and uncertainty grate on Evain's nerves. One day since the hedgewitch confirmed Anton ka Tariel is searching for the summoning chapel. Almost two days since Leth rode off alone into the woods. Helplessness unmoors Evain. For all he knows, Leth is well away from all of this. He could have ridden Daziroth south, to another village. But every moment without Leth in sight fuels Evain's anxiety.

"We should lay him to rest," Arthur says.

Before Evain can snap at him for suggesting a delay, Shae shakes his head. "I sent his soul onward already. His body can wait. This array is dangerously unstable—we need to find the ones responsible."

"Can any of you track him?" Evain asks.

Freya says, "Vara's given us all we're going to get."

Shae separates from Arthur's grasp by about an inch. "There's nothing in range of my detection spells."

"Then we keep moving," Evain says, just before the magic strikes him, and the world rattles around him.

Desperate yearning claws into his soul and twists its thorns around his limbs. Evain's first instinct is to struggle against the summons. Rebel against the command. Then he recognizes the taste of the soul calling to him—the precise timbre of the voice in his ear, pleading across however many miles:

"*Aevendaris.*"

Pure joy ignites under Evain's skin, burning away all his enchantments and control. His fingernails sharpen under his gloves, and a crimson mist blurs his vision. He hears distant shouts from the paladins as red and black smoke billows around him.

He stops fighting, as if his resistance would make

a difference against the summoning's overwhelming power. No demon could resist this call. In a blaze of blood-red shadow, Evain vanishes—

—a moment of pure nothing, riding the edge of the veil, no reality to latch onto, his only anchor his trust the witch's magic will guide him true—

—and emerges in a blast of power. Shrapnel explodes from his point of apparition, and a column of luminous smoke spirals around him. Past the swirling clouds, Evain sees mountains, crumpled tents, fleeing figures. Jagged walls of familiar ruins. Human voices vanish in the roar of magic, the hurricane of dark desire.

And in the eye of the storm waits Leth.

Evain drinks in the sight of him, but concern quickly tempers his joy. Leth's hair whips back from his face to reveal ashen skin and red-rimmed eyes. Blood soaks his left sleeve, dripping onto the stone and scraps of canvas beneath his feet. More scraps of canvas are staked into the cracks between stones. This must have been a tent, before Leth summoned him.

Encircling Evain, the summoning array glows a deep, dull red, its runes burned deep into the stone.

"You came." Leth's voice is clear and quiet, like a blade in the storm. "That really was your name. Why did you give it to me?"

"So you can do whatever you wish with me, of course." The force of the magic echoes through Evain. He clenches his fists, claws pricking his palms through his gloves. "Why did you summon me, Leth?"

As delighted as he is to see Leth, he knows the position he's in. When a witch binds a demon with his true name, it rarely ends well for the demon, unless the witch makes a mistake. And Leth doesn't make mistakes when it comes to magic. Evain is quite possibly about to die, or return to the dark wasteland of his birth realm.

More magic ripples under his skin. The familiar taste of Leth's desire.

"I suppose," Leth answers, "it's so you can do whatever you wish with me too."

The heat in his voice drives Evain forward, but he stops himself before he hits the edge of the array. Then he looks down, and his breath catches.

The array shouldn't be this simple. It's a step above the plain circle Evain once used to seal a rift, but hardly sufficient to safely summon a demon. There are no runes of binding or compulsion. Nothing to hold or command Evain. The spell began and ended with his arrival.

Evain doesn't know what changed. Something must have—there's a desperation in Leth's eyes that has nothing to do with desire. Leth is afraid, but not of Evain.

Whatever it is, Evain knows in his bones they can face it together. He doesn't know what's changed, but he'll seize the chance wholeheartedly.

"This was reckless of you," Evain says. "Whatever I wish?"

Leth's breath hitches. "Evain."

Eyes ablaze, Evain steps easily from the array. Swirling shadows still obscure the rest of the world. Leth's gaze climbs with his approach, forced to look up as the distance between them vanishes. Evain removes his right glove, and when he reaches out, Leth doesn't flinch away from the claws tracing the line of his jaw. Desire burns between them, and Evain leans down to claim Leth's lips.

He doesn't need any runes to bind him to Leth. Just this.

LETH

Leth never wants to forget the sight of Evain responding to his summoning. Eyes burning crimson, hair swirling in the wind. Nothing hidden, more beautiful than ever, his aura spills out to oppress the very air around them. His presence should fill Leth with fear or revulsion—but all Leth feels is relief.

And desire. Evain's kiss burns away all Leth's uncertainty. Evain's tongue sweeps between his lips, warm and wet against Leth's. With a desperate groan, he tastes Evain's sharp teeth. Arousal ignites his blood. Every nerve in his body sings as Evain's lips move against his.

Evain's tenderness is inescapable. Clutching Evain's coat, Leth rises on his toes as Evain grabs his arms. His waist. Evain's claws never pierce his skin.

Then Evain cups his ass with both hands and squeezes. Leth whimpers into the kiss, and whimpers again when Evain lifts him. As the ground disappears from beneath his feet, Leth's legs instinctively hook over Evain's hips.

The strength in Evain's arms, easily holding him up, is almost as exhilarating as the feel of Evain's cock hot and hard against his.

Leth can't see if any of Anton's soldiers are still in the destroyed campsite. The whirling shadows of the summoning are dispersing, but Leth is too preoccupied with Evain to pay attention. He's too enraptured to care about anything else—if Evain wants to fuck him right here, right now, he'll gladly give himself. He wants far more than that from Evain, after all.

If Evain is willing. For all Evain's promises, Leth may still be asking too much of him.

Evain breaks away with a final kiss to the corner of his mouth. "You're hurt."

I'm fine, Leth almost says on reflex. But he's tired of pretending to be fine. Pressing his forehead into Evain's neck, he inhales the familiar cinnamon and smoke scent. "I shouldn't have left you."

"I want to agree, but I remember you had a pretty compelling reason to leave me." Evain's arms tighten around him. "You know I'm still a demon, right? How's your memory?"

"I know what you are." Leth's memory is sharp, but he's not thinking about the last time they parted. He's thinking about carved silver pendants, ravenous kisses, and a paper-wrapped pill forced on a cranky, fevered witch. Eyes stinging, Leth inhales once more. "Set me down?"

"I don't want to," Evain says, but he returns Leth's unsteady feet to the ground nonetheless.

Leth's heart sinks as he recognizes their surroundings. Javius was right; that's the half-arched gate of the summoning chapel to their west. The snow-scoured roof cuts sharp angles against the sky. If Javius was truthful about everything, Anton's in there. But he doesn't have a sacrifice ready anymore, so dealing with him can wait another minute.

The campsite around them is destroyed and deserted. The closest tents were crushed and scattered by the force of the summoning, and remnants of campfires smolder out in the snow. There are signs of retreat to the north. Leth doesn't know if they're truly fleeing or just circling around.

As Leth looks around, Evain pushes up Leth's left sleeve and inspects his cuts, accidental and intentional alike. Transformation shivers through his bare hand, and Evain's fingernails are blunt and human when he touches broken skin. "Tell me who hurt you."

The soothing touch keeps Leth grounded. "I was stupid, and you were right. Anton's trying to summon that demon, but sacrificing one of his soldiers wasn't enough. When I showed up, he decided family would work better."

Evain's eyes blaze red.

"That's not the important part," Leth says.

"I rather think it is." Despite his fury, Evain's hands remain gentle around Leth's arms.

"Anton isn't strong enough to control a demon like that. I have to stop him, or more people will get hurt." Leth takes a deep breath. "But I'm not strong enough either."

"There are rope burns on your wrists." Evain's gaze is shuttered and dark. "Would you be terribly mad if I slit your brother's throat?"

That probably shouldn't sound as seductive as it does.

"You said this demon was beyond both of us." Leth touches Evain's neck, leaving bloody fingerprints. "But that's with you unbound, and me without a contract."

Evain grabs his hand, heedless of the blood. A tremor passes between them. "Don't tease me like this, Leth."

"I'm not teasing," Leth says quietly. "Would you contract with me?"

The chill wind catches Evain's hair like a banner. All the world is gray and pale except the red of his eyes. Evain trembles again, and the yearning in his face mirrors Leth's own.

"No," Evain says, and Leth flinches.

The ruins flicker out of sight, as if part of Leth still kneels in the shadowed chapel outside Fort Tarhaeg. So much has happened, yet nothing has changed. Leth is still a pathetic pilgrim without a god, begging for power and acceptance. He thought Evain was different. He thought Evain wanted this.

Evain's grip tightens on Leth's bloody hand when he tries to yank away. "No, I'm not done. What happens after we stop your brother? Will you break the contract?" His grin is sharp and dangerous. "I won't agree to a temporary contract with you, little Leth. Once I have you, I'm not letting go."

Leth freezes. This time, the shock doesn't hurt.

Evain leans in with a low laugh, surrounding Leth in warmth. His breath burns against the shell of Leth's ear. "A willing contract. You'll get more power from me than any mage has gotten from a forced binding. I'll share my lifespan with you—that's centuries, unless we're careless. But there's a catch. If you ever want to break the contract, I'll have to agree." Blunted fingertips trace a vein in Leth's neck. "And I'm going to be obsessed with you for a long, long time." Evain pulls away and seizes Leth's chin. "I'm madly in love with you, Leth."

Breath returns to Leth's lungs with painful force. Behind Evain's bravado, he sees the same uncertainty he feels in his own pounding heart. "I'm not asking for a temporary contract. And I think I love you too."

A jubilant grin spreads across Evain's face. "Marvelous," he purrs, and leans down.

Array, catalyst, contract. The demon's kiss is the entire binding promise. More power than Leth has ever felt before floods into his body. Evain's hands slide to his waist, and demonic power carves new rivers parallel to his veins, surging up and inward to the wellspring of his heart. Pleasure and shadows weave between his bones in welcome invasion. Locking his hands behind Evain's neck, Leth doesn't resist.

Evain pulls him closer, and Leth presses achingly hard against Evain's body. He feels Evain hard against him too, but more than that, his spirit fills with new awareness of Evain's desire. The rest of the world falls away, and Leth can't believe he ever thought desire was a weakness, not a strength. He's been missing this his entire life without knowing it, and as long as this contract holds, he'll never truly be alone.

When Evain pulls away, a ridiculous smug smile on his face, the contract is complete. The flood of power slows to a trickle, but Leth still feels Evain's lust like a caress inside his soul. A gentle, constant echo of heat that feeds his own arousal.

Leth rubs his blood-stained thumb under Evain's jaw, and the sensation intensifies. "Is this what you feel all the time?"

A flush crests Evain's cheeks. "I'm not sure." He touches Leth's lips, then his own. "I believe we should experiment, and compare—"

A dull explosion sounds from deeper within the ruins. Moments later, the earth shivers beneath them, and black smoke rises again in a torrent against the gray sky. A chorus of birds screams away from the concussion—away from the summoning chapel, and the swelling demonic aura.

Through his new connection with Evain, Leth hears the growl of a ravenous hunger.

"He's done it." Icy horror cuts away Leth's arousal. "I thought we'd have more time. Anton needed a better sacrifice." Nausea crawls through him. Someone else died, instead of him. Shivering, Leth forces himself to focus on strategy, despite the overwhelming cascade of emotions and magic. "Fuck. I need a sword. I don't have my spell beads."

"You need a *coat*," Evain says, laughing despite his ashen pallor. He shrugs off his own red coat. "Wear this for now. I'll buy you a dozen better ones later. Take my gloves too."

"They're too big, I'll lose my grip on the hilt." Leth shoves his arms through the sleeves. The hem nearly reaches the ground on him, and the shoulders are too baggy, but it's warm with Evain's body heat, and he can move in it. "There has to be a sword somewhere—"

"Don't use other people's swords." Evain pulls his right glove back on, then stretches his hand to the side. "You don't know where they've been." Shadows flicker in the air and coalesce into an elegant, dark red blade. He passes it hilt-first to Leth. "I'll teach you how to do this later."

The blade is light and balanced in Leth's grip. It'll do.

"Kiss for luck?" Evain says.

Leth lifts his chin, and with Evain's lips comes a new rush of power. The welcome magic fits perfectly inside Leth's soul. He doesn't have to fight for it.

Clinging to that power and promise for strength, Leth turns towards the broken archway of the summoning chapel. He takes a deep breath and prepares to face his brother once again.

As Leth strides across the frosty courtyard, sword in hand and his own demon at his heels, laughter wails from the chapel. Anton's voice, twisted into a demented cackle. The sound would chill Leth to the bone, if Evain's power wasn't there to keep him warm.

The chapel doors hang open, and Leth's boots pause on the steps. "We need to banish the demon. Not kill it." If they kill the demon in this realm, Anton will keep its powers. Assuming Anton cast that part of the spell correctly.

A set of long shadow-knives manifest in the air around Evain's shoulders. They circle him slowly. "What about your brother?"

"I want to bring him to justice. He deserves a trial in Ostaris." Leth adjusts his grip on his sword and moves forward. "But if it comes to it—don't hold back."

"Understood."

Inside, the chapel looks much the same as before. The walls were built to withstand magical accidents, and the concussion that shook the surrounding ruins didn't shake this one. Light streams from broken windows, bending and fracturing around the figures in the center of the room.

Leth thought he was prepared. He isn't.

Upon the raised circle crouches a demon. His form repels the eye, like a human shape twisted to the limits of recognition. Or a monster twisted almost to the shape of the man. His limbs are too long, his bones too sharp. Red magic wavers through the air between him and the man who summoned him—no less monstrous in his gleeful rictus.

Anton stands at the edge of the black stone platform, his cloak flung back from his shoulders. His laughter rises in fitful geysers, interspersed with pained gasps. Blood spatters what parts of him Leth can see. He doesn't turn as Leth enters; all his attention is on the bloody array painted across the platform.

The array is similar to the one in the cave, but much larger. The blood is fresh. Pieces of another corpse spread out over the entire array. Hands too far away from arms. Ribs too far away from pelvis. A wet, slurping sound echoes as the hunger demon shovels shredded organs into his jaws.

The dead man's head has rolled to the edge of the platform. The skull is dented and misshapen, but Leth recognizes the scraggly beard, the gaunt features and weak chin. One eye is wide open and dead. The other eye is gone.

I guess Anton valued your friendship after all, Javius. You were sacrifice enough.

The irony strikes painfully. Leth's ancestors would spin in their graves to learn both Tariel brothers had contracted with demons. But the roads that led them here are nothing alike, and their contracts couldn't be more different.

Anton and his demon lift their heads at the same time, swiveling to face the intruders. A miasma of power wavers between them. Anton's arms and chest are wet with blood, and he holds his greatsword in one hand.

"You're just in time." Anton's voice echoes through the chapel. He sways where he stands. "He's still hungry. Ozarell! Kill them for me."

"Mortal maggot," the demon Ozarell rasps. "Do not speak my name so lightly." But he pulls himself to his full height and lurches a step forward.

Madness burns in Anton's eyes, searing away Leth's last hope of talking his brother down. Capturing him will have to wait until the demon's gone.

"Handle your brother," Evain says. "I'll take the other ugly brute."

Leth takes one last look at Evain—features carved from finest marble, a wild fierceness in his brow—and lets his desire fill his heart with strength.

Armed with magic, sword, and love, Leth races forward to meet his brother.

Evain

"That's no way to behave," Evain addresses the hunger demon, aiming to draw his attention away from the humans. Ozarell, Anton called him. "You're a guest in this realm. Show some respect." He punctuates the scolding by flinging a shadow dagger at the demon's head.

Ozarell jerks around and snatches the dagger from midair. Blood drips from his jagged bared teeth. Only half a foot taller than Evain, his form is so close to human, but the proportions are wrong. Marble cracks under his feet, and his aura presses heavily against Evain's. His true form must be far larger when not constrained by mortal physics.

"You're a demon," Ozarell says, in an abyssal language Evain hasn't heard in centuries. He cocks his head. "But you reek of humans. How long have you been trapped here?" His rattling voice is punctuated by the ring of steel on steel from the brothers across the hall.

Evain forces himself to focus on Ozarell. He can't get distracted by Leth. "Was I unclear?" Evain flexes his power and flings another pair of daggers. "I'm not here to talk."

Ozarell lunges forward. Beneath him, sacrificial flesh scatters and bloody runes smear. Magic flares red and black as he crosses the perimeter of the array—it doesn't contain him at all. Evain skids across the marble, barely dodging the other demon's strike. Stone shatters where he stood an instant before.

A shadow-knife circles around to deflect the shrapnel as Evain dodges again. Only the power of the freshly sealed contract gives Evain the speed to avoid Ozarell's onslaught. There's a mad unpredictability to his movements that requires all of Evain's attention. Despite Anton's orders, the hunger demon isn't trying to kill him quickly. Ozarell wants to wound and restrain him. He wants Evain alive for his devouring.

Evain lands one knife in Ozarell's shoulder, but Ozarell catches the next before it hits his throat. Laughing like gravel, he brings the knife to his lips. His bloodstained teeth gnaw directly through the blade.

Tipping his head back, Ozarell swallows the shards. "Is that little thing your captor?" Black blood oozes from his shoulder. "Shall I save you a bite?"

Evain throws out his arm in a burst of pure power, deflecting the blow Ozarell aims at Leth—and dodging the next strike at himself. The hunger demon is easier to manage than Evain expected. Part of that is Evain's new contract, strengthening and stabilizing his magic in a way he hadn't thought possible. Part of that is Ozarell.

The hunger demon is unpredictable, but he's not as quick as he should be. Not as strong. His erratic movements aren't always an advantage. His flaring magic lacks the crucial edge, as if not all of Ozarell came through between the realms.

Anton's summoning was flawed in more ways than one. A new, uneasy feeling creeps behind Evain's shoulder blades. The barrier between realms is too thin here. The shivering echoes of the demonic realm aren't just from Ozarell's aura.

"Ozarell!" Anton roars from across the chapel. "Forget the demon. Kill Leth first! That's a fucking order!"

Swearing, Evain interposes himself between Ozarell and Leth again—but Ozarell pauses. "I'm not strong enough, Master Human. May I take more power?"

"Don't listen to him," Evain shouts, whirling around. Leth has Anton backed against a wall, his sword pointed at his throat. Though his arm is steady, Evain sees the tension in Leth's shoulders. Anton's sword is on the ground ten yards away.

But neither Evain nor Leth can stop Anton from snarling, "Yes."

Dark laughter rumbles through the broken chapel. Ozarell vanishes in swirling smoke and reappears at Anton's side. The force of his teleportation sends Leth skidding back, and Evain instinctively races forward to catch him.

Evain takes hold of Leth's shoulders as Ozarell grabs Anton by the arm. When Anton finally starts to struggle, it's too late. Ozarell's teeth sink into his upper arm, tearing through layers of clothing like they're paper, and rips away a mouthful of flesh.

Anton's scream drowns in the thunderclap of power. Ozarell throws him aside and flings back his head, chewing with hideous relish. Evain's bones rattle, and he barely keeps his feet. Pressing his cheek against Leth's tangled hair, he grits out, "I know the atmosphere's all wrong, but I need to kiss you again."

"Go ahead," Leth says faintly, raising the dark red sword again. He's poised for combat as Evain pulls back his hair and seals his lips to the heated skin of his neck.

Fresh magic floods into Evain, more easily than it ever had before the contract. The stream of power continues even when Evain breaks away. He channels it into a shield just before Ozarell swallows Anton's flesh and lunges towards them.

Demonic power clashes, and marble fractures under their feet. Fueled by Leth's intense attraction, Evain knows he's stronger than Ozarell. But he's constrained by the fact that he can't aim to kill—and that he cares about protecting the mage he's bound to. He has to fight carefully, while Ozarell relies on brute strength and madness.

And Leth is tiring fast. Evain sees it in the pallor of his face, the new caution in his movements as he conserves his energy. He isn't used to wielding Evain's power.

Evain doesn't have time to wear Ozarell down until the hunger demon is weak enough not to interrupt a full banishing spell. He needs to finish this fast, before one of them makes a mistake.

"I'm going to drop the shield," Evain says. "Can you distract him for three seconds?"

"I'll give you five."

Despite his clear exhaustion, Leth is already darting forward when Evain drops the shield in a shower of blood-red sparks. Evain flings the last of his shadow-daggers towards Ozarell's face without bothering to check whether any of them hit true. He focuses all his attention on the empty air above the summoning platform. Above the smeared runes and gore, the barrier between realms has thinned. If it was woven cloth, it would be fraying.

Evain lashes out with blood-red magic. Seizes hold of a thread, and pulls.

The air unravels.

In an instant, the new rift overwhelms the chapel hall with its corrosive aura. Smoke swirls between its torn edges, a yawning mouth of darkness and green fire.

Evain braces himself for the fight of his life, but the familiar pull never hooks into his soul. Both his feet stay firmly planted on the cracked marble of the mortal world. His contract with Leth holds him steady.

He belongs in this realm.

Ozarell doesn't, and his contract with Anton is a flawed and patchwork thing. The hunger demon shrieks in delighted laughter, the grating sound cut short when the rift flares out and swallows him. Ozarell's return to the demonic realm snaps the forced contract apart— painfully, by Anton's hoarse cry.

Sealing the rift afterwards is easy. Evain simply touches his silver pendant through his shirt and focuses on the magic. In an instant, the air is whole again. Corrosive energy ebbs away, leaving only the silent wreckage in its wake.

Shaking away the after-images of green fire, Evain staggers back towards Leth, who stands, sword in hand, over his brother.

Evain deliberately steps on a piece of broken marble, using the soft crunch as a warning so he doesn't startle Leth with his approach. He touches Leth's elbow, then curves his hand around Leth's wrist. His human's unsteady pulse flutters beneath his fingers.

Anton sits slumped against the wall, diminished. Blood smears the stone behind and above him, and still pulses sluggishly from his torn arm. His face is pale under the soot stains. A choked sound rocks through him, and Evain wonders if the man is dying, until he realizes Anton is laughing instead.

"It appears we're the same after all," Anton says when his laughter dies. Ignoring Evain, he focuses on Leth. They have the same hazel eyes. "We can't have Valor, so we caught ourselves demons instead. What did you give up for your contract, little brother?"

"We're not the same," Leth says, steel in his voice. "I gave up nothing."

Evain's hand tightens on Leth's trembling wrist. He doesn't care if Anton dies, but Leth will. "He's bleeding out."

Anton tips his head back against the bloody wall. "That's the second time you've broken my contract. First Valor, now this. You used to be so sweet when you were younger. How did you turn out so selfish? You can't stand me being stronger than you, can you?"

"You killed your subordinates." Leth flings his arm back, pointing to the mess of a corpse behind him. "You killed Javius. He was a piece of shit, but he was loyal to you. Do you even care?"

Arm falling limp to his side, Leth leans against Evain.

Anton's gaze finally flicks away from Leth. His expression doesn't change as he looks over the gruesome remains spread across the chapel floor. "Of course I care." His gaze returns to Leth and Evain one more time. To Evain's hand around Leth's wrist. "It wouldn't work if I didn't care."

His eyes close, and his shoulders slump.

"Anton!" Leth breaks free of Evain's grasp. Dropping his sword, he falls to his knees at his brother's side.

"Careful." Evain steps forward. "You should let me—"

Anton's hand closes around a broken shard of stone, and swings towards Leth's neck.

LETH

Anton jerks, then slumps back with a wet cough. Blood spills from his lips, and tendrils of shadows rise from the hilt stuck in his chest. Leth crouches stunned as he processes the shard of stone in Anton's hand. The blade in Anton's heart.

Once, when Leth was six and Anton was twelve, they sparred with wooden swords under their mother's watchful eye. Leth committed too hard to a feint, and Anton took the opportunity to unbalance him with a bruising elbow to his side. The blow knocked Leth onto his back, and he struggled for breath as their mother scolded Anton for the dirty move. "Your brother isn't ready for that," she said. But Anton just reached a hand towards Leth. "He's ready," he told their mother. Then he turned his smile to Leth. "Get up and prove it."

Leth doesn't know whether the memory is painful or sweet.

Either way, his memories will have to be sufficient: there are no final words from Anton ka Tariel. The dagger evaporates into shadow, leaving only a gaping hole between his ribs. Blood pulses out. With one more wet choking sound, the glare dulls from Anton's gaze. He sags against the wall.

Ribs seizing around his lungs, Leth scrambles to his feet. Each breath he takes is too quick and too shallow. Knives in his throat. His vision darkens and his joints soften, but when he falters, he lands in Evain's embrace. Strong arms wrap around him and half-carry him forward. Away from the dead men, to the chapel doors.

When they reach a stretch of unbroken marble, Evain pulls Leth closer in. One hand cradles his head, and the other rubs soothingly down his back. Gradually, the gentle friction draws Leth back into himself. Evain's warmth, his steady heart and the anchoring magic between them, slows Leth's breath until it's bearable again.

Leth closes his eyes and leans his forehead against Evain's chest. His hands hurt, from clenching Evain's shirt so tightly.

"I'm sorry." Evain's lips move in Leth's hair. "That's all the justice he's going to get."

The adrenaline of the fight, the summoning, the contract rushes away. All Leth has now is numb exhaustion—and a knee-weakening sense of relief. Is that wrong of him?

"I don't know what to feel," Leth says into Evain's chest. His eyes hurt, but he hasn't cried. Should he be crying now? His brother is dead. Maybe someday, Leth will know whether to grieve for him or not.

Long fingers soothe through his hair, plucking gently through the tangles. Evain comforts with touch instead of words. The pressure against his scalp and the firm massage against his spine keep Leth from spiraling away.

He's alive, and he's not alone. He'll figure out what else he's supposed to feel later.

They hold each other at the chapel's threshold until approaching hoofbeats interrupt the peace. Evain turns to face the courtyard and complains, "This really isn't the time." He leaves one arm around Leth's waist, and demonic shadows eddy around his other hand. "I'm not tapped out yet, but if there's more than about five of them, you'll have to kiss me again."

"The rest of the Dravans ran off into the ruins." Leth's hand flies to his hip before he remembers he isn't wearing a sword. "There's around thirty of them."

"Excellent. You'll have to kiss me at least twice."

But they need neither swords nor kisses to face the oncoming threat: only three horses and two riders canter across the chapel courtyard. Glossy black Daziroth leads the pack, his tail proudly raised. Behind him rides Haldis, straight out of a tapestry with her straight back and drawn sword, and Marta, a glittering marshmallow of celestial magic in her layers of coats.

Leth's hand falls from his nonexistent sword hilt, and the shadows dissipate from Evain's hand. After a moment, Leth says, "Did your horse… bring reinforcements?"

"Daisy's not really a horse," Evain says faintly.

"Oh." Leth has exceeded his capacity for surprise,

ascending instead to dazed acceptance. "That makes sense, in retrospect."

The Sephinians rein their horses in at the foot of the steps. "Mother's Grace!" Marta's hood has fallen back, and her curly hair forms an uneven cloud behind her head. She dismounts in a splatter of snow. "I knew Daziroth was leading us to you. Haldis owes me ten gold."

"I never agreed to that." Haldis looks as pristine and forbidding as ever, except the windswept flush across her cheeks. "Are you two all right? What's going on up here? We saw Dravans skulking in the woods, but that damned horse wouldn't let us stop."

Daziroth trots up the stairs to rub his entire face against Evain. "A little late, aren't you?" Evain mutters, staggering with the blow. But he pets the stallion's nose even as he scolds him.

Leth tugs the too-big coat closer around him, feeling the cold more without Evain's arms around him. "We're all right," he says, while Haldis dismounts too. "As for the Dravans, that's a bit complicated."

Suddenly, Marta swears. Divine magic blazes around her. "Leth, get back!"

For a wild moment, Leth thinks Anton isn't dead after all, or Ozarell wasn't banished. But the chapel behind them is silent, and the only people around are Leth himself, Evain…

Evain, with blood-red eyes and too-sharp teeth.

"Wait!" Leth flings himself between Evain and the paladins. He spreads his arms out empty-handed, without sword or spell beads. "It's not what you think."

Magic gleams poised around Marta, and Haldis holds her greatsword with both hands. Their horses shy backwards. "He's possessed," Haldis says. "Get back, we'll take care of him."

More magic tingles under Leth's skin. Evain's desire gives him the strength to stand firm. "Evain isn't possessed," Leth says. "He's a demon. He's always been a demon. But he's different from the others."

A heavy arm drapes over Leth's shoulder, and Evain's smiling voice sounds right next to his ear. "I wouldn't normally make things difficult, but I'm bound to Leth now. Banishing me too hastily would hurt him, and I can't allow that."

"Marta?" Haldis asks, her sword unwavering.

Pearl-white magic shimmers again. Marta's eyes widen. "He's telling the truth. I can sense the contract."

Leth doesn't move. "I won't let you hurt him. Evain's good." Hot breath tickles his ear as Evain laughs, making Leth's cheeks burn. "Insufferable, but good."

"I'm very good," Evain confirms.

Marta blinks, then laughs. "*Quite* the contract, it seems."

Haldis rolls her eyes but lowers her sword.

)O(

A GREAT DEAL of explaining later, Marta and Haldis depart to round up the leaderless Dravans, and Evain sends Daziroth to fetch Freya, Arthur, and Shae. The Varans will be able to interrogate the living under truth spell, in preparation for whatever military and legal inquiries will await in Ostaris. The necromancer will be able to lay the dead to rest.

And Evain leads Leth through the summoning chapel, up a winding set of stairs, to the roof. A balcony walkway runs along the back of the building, facing the edge of the ruined city and the forested slope behind it. Snow shaken from the slanted roof piles on the walkway.

Leth brushes snow from the stone railing and leans his forearms against it. Evain leans next to him. Their elbows touch.

From this height, the valley is serene. Diamond snow and velvet forest, silver-blue sky painted with paler clouds. There's a beauty to the landscape that no wild rifts can diminish. Leth thinks he understands why Lyrisenia's people have lingered here so long after their empire fell. Belonging somewhere can be worth the risk.

Or maybe everything just looks a little more beautiful when he has someone standing beside him. His grief and hurt ebb away for now. They'll rise again soon enough, but in this moment, Leth can breathe.

"I imagine you have some questions," Evain says after a while.

"A few." Leth rubs his hands together, feeling the cold again now that he's not fighting for his life. He considers where to start. Maybe something easy. "How old are you, really?"

"I'm not sure." Evain leans closer. One of his hands settles on Leth's waist, and warmth radiates where they touch. "Time passes differently in my home realm, but I believe I was around fifty when I crossed over through a rift. I know I've been in the human realm for around two hundred and fifty years."

Another thing that should be stunning, but makes sense, in retrospect. "Why do you want to seal the rifts?" Leth asks next.

Evain moves again, this time to stand behind Leth. He reaches around and clasps Leth's hands together in his. "I should probably say that it's the right thing to do. That my deep sense of justice and goodwill is driving me. Would you believe that?"

Leth leans his head back against Evain's shoulder. "I might."

"You shouldn't." Evain sighs. "The truth is, I'm very selfish. I like your world quite a bit. Most of my fellow demons would ruin all the things I like about it, so I have to do my best to keep them out."

"Our world," Leth says quietly.

"Hm?"

Leth hooks his fingers between Evain's, interweaving them. "You've been here long enough. I think it's your world too, by now."

Evain breathes deep, a full-body movement against Leth's back. Then he spins Leth around and presses him against the railing. Heart pounding, Leth gets only a glimpse of burning red eyes before Evain leans down.

The kiss is ravenous. Tender. The terms of the contract are fair: a heart for a heart.

EVAIN

"I still think it's unfair that I have to wait outside." Evain lounges against an ornate windowsill. The whole of Ostaris stretches out behind him. Springtime in the capital makes for a breathtaking view, but Evain only cares about the wooden door at the end of the hall. The two soldiers guarding the door watch him warily in return. "Can't you pull some holy strings, O Great and Benevolent Prophet?"

Evain waits in the antechamber of the Charaini High Council's meeting hall, located in a rather boring wing of the Ostaris palace. Ronan sits on a velvet bench across the room, dressed as plainly as usual. His only ornaments are the dice bag on his belt and the golden ring on his left hand. Karis, meanwhile, is dressed all in white, with gold embroidery at every hem and seam. He stays standing next to Ronan, as if afraid to snag the gold thread if he sits down. The Varan regalia makes his amber eyes brighter than ever.

The soldiers on duty don't look happy to see *any* of them.

Behind that wooden door, Leth is giving his last required testimony under truth spell before he's allowed to leave the city again. The interview is only a formality; everyone involved has already been questioned at least once, and only a few of the remaining Dravan soldiers are bound for criminal trials. Most were truly unaware of the extent of Anton's crimes. But apparently the death of a Charaini general requires a lot of bureaucratic processing.

"I tried." Karis wrinkles his nose. "I wanted to cast the truth spell myself, but the council decided our friendship constituted a 'conflict of interest.' Captain Tanner's good, though."

"Are you worried about Leth?" Ronan asks Evain. "Or worried about what he might say?" he adds meaningfully.

Ronan and Karis are part of the slowly expanding circle of people who know Evain's true nature. There's a new caution in the way Ronan treats him, which Evain doesn't mind. Karis accepted it with surprising ease— apparently Radiant Vara doesn't care either.

"Neither." Evain gives a dramatic sigh, playing with the ends of his half-bound hair. "I just like looking at him. He's just so…"

"Gods help me," Ronan says, while Karis stifles his laughter. "I can't wait until you leave town again."

"What are your plans after this?" Karis glances sidelong at the guards. "The plans fit for polite company, at least."

Evain has quite a few plans he shouldn't mention, in that case—not that he wants to. Leth's flexibility is a secret for Evain's knowledge alone. "We're returning to Lyrisenia first, to seal a few more rifts and make sure the crown's mages are doing it properly. I want to teach the array to more Lyrisenian witches too. After that, Leth wants to travel."

"You should take him on one of those Etenian pleasure boats you always talk about," Karis says.

Evain lifts an eyebrow. Leth had expressed more interest in Ellaroc's arcane libraries, but a month cruising Etenian harbors in luxury isn't a bad idea. "Do you think he'd enjoy that?"

Karis's amber eyes sparkle mischievously. "No."

Ronan mutters another curse. "I'm not involved in any of this."

Before Evain can solicit more excellent vacation ideas from the Voice of Vara, the soldiers on guard jump to attention and open the door. More guards come out first, escorting a trio of finely dressed people. Two council members, plus Telvin the herald. Telvin, clutching a book and writing set to his chest, hurries down a side hall. The council members stop to bow to Karis—who smiles beatifically—before retreating with the guards.

Evain doesn't watch them leave. His gaze arrows through the open door, alert to any sign of movement. He hears low voices before another woman walks out, shoulders broad under a Charaini green cloak. Her hair is cropped short and she's almost as tall as Evain, but there's a definite familiarity in the line of her nose and the color of her eyes.

The woman slows as she passes Evain, looking him up and down, but in the end doesn't say anything. She salutes Karis before striding around a corner.

"You enjoy that too much," Ronan says, standing up.

"I enjoy it exactly enough." Karis grins and tucks his hand into Ronan's.

Finally, Leth emerges from the doorway with Edith Tanner talking at his side. Leth nods to her without saying anything. He looks tired, but his footsteps are lighter than they were when he entered the council chamber. Like there's a weight off his shoulders. When his eyes meet Evain's, a small smile lights up his face.

Evain's heart flips over a few times.

Leth looks good today. He looks good every day, of course, in Evain's expert opinion. Today Leth wears a pale gray shirt, loose sleeves narrowing at his wrists, under a dark red, sleeveless coat that Evain had custom-fitted for him as a New Spring gift. Neither of them celebrates the Harvest Lord's holy days, but Evain will take any excuse.

More color gleams in Leth's hair. Ruby and turquoise beads, drops of amethyst, braided in with his usual onyx spell beads. Evain has been giving him one every few days for the past month. After the first five, Leth said he was being excessive. But the accusation came between heated kisses, so Evain thinks he's not anywhere near excessive yet.

And Leth lets Evain braid the beads in for him every morning, when the sun's barely up and Leth is still soft and sated from the night before.

Now, Leth's face reddens slightly. He says something in reply to Tanner, who nods and goes to talk to Karis.

The distance between Evain and Leth lessens until Evain can count each of Leth's eyelashes—lowered, as Leth averts his gaze.

"Is it over?" Evain asks. "Are you free from the clutches of bureaucracy?"

"It's over." Leth's voice drops to a whisper, so only Evain can hear: "Stop doing that."

"Stop doing what?" Evain's fingertips hover half an inch beneath Leth's chin. He's not sure whether he's teasing Leth or restraining himself.

"Looking at me like that." Leth tucks his hair behind his ear, and beads click together. "I can *feel* it."

"Can you?" Evain's smile broadens, and he finally lets his fingers rest against Leth's pulse. The quickening against his fingertips matches the rush of magic inside his own veins.

The contract lets them each feel the other's desire—but Evain has a few more centuries' experience handling the sensation. Leth is still getting used to the influence of Evain's lust for him.

"You look a little out of sorts," Evain says. "Was the truth spell difficult? Do you need to do anything else here, or can I take you home to rest?"

He's a little too loud on the last bit. Tanner's the one who answers from across the hall, "Radiance, yes, please go home and stop flirting in the council chambers!"

Leth jerks away, flushing even brighter red. "Thanks for your time today," he tells Tanner, while Karis entirely fails to hide his laughter. "Ronan, Karis…"

"Let's have dinner some night before you two leave," Ronan says. "Evain can cook."

Evain doesn't mind being volunteered. He sweeps an exaggerated bow before taking off to catch up with Leth.

🌒○🌘

"WHO WAS THE soldier in that meeting?" Evain asks as they near their neighborhood. Karis offered them space in the Bright Cathedral when they returned earlier that spring, but Evain declined. He picked a house to rent based on the size of the master bedroom and bathtub, in one of the nicer neighborhoods in Ostaris. Trees tended by Maizan acolytes bloom orange and blue along the streets, filling the air with sweet spring fragrance. Leth says he's never seen the flowers as bright as they are this year.

Now, Leth answers, "My cousin Oria. She's next in line for our family title, now that I've officially stepped out. And I'd bet Marta twenty gold that Oria will be promoted to general by the end of the year too."

"I won't tell Haldis." Humans can be so predictable. "So, the Unbinding didn't change everything after all, did it?"

"Yes and no," Leth says. "Nepotism is still alive and well, but Oria is bound to Songbird, now."

All right. Not so predictable. "Songbird?"

"Songbird." Leth laughs too. "I know, I don't know how that's going to work either. I just know the army is going to get a lot more theologically diverse in the coming years."

Blossoming trees give way to the gate of their rented house. The two-story building's garden courtyard is too small for horses, so Leth's Star is stabled at the Bright Cathedral while Daziroth hunts rabbits in the forest outside the city. Magic heats with renewed vibrancy under Evain's skin—Leth's imagination always wanders when they near the privacy of their own home. Evain manages to restrain himself while Leth unlocks the door, but his control snaps before Leth can open it.

They hit the door with a thud as Evain spins his Leth around, seizing Leth's lips in a wet, open kiss. Leth groans, and Evain delves deeper to chase the sound. Anyone could see them through the wrought iron gate, but Evain doesn't care. He wants the whole world to know that Leth ka Tariel belongs to him.

His hands slide from Leth's waist to his thighs. cupping beneath his ass. Evain never tires of how perfect Leth feels in his arms. So tough, but the perfect size to hold, to lift, to shove against a wall or toss onto a bed.

That Leth *allows* him to do all of that is the hottest thing Evain's ever experienced. And that's saying quite a lot.

Evain bites Leth's neck without artistry. Strands of hair catch in his teeth as he digs his tongue into Leth's carotid. Whimpering, Leth rocks his hips, and friction jolts between their erections. Evain sucks harder against Leth's neck, inhaling the scent of his hair, and throws one hand to the doorknob. He keeps kissing bruises as he works the door open.

They stumble inside, and Evain releases Leth's neck to kick the door closed. When he scoops Leth up, Leth's legs wrap around his waist, and Leth's hands brace against Evain's shoulders. Their eyes meet, and possessive pleasure courses through Evain. He can't tell the difference between magic and the visceral, physical reality of Leth's lips meeting his. Perhaps it's the same thing. Slow pressure and gentle movement invite Evain further inside in an active, demanding surrender.

Evain can't believe he used to think Leth was tedious. He used to think a contract would tie him down—instead, Leth allows him to soar. *Our world*, Leth told him, in the cold heart of Lyrisenia's winter. Evain never felt at home until Leth wanted him to stay. Until Leth's love flowed stronger than wild magic through his veins.

He nuzzles into Leth's neck. "Should I fuck you against the wall, or should we go to bed?"

Leth's hands tighten around Evain's shoulders. "I don't care. I just want you now."

"Bed, then." Lust surges through Evain, along with a bone-deep sense of home—not the rented house, but Leth himself. Evain's anchor and purpose in a world he finally belongs to. "I want to take my time with you, today."

LETH

etween the front door and the bedroom, Leth's feet don't touch the floor. Evain carries him all the way upstairs, kissing him every step—his lips, his neck, his ears. Evain's teeth sink into Leth's shoulder, sharp pressure through layers of clothing, and the pain mixes with sheer, supernatural pleasure in an intoxicating cocktail.

Leth never thought being carried off by a demon would be so reassuring. But it's easy to let go, knowing Evain will catch him.

Evain's lust for him is a tangible pulse of magic and pleasure. Leth has practiced channeling the power, coiling it safely inside his soul for later use, and he hasn't exploded any nearby lamps in weeks. But he may never get used to the heights of lust Evain's mere thoughts drive him to.

Even if he gets used to it, Evain will just think of new ways to drive Leth wild.

"Have you been training harder?" Evain squeezes Leth's ass, the tips of his fingers dipping between his cheeks. The enchantment falls from his eyes, revealing their true crimson. "Your ass feels even firmer than it used to."

Not unless riding Evain's cock counts as exercise. Which it very well might, given Evain's stamina.

Evain drops him on the edge of the bed and leans forward to cover him with another kiss, then drops to his knees to start removing Leth's boots. Except he spends as much time caressing Leth's calves through the leather as he does unfastening buckles. Toes curling at the muted sensation, Leth wants to complain about Evain taking too long, but that's a guaranteed way to make Evain slow down even more.

His fingers clench in the unfamiliar texture of the bedspread. "New sheets again?"

Evain slides one boot away and fondles Leth's ankle through his sock. "I thought you'd look good on purple. Are they soft enough?"

A flash of red eyes and a sudden surge of lust prevent Leth from answering. Curling in on himself, he gasps for breath. His nerves resonate in response to phantom hands exploring his body, playing with him. Evain still kneels between his feet, but Leth feels a broad, invisible palm sliding over his cock. Wicked fingers circle his nipples, teasing them into hot peaks under his shirt.

"Can you feel that?" Evain handles the second boot more quickly. "I've been wondering if I could convey more specific sensations via our contract. For example, right now I'm thinking about spreading your thighs wide open and sucking on your balls. Rolling them over my tongue, while your cock twitches and leaks. Can you feel that?"

"Fuck." Leth trembles. "*Evain.*"

Evain sets the second boot aside and rises up on his knees. He tugs Leth into a light, teasing kiss, then starts to work on his coat buttons. "What about this? Can you tell what I'm imagining doing to you now?"

The wet, imaginary heat around Leth's balls vanishes, leaving only the very real ache of his cock straining against his trousers. Concentrating is difficult. "I don't think so."

"Interesting." Evain shoves Leth's shirt and coat down his shoulders, trapping his arms in the sleeves. "So, it only works with things I've done to you before. Things your body remembers. That makes sense."

Leth's curiosity is piqued by the theory. He's been digging into the Varan and Sephinian libraries the past few weeks, trying to determine the ramifications of his contract with Evain. Very few mages have ever bound a willing demon without restrictions; fewer still have been as recklessly in love with one as Leth.

He's also desperately curious what Evain is imagining that they haven't done before. But theorizing and research will have to wait until his mind is clear, when he can think about anything besides Evain rocking to his feet and removing his own clothes.

They're both fully naked in much less time than it took Evain to unbuckle a single boot. Evain keeps talking, a constant flow of filthy affection, as he procures a half-empty crystal bottle. Then he shoves Leth back against the mattress.

"On your stomach, handsome," Evain says, and Leth rolls over. Settling behind him, Evain pulls Leth's hips upwards at a sharp angle.

Leth bends easily with Evain's urging, clutching the new purple sheets as Evain's lust washes over him once again. He's completely exposed, but it's impossible to feel shy when the contract links them like this. Leth needs Evain's attention the same way he needs Evain's palm sinking into his ass, thumb running dry over his hole.

"Do you want to come before I fuck you, or while I fuck you?" Evain asks, as casually as if he's asking what Leth wants for breakfast. His thumb presses almost inside Leth with a teasing burn.

Evain is an obliging lover, and he enjoys giving Leth choices. A month ago, Leth would have chosen one of the options—they're both appealing, or Evain wouldn't have offered them. But Leth's becoming more and more comfortable asking for what he really wants.

"Both," Leth says breathlessly, pressing his forehead to the mattress. His face feels like it's on fire. "Use your fingers first."

Evain's hitch of breath is gratifying, and Evain's laugh pours like molten honey. He leans over to kiss Leth's tailbone. "Mm, I like you greedy. I can't believe it took me so long to learn how insatiable you are." Evain squeezes his ass one more time before Leth hears the familiar click of the bottle opening. "Though in my defense, I believe I still figured it out before you did."

"Probably," Leth admits, before Evain's slick fingers scatter his thoughts.

It's easy to believe Evain has centuries of experience sliding his fingers into people's asses. And it's hard to be jealous of long-gone partners when that inhuman talent is applied to Leth's sensitive nerves. Evain knows just where and how to push, just when to quicken and slow. With only the first finger, all Leth's awareness narrows to that point of connection. The new silk sheets dampen under his cheek as he pants open-mouthed. His thighs tense.

Evain knows exactly where his prostate is—a fact made clear by the way he carefully avoids it, teasing Leth into a breathless, overwhelmed mess.

"I was right." Evain's own breath is barely steadier. "You look gorgeous on purple. Look at how it brings out the flush on your cheeks. Your ears are bright red too. How's my technique? Tell me how you feel."

Evain finally hooks two fingers down to massage into Leth's prostate, drawing a high moan from the depths of Leth's soul.

Leth rocks back onto his hand. "You know how I feel."

"You feel *tight*." Evain's fingers twist deeper. "You clench around me every time I talk, did you know that? I could probably just talk you to orgasm, couldn't I?" His next move sends stars shattering in Leth's eyes, and his ears buzz so he can barely hear. "Fuck, you're so tight, you'd break a weaker man's fingers in here. Luckily I'm very strong." Evain's other hand slides possessively along Leth's back. "I can keep going for hours."

Dazed, Leth doesn't know whether those hours pass or not before Evain drags him over the edge.

The pleasure sharpens in an instant. Evain's fingers press with purpose inside him, and he breathes Leth's name like an unholy prayer. Leth seizes up, his orgasm punching through him. His untouched cock spills onto the new purple sheets, and his entire body echoes with bliss.

He's still shaking when Evain withdraws his fingers and replaces them with the head of his cock. Evain slides in with one long thrust, opening Leth wider and deeper than his fingers could reach. The pleasure is so intense it almost hurts. No space to breathe between one sensation and the next—exactly what Leth wants. He wants to be overwhelmed and overstimulated. He wants to lose control.

Evain pauses for a moment, their thighs nestled together. His silken hair falls against Leth's trembling spine as he kisses Leth's shoulders. His hands slide up Leth's body, along his arms, and settle over his wrists.

"How's this?" Evain asks.

Sometimes Leth likes his wrists held, sometimes he doesn't. Today he does—and he's too overwhelmed to answer out loud, but his spiking arousal must be clear through their contract. Evain's grip tightens in response, and Leth's cock twitches with his full-body reaction. Groaning, Evain rolls his hips into Leth's It's almost too much. It's perfect.

Shifting his grip, Evain pins both of Leth's wrists with one hand. Leth's stomach flutters in anticipation when Evain's other hand grasps Leth's hip for leverage—and then Evain really starts to move. Long, steady thrusts ignite Leth's body, every movement ricocheting through his nerves. The bed creaks. Leth's balls tighten, his arousal nearly painful so soon after his last orgasm.

Either Evain falls into another language, or Leth is beyond comprehension, or both. Leth can't understand what Evain says next, but the words don't matter. All Leth needs is the warmth of Evain's voice, guiding him through the storm beneath his skin.

The storm breaks when Evain's hand falls to his cock. Lightning arcs along Leth's spine. He comes again with a whimper on the piston of Evain's cock and knows by the surge of ecstatic magic that Evain finds his release too.

Afterwards, Evain rolls onto his back. Leth leans over him, and the slow, gentle kiss lures him back to coherence. "I love you," Leth says.

Evain's red eyes glitter. "Love you more."

"Really?" Leth tucks his hair behind his ear, fingers bumping against his braids. His old onyx spell beads, and the new trinkets from Evain. "Maybe you do."

Laughing, Evain hauls him down to nestle against his side. Leth melts into the embrace, his entire body loose and languid. Moments like these, it's easy to imagine the next hundred years at Evain's side.

Leth has already set a new spell into one of the ruby beads. A summoning spell, so he can call Evain to him at any time, any place in the world. He thought long and hard as he prepared the enchantment, and in the end, he didn't include any elements of compulsion.

He doesn't need them. Whenever he calls, Evain will answer.

Epilogue

LATE SUMMER

Nearly two dozen people gather in the green orchard. There are a few River-swords, a few Lyrisenians, and a few very blond, very tall people. The late summer morning is warm as the sun nears its zenith, but the canopy of leaves keeps the orchard comfortable.

Motes of gold and pearlescent light dance between the branches, increasing in number as Marta and Freya send more Grace and Radiance upwards. Two tables sit at one edge of the orchard, one covered with food and the other with beverages under Tally's watchful eyes. There's still some time before the vows will be recited at high noon, when Radiant Vara's vision is strongest.

"Congratulations," Leth says. He only has one hand free to pick at the appetizers. His other hand is held captive by Evain. "This place is beautiful."

Shae's smile in reply is a little melancholy. "The trees were all dead a year ago. But I really wanted to hold our wedding here, so Tally's been helping me and Arthur restore the orchard."

Arthur waves a tiny pastry in greeting. "Don't give me any credit. I mostly just serve as an energy source."

"Don't sell yourself short," Shae says breezily. "You carry heavy objects too." The brief hint of melancholy is gone, leaving Shae the most relaxed Leth has ever seen him. He's wearing a simple, pale green shirt, and all his rings glitter in the sunlight. Arthur's shirt is white, following Charaini wedding tradition instead of Lyrisenian.

Leth was a little surprised to realize the service won't even have an officiant, but the lack of ceremony suits Arthur and Shae. All the guests are dressed casually too, even the paladins abandoning their usual regalia. Freya, Marta, and Haldis are attending as friends, rather than representing their orders. Leth personally prefers weddings with a bit more formality, but there are advantages: Evain's loose cotton shirt shows off a distracting expanse of collarbone.

"Radiance," Arthur says suddenly. "I need to stop Freya from seducing my brother. She could at least wait until after the ceremony." Handing the remaining half of his pastry to Shae, he heads towards Freya and one of the tall, blond people. Moments later, Shae steps aside to talk with Bricks.

Evain's thumb strokes the inside of Leth's wrist as they move towards the beverage table, where Tally and Darren are arguing over whether to open Tally's special brew before or after the vows at noon. Marta and Haldis join them there, and Evain bets Marta five gold that Freya is actually trying to seduce Arthur's parents instead of his brother.

Other than that, Evain doesn't say much. He seems distracted.

A year ago, Leth would have been subconsciously jealous of everyone else Evain spoke to, or even looked at. But for one thing, Leth has become very secure in Evain's attention. It's impossible not to be when he feels every flare of Essvain's lust beneath his own skin. For another, Evain isn't actually flirting with other people today. If anything, he's paying more attention to the floating lights and flowering vines than he is to any of the other guests.

"What's wrong?" Leth asks when they're alone for a moment. An illuminated tree stands between them and the rest of the party.

Evain's attention snaps towards him. A smile curves into his eyes, and he strokes the inside of Leth's wrist again. "Nothing's wrong."

"You keep looking around, and you've barely said anything," Leth says. "I'm not used to being the talkative one."

"Oh, I've just been taking mental notes." Evain lets go of Leth's wrist to curve his hand around Leth's waist. Tugging Leth closer, Evain murmurs directly into his ear. "I have to make sure our wedding is *much* more impressive than anyone else's."

"Are you always this competitive?" Evain's voice melts Leth's brain into a puddle of lust, and he takes a moment to process the rest of the implications. "Wait, our what?"

"Don't worry about it." Evain kisses the corner of Leth's mouth. "Come on, it's time for their vows."

Desire rippling through his veins, Leth grabs a fistful of silken black hair to hold Evain in place. "You're insufferable," Leth informs him, rising on his toes and dragging Evain down to kiss the smirk from his perfect lips. The moment is brief, but so heated that when Leth pulls away, Evain's dark eyes flicker red. "All right, now we can go."

This time Leth is the one who takes Evain's hand and holds him tight.

A Gift at the Altar

A RADIANCE SHORT STORY

The chapel's crumbling exterior is unadorned. Anonymous and abandoned, like the rest of its village, to the Lyrisenian elements. Once-narrow windows have widened with intrusive flora, blurring the lines between the worship hall and the autumn wilderness. So, Leth doesn't recognize the chapel's dedication until he sees the carved friezes inside.

Wolves. Warriors. This is a chapel to Ka Dravos. There are friezes instead of statues, and the floors are dusty flagstone instead of marble, but the black marble block of the altar looks nearly identical to the Tariel family altar.

Evain's footstep is the only warning before a gentle tug on one of Leth's braids. "All right there?"

"Just surprised." Leth wars with himself for a moment. He's trying not to minimize his emotions. "I haven't been in a Dravan chapel since I left the Dravansword in my family's."

Still minimizing. Leth can't help it. *Since Ka Dravos rejected me* is too maudlin for such a lovely autumn day. *Since Ka Dravos found your demonic stain on my soul* sounds too much like blame.

He and Evain have been scouting out ruins the past few weeks, partly on behalf of Charaini-Lyrisenian rift-sealing teams. Partly spinning increasingly plausible what-ifs about finding somewhere in Lyrisenia to settle down. Somewhere to come home between travels. They can build their own house—if one asks Leth. Or their own castle—if one asks Evain.

Leth would much rather dream about future castles than dark memory chapels. Strange, how heavily he leaned on faith as a crutch. He used to think he would stumble without it, but now it's the reminder that knocks him off balance.

"He never deserved you," Evain says, because he knows what Leth's thinking anyway. "Come here."

Leth spins around at Evain's impatient tug. Gloved hands trace sparks of desire along Leth's jaw, holding him in place for a kiss. It's sweet. Grounding. Evain isn't using any of his magic, but Leth still warms with every touch.

When Evain's hands fall to his ass, Leth rocks forward in a heady blend of obedience and chasing his own desire. Evain wants him to do exactly what he wants to do. What he *truly* wants, not just what he's supposed to—

Leth falls back on his heels, breaking away. "We shouldn't. Not here."

Evain tilts his head, long hair shifting over his shoulder. "Why not?"

"It's improper. Ka Dravos teaches restraint."

"Ka Dravos isn't here." Evain takes one step back, but his gaze is so intense, it feels like he's drawn closer instead. "You don't belong to Ka Dravos now."

Leth hugs himself through his new coat. Dark purple. Evain likes him in purple. And red. Black. Gold. Most colors, really. Evain likes dressing Leth up and stripping him down, hiding him away and parading him in front of everyone else who isn't allowed to touch him.

"I never really belonged to Ka Dravos," Leth says, both because Evain wants to hear it and because it's true. "I only belong to you."

Desire washes through their contract, as breathtaking as Evain's wicked grin. "That's right, little Leth. But I think you need a more physical reminder." His smile widens. "Shall I remind you outside, or in here?"

That's one of the thousands of reasons Leth loves Evain. As much as Evain thrives on shocking Leth, on surprising him, on pushing Leth to heights he never imagined he could reach, if Evain isn't sure of a boundary, he asks.

Suddenly, a little impropriety doesn't sound so bad after all. Leth's last memory of a Dravan chapel is fleeing in disgrace. Maybe it's time to overwrite that memory with something very different.

"Here is fine."

"Oh, good." Evain tugs at Leth's belt. "Give me your sword and coat, then bend over that altar."

The order races hot through Leth, his own desire flaring to meet Evain's. He unbuckles his sword belt and hands the whole thing over with his coat, then approaches the altar. There's a puff of dark smoke at the edge of his vision, probably Evain tucking their unnecessary belongings into a demonic pocket dimension.

Possibly Evain retrieving a few more immediately necessary items, too.

Up close, the altar is easier to differentiate from the Tariel chapel altar. The marble isn't a true black, and the paler gray markings are wider. Softer. Just as cold, though, as Evain's strong hand pushes him onto the dusty surface.

"On your elbows, just like that," Evain purrs. "Your ass looks so delicious at this angle. Presented so nicely for me."

A kaleidoscope of sensation spins through Leth. Memories of Evain's fingers, cock, tongue, caressing every sensitive part of him. Leth whimpers under the contract's effects, achingly hard even though Evain has barely touched him.

"I'm thinking about last week right now." Evain unlaces Leth's trousers with maddening patience, even as sense-memory fingers toy with Leth's nipples. Twisting, teasing, to the edge of pain. "That was fun, wasn't it?"

Evain doesn't need an answer, which is good, because Leth is too overwhelmed already to give one. He can't believe they're doing this here. Every intoxicating word and touch feels so much filthier beneath the carved stone eyes of Ka Dravos's wolves. Leth's younger self would be appalled at how eagerly he welcomes his demon's touch.

Leth doesn't regret any step that brought him to his current life, where he's meant to be. But sometimes he wishes he could tell his younger self to care about himself. Just a little more.

"I have a present for you," Evain says as the sense memories fade into the contract's normal shared desire. Leth's trousers are down around his knees, Evain idly massaging the flesh of his ass. "Meant to give it to you tonight, but I think now is better."

"What's the occasion?"

"Edren has something coming up. Wait, no. Kan Halla healed some pauper on this day three hundred years ago. It's a big festival in this one village in Etenia."

Sure. Leth can't even remember today's date, he's so desperate for more. "Please tell me it's something relevant. If you stop to braid another bead in my hair…"

Leth doesn't even have the wit to come up with a proper threat. He just needs Evain to keep going, keep pushing him forward. If Leth slows down, the shadows of worry and shame might catch him.

Evain laughs. "Don't worry, it's extremely relevant." His hand leaves Leth's ass, then returns gloveless and newly slick. "You'll have to look at it later, though. I want to see how it looks in you first."

Which is Leth's only warning before the slick, blunt object pushes into him. He gasps, arching into the slight burn—quickly eased by the salve. No stretching first, but the plug isn't too large. Barely as thick as Evain's cock at the widest part, and the neck is comfortably narrow before the flared base.

"What color's this one?" Leth asks. Their collection already includes half the rainbow.

"Emerald green." Evain leans over Leth's body, pressing him closer to the altar. Pressing the plug more firmly into Leth's prostate. "Jewel tones always look so good on you. My perfect little treasure."

The marble warms with the heat of their bodies. The plug is nice, but Leth needs more. He doesn't have to ask before Evain takes hold of his cock. Firm, confident strokes that never fail to buckle Leth's knees.

"Oh, I forgot to mention," Evain says, clearly and joyfully lying, "the plug is enchanted."

Which is when the plug begins to vibrate.

Leth yelps with the shock, then collapses whimpering atop the altar. He might have slid to the floor if not for Evain covering him. His cheek presses to warm marble, and Evain's every filthy whisper burns his ear.

Every wordless sound Leth makes triggers a new wave of *need* from Evain, as unrelenting as the vibration. Leth comes what feels like mere seconds later, a glorious unraveling.

The enchantment ends, and the plug stops moving. Evain growls and flips Leth around. Smears Leth's own come on Leth's face—stares for one heated, pulsing moment—then leans down to kiss and lick away every drop.

Leth just slumps against that altar, savoring the afterglow. They're done for now, he can tell. Evain hasn't come yet, but the centuries have made him more patient than Leth would have expected.

The entire chapel is quiet and empty except for them. A ruin, long abandoned. Its history is important, but it holds no power over Leth. Not when he would far rather worship someone who worships him in turn.

"There, that's better." Evain hikes Leth's trousers up again. "Now we can explore the rest of the ruins."

Leth would ask if Evain was forgetting something, but there's no way Evain is forgetting anything. "You want me to walk around with this?"

Beaming, Evain laces Leth's trousers. "I want you thinking about me every moment we're in this chapel."

"I don't need a toy for that." Leth lifts on his toes to caress Evain's face. The movement jostles the plug inside him—and suddenly, Leth clearly, viscerally understands the appeal. "Um. But I'm happy to indulge you. Of course."

"Of course," Evain says cheerfully. He waves through a tendril of shadow, pulling out Leth's purple coat. Sliding it over Leth's shoulders, Evain adds, "Now, I saw some interesting carvings on those walls, down by the floor. If you could be so kind as to bend over and examine them—"

ABOUT THE AUTHOR

Tavia Lark writes m/m fantasy romance and erotica. Her favorite romance tropes include hurt/comfort, sharing a bed, and enemies to lovers. She writes from a sunny little apartment with the constant "help" of her fluffy cat. He just really likes typing, okay.

KEEP IN TOUCH

Website: www.tavialark.com
Newsletter: www.tavialark.com/list
Patreon: www.patreon.com/tavialark
Group: www.facebook.com/groups/tavialark